Disconnected

Volume I

About this book

Dear Reader,

this book has been written by an autistic writer, which means that it is different in ways that may seem confusing, or even 'wrong.'

Autistic people (also known as people with Autism spectrum disorder—ASD) have unique brains. They think differently than neurotypicals (also known as the 'normal' people), concentrating on other aspects of things than the majority. Sensory sensitiveness helps them see, hear, and taste things deeply. They constantly collect data from their surroundings, going from the small to the big in order to try to make sense in the chaos. Autistic people also have distinct speech patterns and facial expressions compared to neurotypicals. This is why there is a noticeable difference in how an autistic individual speaks; in how they build up a story and then tell it.

It can become confusing for neurotypicals to follow their trains of thought, getting lost easily. It is said that autistic people speak a different language, even though they use the same words as those around them. This, then, often leads to friction between neurotypicals and autistic people, leaving the latter confused and hurt.

This book has not been moulded especially for neurotypicals. The author wants to represent their way of thinking, even if it may initially be confusing for most. However, it is the way the author operates; it is the way they see the world around them. It is impossible for them to write like a neurotypical, and they decided that being true to their nature was more important than the social pressure of fitting in.

They are different; therefore, this book is different. Perhaps, it may be confusing or puzzling at the beginning. But given the chance, difference can bring joy and foster a deeper understanding of new perspectives.

Enjoy the journey.

N. Saraven

DISCONNECTED

vol. I

N. SARAVEN

ISBN: 978-3-8192-4712-5 (paperback)

Cover image based on Adobe Stock #101426449

Typeset in Gentium Book Plus
with manual fine-tuning.

Publisher: BoD · Books on Demand GmbH,
Überssering 33, 22297 Hamburg, bod@bod.de

Printed by: Libri Plureos GmbH,
Friedensallee 273, 22763 Hamburg

www.saraven.net

Contents

Chapter 1

Walking home in the dark was the only thing, Neila liked about going out. Despite spending a pleasant dinner with a friend, she could hardly wait to get home. This late, the calmness and emptiness of the suburban streets had finally managed to calm her down after visiting the city. Neila lived in a fairly peaceful and safe area, about a fifteen-minute train ride from the main station. After a certain hour, hardly any cars occupied the roads; and almost never any other pedestrians.

A louder motorbike passing by brought Neila back to the present, making her raise an eyebrow. *Apparently, it's still not suburban enough,* she thought grumpily. Truth be told, she considered herself fortunate, living in a relatively small town, far from the 'big city life.' It was still too large and noisy for *her.*

But, at least, nothing's likely to happen, and I can get home in peace, she added in her head, even if it truly was a beautiful night. The starry sky stretched endlessly; the thirteen degrees Celsius felt comfortable. Since it was the middle of April, the days warmed up nicely, only to be followed by the occasional frost at night.

Overall, it was the perfect time for having a friend over for a visit, whom Neila had just seen off at the train station. For some reason, that particular friend preferred the night train. Unlike Neila, who would never travel for that long on any vehicle. Airplanes were much more comfortable, if not eco-friendly.

In any case, Neila now decided to take a small path that led amidst the houses. Here, only a row of huge cobblestones represented the 'road' in the grassy ground. Bushes served as fences between the buildings; trees gave shades during the summer. In the dark, though, they looked like grumpy guardians, overseeing the people who might wander there.

Feeling a sudden urge to quicken her pace, Neila hurried towards her apartment. Despite loving to be outside, there were people, which she preferred to avoid. Luckily for Neila, only a few more buildings stood between her and the flat. After turning left at a large tree, she could spot the inviting windows of her home.

"Please, I require assistance," Neila heard a weak call, making her halt and look around. Now, she could also hear a hiss, accompanied by laboured breathing. Whoever called to her, must have been in great distress.

Neila finally spotted the man at the bottom of the tree she had just passed. Taking a step back, scared, she stared at the stranger with widened eyes, not knowing what to do or say.

The man was sitting on the ground, leaning against the tree. In the dark, not much could be seen of him, making Neila even more afraid. Since she did not move a muscle, he now turned to her again.

"Please," the stranger repeated hoarsely, "time is of the essence, I believe. That elderly woman, who passed by a moment ago, might have called the authorities. Would you please be kind enough to help me to a more secure place?"

Neila blinked, still frozen in surprise. Feeling the waiting glance on her made adrenaline rush through her veins. Finally, a sudden jolt snapped her out of the numb state. Despite her mind screaming *Don't get involved, just run!,* Neila stepped to the stranger and crouched down to see what to do.

The man's breathing sounded hoarse, and he held his right side. Neila could see blood in the faint light, indicating a serious injury.

This is crazy! Neila's rational mind screamed, making her heart throb even faster. *Where the hell did he come from?! I didn't see him until he spoke! Just leave him already!*

Yet, Neila's body obeyed her not.

"Can you walk?" she asked, feeling, as though her soul left her body, watching everything from afar.

"I believe so, yes," he answered.

Neila now grabbed his left arm and put it around her shoulders to help him up. Anxiety still ruled her mind and soul, making her feel, as if being electrocuted from the inside out. Her senses had gone haywire, making the walk as difficult as it could get. Neila grunted under his weight, but held him tight. Hissing and groaning, the man took a step forwards, then another.

The pair moved slowly. Even though Neila's apartment was close, it proved to be just farther away than they both would have liked. The single row of cobblestones also helped little to none. The spacing between the rocks made the path uncomfortable for most people, whose every third or so step ended on the grass in-betweens anyway.

Still feeling like a zombie, Neila suddenly missed a step and stumbled, almost tipping them both over. With a lot of grunting, hissing in pain, and groaning, they barely found their balance once more.

"Sorry," Neila panted.

"You needn't worry about it," he replied with a strained voice. "It is not like anything hurts. How much farther?"

"Just that building in front," she pointed at the house only around ten metres away.

They said nothing during the rest of the walk apart from his not-so-silent suffering. At the door, Neila helped the stranger lean against the wall while she opened the front door to the staircase. Luckily for them, she lived on the ground floor.

At the apartment door, Neila tried to open it, but dropped the keys. For some reason, her hands shook terribly. It took her three attempts to get the key into the lock.

When they finally could get inside and shut the door, Neila guided the man to the living room, then helped him lie down on the couch. While he struggled to a more comfortable position, she hurried out to the corridor again. After throwing off her jacket and shoes, Neila paused for a moment, breathing heavily.

"What the hell am I supposed to do now?" she whispered, horrified.

Chapter 2

Neila knew, she needed to pull herself together, but her throbbing heart and overwhelming anxiety made this difficult. In the overall silence, the unknown man's painful grunts served as a good reminder for her to concentrate on the problem at hand—an injury that demanded attention. Just when she was about to move, she heard a faint call.

Neila hurried inside the living room.

"Miss," the man said, with a hand still clutched around his wounded right side. "Could I trouble you for a glass of water, please?"

Neila blinked, but obeyed immediately. With a shaking hand, she then handed him a full glass. Watching the stranger drink, Neila had no idea about how to proceed. Anxiety rampaged inside her body freely, making her almost tremble.

After finishing the drink, her 'guest' gave a somewhat content exhalation.

"Thank you," he said, handing the empty glass back. "Would it be possible for you to attend to my wound as well? It would need cleaning, I think."

Neila's eyes widened at this while almost dropping the glass. In her upset state, she was unable to reply anything. A myriad of thoughts rushed through her mind, starting with the fact that she had no idea how to tend to a more serious wound. A simple cut was one thing, but, judging from the still streaking blood between his fingers, this was something graver.

How am I supposed to deal with THAT?! I don't even have proper clean water for that kind of washing! Neila thought, now getting desperate besides anxious. And even her cleanest towel would be far from sterile.

However, it's a start, isn't it? I cannot make it much worse, or? she asked herself, rooted to the spot. Then, the 'what-if-he-dies-here' thought made her brain freeze completely, yet everything still swirled inside like a tornado. Several other aspects came to mind, all good angles to approach the problem. Choosing just one of them became nigh impossible now.

The man flashed a puzzled frown, bringing Neila back to the present enough to do what he asked. Nodding, she hurried out again. After fetching some clean kitchen towels from a cabinet, a bucket of water, and rubber gloves, she sat down next to him on the couch. Taking a huge breath while putting on the gloves, she grabbed a towel with her right, then carefully pried his hand off the wound.

At first glance, the injury did not seem severe. The wound was a cut, but knowing more was impossible with his clothing stuck into it, forming a makeshift bandage.

"I need to take a closer look and your shirt is in the way," said Neila, now pulling on the fabric a little to try to get the shirt free from the trousers. However, he grabbed her hand with his bloody right, making her wince.

"It's easier if you cut that part out," the man said, letting her go.

"Are you serious?" Neila asked, dubious. When he just nodded, she shrugged and quickly fetched a pair of scissors.

After carefully cutting a quite large hole in the fabric, she gingerly removed the cloth. The man clenched his jaw in pain and sometimes growled. Neila tried to be careful, but she, too, knew, how truly painful a fresh wound could get when anything stuck into it.

Putting the bloody piece on a towel on the ground, Neila now could see the wound in full.

"By the gods!" she whispered with widened eyes, staring at the palm-sized, deep cut. Blood still leaked, so Neila put a dry towel just under it, then grabbed another, which she soaked in water.

Just as she was about to wash the dried blood from around the wound, she paused. With a shaking hand, she still felt unsure about this. Unclean water could easily cause an infection, especially in such a deep wound. Although, what she had now was clean enough, courtesy of the modern world. A proper boiling could never hurt, though.

"Is it that terrible?" asked the man, snapping Neila back to the present.

"Well, it's not pretty. You need to go to a hospital! This cut certainly needs stitches. A lot," she said, still unsure about how to continue.

"I will be fine," argued the man with a faint smile, although, his pale skin and painful grimace told otherwise. "I just need a little time to rest, that is all."

"You will need *a lot of* rest, believe me," she argued, and started to clean around the wound, making him clench his jaw once more. "I'm far from anything professional, but you're lucky that it hit your ribs instead of the insides. In any case, this will hurt, so if it helps, try to take your mind off it."

Neila washed the cloth in the bucket beside her. Before continuing, she caught his left hand clutching the armrest of the couch.

"Well, you can start with telling me your name, perhaps," she said, trying to occupy his mind with something else than the pain.

"I am called Loki."

Neila halted, glancing at him.

"You're joking, right? Loki?"

"Yes."

"As in the Norse god, Loki?" she asked, dubious.

"I *am* Loki, not *as in*. Is there a problem with this?"

The man looked truly curious and obviously did not understand Neila's reaction. Her chuckle even made him flash a frown, although, it quickly was distorted by pain again.

"No, no problem, at all," she said with a half-smile, not even looking up from washing the wound. "After all, who am I to judge? If you wanna be Loki, you can be Loki. Although, you don't look like a giant."

"I am not going to dignify that with an answer," he grunted, annoyed.

After finishing with as much as she dared to do, Neila leant back a little to examine the wound.

"You really need to go to a hospital. I am no medic by any means; you need a proper doctor to deal with this," she announced, now starting to scrape the man's hands clean. "But, the bleeding's stopped, at least," she noted, then put the last clean towel over the wound.

Instructing him to hold it in place, she hurried away to find a bandage. Coming back, Neila told him to sit up so she could wrap a gauze around his torso. With a withheld breath, he obeyed. Seeing her disagreeing grimace, he broke the momentary silence.

"As I said before, I will be fine after a little rest," Loki said faintly. "Can you give me sanctuary for the night?"

Neila blinked in surprise. Then, fear appeared in her eyes.

"Sanctuary? What the hell happened to you? Are you in trouble?" she asked, worried. Not for him, though, which fact Loki could surely see as well.

"It was a misunderstanding, nothing more," he replied calmly. "They would not find me here, believe me. I've rather meant that I would need a more comfortable place to rest than at the bottom of a tree."

"I ..." Neila started, but words fell off her mouth. Seeing the fear in her eyes, Loki continued soothingly.

"Everything is perfectly fine; you are safe. My wound is a result of an accident. A miscalculation, if you will."

"That's why your skin is purple around it?" Neila asked with an almost cynical tone. Loki gave a faint chuckle.

"No. That is because of the poison. It—" he answered, but she cut in.

"Poison?!" Neila cried out. From her look, it was obvious that she now worried for herself being poisoned.

"You need not worry, it will not affect you. You were smart enough to use gloves in the first place," he said, now laying his head back on the couch. Pain distorted his features again and he continued with a strained voice. "It makes the blood thicken almost instantaneously. As it would spread, the blood would literally clot inside your veins."

"What kind of poison is that?" Neila asked with widened eyes. Then, she flashed a frown, looking at the many bloody towels. "How did you bleed so much, then?"

"I've managed to ... force the bleeding, in a manner of speaking, so I could get rid of the poison," he replied, obviously simplifying things. Which now raised Neila's interest in the matter. But, before she could enquire about it, he asked for another cup of water.

Neila took off her gloves and cautiously put them on the water bucket, then hurried to the kitchen. Loki glanced after her, curious.

A very delicate situation started to form, Loki knew that much. Coming to Miðgarðr was not a thing anybody would do just because they had free time. It was not recommended in the higher-level realms by any means, and with good reason.

Yet, here he was, almost at the mercy of a mere human female. It would be lucky, if he would not get into any more trouble than he already was. Last time Loki tried to just talk to a human, they almost lynched him then and there for whatever reasons. Apparently, he had a very bad reputation.

Granted, that happened a few hundred of their years ago, but still ... he thought, now glancing up to the returning host again. While drinking, he could not dismiss one thought, though. *She was the only one, who responded to me. Perhaps, everything would be fine this time around,* Loki said to himself.

Watching her putting the gloves on again and packing up the bloody towels, there was something strange about her. What? Loki could not really guess. *There WAS a time when Miðgarðr was a part of the higher levels. Perhaps, the blood has finally returned.*

In any case, he finished the water slowly, then leant back again to rest. If he looked half as bad as he felt, the situation might be more complicated than he thought.

A cool hand on his forehead made him glance up again.

"You look too pale, and you're burning up. You must go to a hospital!" Neila declared, sitting down on his right again. However, this time, she sat as far from him as the couch allowed it, watching inquiringly.

"I do not like to repeat myself," muttered Loki at this. "It is because of the poison. It will be gone in a little while."

Neila now held both her hands up as a sign of surrendering.

"All right. But if you die, I will make sure to bring you or your ghost back for a proper scold."

Loki glanced at her, confused, making her flash a frown as well. He did not seem to understand the joke. Before she could open her mouth, he continued.

"That will not be necessary," Loki said with a faint smile. "However, I do not even know, whom to thank for this kindness."

"My name is Neila."

"It is a pleasure meeting you," he bowed his head a tad. "I'm eternally grateful."

"Well, don't get carried away, it was nothing," she dropped her gaze, blushing. "Anybody would've done the same, I'm sure."

"Since nobody else did, I would highly doubt that," he argued, musing. "In fact, that elderly woman only scolded me for being irresponsible and said that I should not have partied 'so hard that I couldn't handle it.'"

Neila made a well-yeah head bob.

A momentary silence fell on them, in which Loki tried to relax with closed eyes, while Neila glanced around, probably trying to figure out what to do. In the end, she broke the stillness.

"Well, I'll make some tea. Would you like some? Or something to eat?" she asked, standing up.

"No, thank you."

Neila left him in the living room. While waiting for the water to heat up, she could not wrap her head around the situation.

"Maybe I've gone mad, taking in an injured and obviously delusional stranger like that," she mumbled. "That must be it. No other reason exists to just jump into the middle of something dangerous."

Sighing, she finally started to calm down, feeling her 'reasonable mind' returning to her body.

"Maybe, it's a good thing. I've never seen or heard of a comic con war before," Neila continued her monologue.

Chapter 3

"Sooo ..." Neila entered the living room, carrying a pot of tea and a mug. Settling down at the table beside the couch, she glanced at Loki, who now opened his eyes again. "Should I ask or just roll with it?" she asked, measuring him from tip to toe.

After calming down a bit, Neila could properly examine the stranger. And she had to admit, Loki was a handsome man. Incredibly so, even if crazy to dress up like that. *He must be a huge fan,* Neila thought. However, this theory did not quite add up. Whenever she caught his eyes, a chill run down her spine.

Truth be told, Neila did not recognise the material of Loki's clothes. Not that this was a surprise, given her limited knowledge of fashion and fabrics. Yet, the overalls-like something on him seemed too strange for a mere comic book or movie fan.

And that hair, she mused further. *He must have spent an eternity in front of the mirror to get that anime hair!*

Neila liked Japanese animation, and always admired those incredible hairs in them. No real-life hair sculpting could get close to the animes, no matter how talented the dresser was.

Nevertheless, Loki somehow managed to create a masterpiece, looking incredibly good and real. His shoulder-long, black hair seemed to have a gravity-defying mind of its own, never flattened by things like the couch. This perfection was paired with the most striking dark-blue eyes Neila had ever seen, which just emphasised his skin tone. Interestingly enough, he did not just have the 'normal' Caucasian complexion. Something subtle lay in the background, almost literally under his skin, making him look ... different.

Could he really be ...? Neila now played with the thought. When his eyes met hers, though, she dropped her gaze immediately.

"Should you ask what?" Loki asked, confused by her enquiry.

Neila raised a questioning eyebrow in response, but let it slide. If he wanted to stay in character that much, it was pointless to struggle.

"Never mind," she fluttered a hand, then poured tea in her mug. Loki watched her, measuring, making Neila fiddle in her seat.

"I'll be out of your way soon," he grunted, earning a questioning look. "You can go on with your chores as you wish, no need for you to do anything further."

"Yeah, because I could sleep with a bleeding stranger in the next room," Neila scoffed. Seeing his confused look, she just rolled her eyes disbelievingly, then sipped her tea. Before he could say anything, she continued. "Besides, you need a fresh ... erm ... bandage in a few hours. So, you won't get rid of me that easily."

"As you wish," he agreed, leaning back his head and closing his eyes.

Neila sipped her tea quietly, sometimes glancing at Loki. Obviously, he tried to rest, if not sleep. If he were, indeed, running from something or someone, it would be unlikely that he would actually sleep with a stranger beside him.

Her musing thoughts must have been too loud, though, since Loki looked at her when she finished her tea.

"If you have questions, just ask."

Neila blinked in surprise, but then shrugged, deciding to take him up on the offer.

"So, how did the God of Lies end up in my living room?"

"The god of lies ...?" he echoed with a spark of anger in his eyes.

"Well, that is one of your ... erm ... titles?" she replied.

"What titles?" he snapped, sitting up straight. "I am but a mere citizen of Ásgarðr."

Neila raised an eyebrow dubiously at this. Loki spoke with a heavy Nordic accent, and pronounced Norse names like she had never heard before.

"Sooo, you are not Loki, God of Mischief, the giant who may or may not be an Aesir?"

Loki blinked, getting more upset, it seemed.

"First of all, 'Æsir' is plural. I am an Áss, as a male, and Ásynja is the female form."

"Ice ...?" she muttered, interrupting and trying to mimic the word, earning a disapproving glance.

"And secondly, is THIS what humans say about me now?"

"There are a lot of myths about you, yes, and I believe, most of them are not very flattering."

"As in what?" he demanded with flaring eyes, making Neila slid back with her chair, almost fearful. Seeing this, he tried to calm down. Pain distorted his features as he leant back again. Resting his left hand on the bandage towel, Loki took a few deep breaths.

After the air cooled down a little, Neila continued.

"Well, I only dabble in Norse mythology. As far as I know, you've killed Odin's favourite son, Baldur. Or, at least, played a big part in his death. Which then made you an enemy of the Aesir, and they chained you up with a snake above your head. It also caused the war between the Aesir and Vanir, and so on. But even before that, you've caused a lot of trouble, shape-shifting all the time and all that; had a ton of strange offspring, and so on. I like Fenrir the most, though, who will kill Odin and swallow the Sun when Ragnarök comes," said Neila, musing.

Loki seemed baffled by all of this.

"Ragnarǫk?" he echoed, utterly aghast.

Neila now flashed a questioning frown.

"Yeah, the end of Asgard and the nine realms? This is pretty common knowledge, I would say."

Seeing Loki's widened eyes, she now looked more suspicious than anything else.

"Where did you people get all this?" he then asked, making Neila confused.

"From the myths?" she answered dubiously. "It's in the Norse culture and all. Even today, soldiers want to get into Valhalla, and not Heaven."

Loki relaxed now, musing while holding his wound. Neila was just about to ask when he gave a disbelieving scoff.

"I honestly cannot believe, how little you have understood from everything we have ever told you," he swayed his head. "What else do you say? Do you know anything else about Ásgarðr?"

"Well, yeah," Neila said, unsure now. Suddenly, she turned rather defensive again. "To be fair, Loki ... I mean, YOU are a hero in several stories as well. Before that Baldur shenanigan, that is. You, in fact, have saved the Aesir several times with your ... uh ... different way of thinking," she continued with a somewhat forced smile.

"Well, that is at least something," he muttered grumpily. "It is a shame that it is unlikely to be true."

"But, you've said you are Loki, so ..."

"Should that mean anything?" he asked. "As I said, I am but a mere citizen, nothing more."

Neila raised a questioning eyebrow again.

"If that's true, then that's just sad," she announced sarcastically. "Loki's my favourite Norse god, but if you say you are nothing like that, then ..." she shrugged. Seeing his confusion, she finished, "that's just sad."

"Well, after such a colourful introduction," Loki grunted, insulted. "Who do YOU think I am? Or should be?"

"The God of Chaos, of course," Neila answered immediately. "The giant, who lives in Asgard, brother of Odin, or, in some interpretation, of Thor; father of—" she started again, but was interrupted.

"I am NONE of those things, nor would want to be!" he cried out, which turned into a painful hiss. Holding his side, Loki continued. "I have NO relation to any of the Æsir, least of all Þórr! How insulting!"

"Is being the brother or uncle to the Lord of Thunder insulting?" she asked, baffled.

"The lord of thunder?" Loki echoed, bursting into laughter. "Oh, that is absolutely hilarious! He would surely laugh until he cries," he continued, with laughter still in his voice. However, his wound reminded him of reality, prompting Loki to calm down and lean back. Still smiling, he then glanced at the stunned Neila, asking, "so, where do you think I am from?"

"Erm ..." she stammered, confused. Whatever she anticipated about him, it was surely not this. "Well, you're a giant, so a Jöt-something or other. I am not good with names. Giants have this Jöt-something name."

"Are you referring to Jǫtnar?"

It took Neila a second to decipher his strange pronunciation again.

"Yes! Thank you. So, in their world, that erm ..." she was looking for the word.

"Jǫtunheimr."

"Yes! One of the nine realms, connected by Yggdrasil—" she wanted to continue, but was interrupted again.

"Oh, no, not that tree again!" Loki sighed, annoyed. "Now, I think I understand, what happened."

Mumbling something inaudibly, he just slowly swayed his head.

"So, could you enlighten me, then?" Neila asked after a minute.

"I'm afraid, I lack the energy to explain everything right now, I am sorry," he said, wearily massaging the bridge of his nose. "I am in need of rest."

"Of course you are," echoed Neila sarcastically, earning a disapproving glance from Loki.

But, seeing the pain in his eyes made her drop the matter. Truth be told, he looked horrible. Sweat still beaded on his forehead, his eyes sparkled rather feverishly. Neila approached him now, placing a hand on his forehead.

"You are still running a fever. Would you like a pill or something?" she asked. Hearing the genuine worry in her voice made Loki flash a smile as he dropped his head back on the couch.

"Nothing, thank you. Just a cold cloth will suffice."

This time, Neila fetched a hand towel and rinsed it in the coldest water the tap could produce. Also, she filled his glass once more, just in case. After putting the glass down on the table in arm's length of Loki, she placed the cold towel on his forehead.

"Thank you kindly."

"Don't mention it," she smiled, then settled down on the other end of the couch again, eyeing him intensely.

Neila just could not decipher, what felt wrong with this whole situation. First, she thought, whoever this man wanted to be, he did not do his homework. In fact, she started talking about the Norse mythology in the hope of catching him in a lie. Or rather, getting proof that Loki knew as much about Æsir history as humanly possible. Neila would not be surprised, if he could even speak the language, as far as anybody knew, how. That accent surely was convincing.

But the complete denial of the myths caught Neila off guard. If somebody were just a fan of the recent movies, he would still know *some* things, if incorrectly. Catching a bad impersonator would have been easy, even for her.

However, Loki possessed the knowledge. At least, Neila believed so; and his reactions seemed genuine. Being a socially anxious person herself, she learnt to read others' body language. Knowing about micro-expressions and illustrators helped her a great deal, although, not nearly enough to have a 'normal' social life.

Humans tended to say the exact opposite than their tone and body language suggested, then denying the whole thing when confronted about it. And, of course, an anxious person such as Neila had no confidence to stand up against *that* kind of anger and 'bullying.'

On the other hand, she saw no controversy in Loki's behaviour and words. If this should not have been strange enough, she just could not get enough of his hair.

That is impossible! How the hell does it do that?! she asked herself, watching as he raised his head to drink a little. That magnificent anime hair just could not get flattened! No tuff 'misbehaved' or got out of line, they stood in their place perfectly, as if Nature itself ordered them to do so.

Loki seemed not to mind her inquiring glance, so Neila also leant back comfortably. Her thoughts wandered off as the excitement of the happenings started to fade away. Neila was never a late-night person, thus her eyes now stung. With her blinks becoming longer and longer, she drifted off from the present.

Only the smaller lamp was on by that time, although, Neila could not recall when she turned off the main one on the ceiling. She must have had, though, otherwise how could it have turned itself off? In any case, the soft yellow light almost allowed her mind to relax.

A faint noise made Neila jerk her head up, looking around.

"I am sorry to wake you," apologised Loki immediately. Apparently, he shifted position.

Neila flashed a frown.

"I wasn't sleeping," she said, sternly believing; she would never be able to actually fall asleep beside a stranger, who claimed to be one of the most controversial gods in all mythologies.

Loki just gave a well-all-right grimace, crossing his legs on the chair before the couch. Neila glanced at the chair, baffled. From her look, she obviously had no recollection, when did that get there. Seeing this, Loki raised an eyebrow, but explained not.

Confused, Neila looked at her watch. It was one in the morning. Somehow, more than two hours had just 'disappeared.'

"I ..." she stammered, glancing around, still confused. Then her eyes caught the bandage. "We need to change the bandage."

Loki tried to argue, but she was already up and on her way to fetch another clean towel.

Waiting patiently, Loki did not really want to correct her in any small thing. Neila was kind to him and obviously had a difficult time with the situation. Humans were easy enough to read, they could hide nothing of their thoughts or emotions.

Not even a thousand of their years was enough for them to learn that, apparently, he thought, watching her thud down beside him.

Listening to her instructions of sitting straight only half-heartedly, Loki mused further about his 'host.' Neila was a gem, he knew that much immediately. Not many would have the strength of soul to interact with him, an Áss. Several times now, he had visited Miðgarðr, and they almost always ended in insulted and hurt humans. Fear and insecurity still drove them to aggression, so seeing Neila actually helping him was a pleasant surprise.

Also, she seemed genuinely interested in him, and respected his wish to rest. Without that time, Loki would not be able to leave soon; and the misunderstanding had to be cleared as soon as possible. A tricky situation, it was—they wanted him caught and to pay, while Loki needed to get around them to do what was necessary to close the deal. After the unfortunate last time, though, the Áss felt unsure about how he could avoid them and get back to Ásgarðr.

A surprised inhale brought him back to the present. Loki glanced at Neila, who just sat there, staring at his side with widened eyes and mouth agape.

"What the hell?" she gasped, now leaning in closer to tap around the wound. "Impossible!"

The formerly almost gushing cut was nothing more than a cat scratch. A bad one, little bit infected, but basically superficial.

"I have told you that I only needed a little rest," Loki said. "The poison slowed the healing down. Otherwise, I would not have been in need of help at all."

Seeing her bewilderedness, he could not withhold a smile. As she looked up into his eyes, Loki saw the bafflement turning into realisation.

"You ..." Neila stammered.

The tornado of feelings inside her soul could be seen perfectly in her tricoloured eyes. Bafflement, fear, confusion, anxiety. Then, excitement emerged, catching Loki's interest.

"You *are* a god!" she cried out, turning him rather disappointed.

"Please do not call me that. None of us appreciate being called a god. It's ... demeaning and misleading."

"How did you do that?" Neila asked, obviously hearing nothing of what he had said.

Loki just gave an annoyed sigh.

Why do lower-levels always have to do this? he asked himself. Even some humans learnt to use the mind for healing, Loki knew as much. Although, his last information was a few hundred years old, so it might not be accurate anymore. Regardless, seeing Neila's almost childish excitement started to remind him, why higher-levels did not often go to disconnected worlds.

"Every higher-level person can do this, it is not as exciting as it may seem," he said with a sigh.

"Higher-level person?" she echoed, puzzled.

"Yes. The ones, who live in higher-level worlds."

Neila just blinked, making Loki sigh again.

Why do I always do this? he wondered, annoyed. *Look what happened last time! You cannot take pity on every such creature! All you have to do is leave,* he chided himself.

The sparkling tricolour gaze made the Áss change his mind, though, leaving him even more annoyed with himself. Truth be told, Loki had a fondness to such a complex soul, especially amidst the lower levels. Neila's begging expression now caused almost as much pain as his wound earlier.

This will end badly. Very badly, he thought with a grimace. *But, we will see, how much more evolved she is, if at all,* he mused further.

Taking a huge breath, Loki forced a smile and continued.

"You are familiar with the nine realms, if I am not mistaken," he began, earning an eager nod. "Well, forget about that tree business, it is as offensive as it is primitive. I cannot fathom, how you people could misunderstand such a simple metaphor."

Neila flashed a confused frown, making him get back on track.

"It is not important; much time has passed since then," he smiled. "The nine realms you speak of are, in fact, real worlds, ranked by the ninth, the most evolved ones among us. Ásgarðr is the seventh, and Miðgarðr is the third. The first three had lost the connection to the rest a long time ago. Hence humans know basically nothing about any of this," he explained with a shrug.

Neila blinked, looking equally excited, shocked, and confused. Unable to decide on a feeling, she remained silent while trying to comprehend.

Loki took another deep breath, but then his body tensed as his gaze looked into the distance. The Áss seemed to see or hear things that were not there; or sensed something in some way. In any case, he then jumped to his feet, startling Neila.

Baffled, Neila watched him close his eyes for a moment. Suddenly, she felt *something* around or inside herself, like a buzz or strange pressure in her mind. Looking to find what was happening, she dropped her mouth when she caught the cut-out spot mending itself on his side. The scratch looked even fainter now, not at all life threatening like before.

Then, Loki turned to her.

"I am terribly sorry, but I must take my leave now," the Áss said, bowing gracefully. "I am eternally grateful for your kind heart. Here,"—Loki handed a coin to Neila, who took it by reflex—"a little memento, to remember me by. I wish you all the best, and, perhaps, our paths will cross again."

Without further ado, he turned and headed for the terrace door on the left. Neila's jaw dropped again when he stepped through the door, as if it were not there at all. Then, literally in a blink of an eye, he vanished.

Neila felt too stunned to do anything, so she remained on the couch, staring at the terrace door. Then, her gaze wandered to the coin in her hand. For the first time in her life, every thought eluded her, leaving her mind blank. What was there to think after meeting a god ...?

Chapter 4

Neila opened the oven to determine whether the lasagne she made needed a little more time or not. Fortunately for her rumbling stomach, it looked perfect. After turning off the oven, she picked up a pot-holder and swiftly put the lasagne on top of the stove. On the counter, a plate and a pot of tea already awaited on the tray. After cutting a nice piece, Neila positioned it on the middle of the heated plate, then picked the tray up and headed for the living room.

Neila could hardly wait to dive back into the series she had just started yesterday. It was about Vikings, a historically-as-accurate-as-it-could-get show about how they almost managed to conquer England. Only one Saxon kingdom remained free, and Neila was keen to see, how it repelled attack after attack.

The series reminded her of Loki and the entire 'incident.' Since then, two perfectly uneventful weeks had elapsed, so Neila slowly returned to her normal life. Had it not been for the coin he left behind as a souvenir, she would certainly have questioned the whole thing ever happening. Even the need to replace several kitchen towels proved little, should Neila be going crazy.

Well, it's over now, and nothing remotely similar will happen, ever again. So, forget about him and concentrate on your upcoming story, Neila chided herself. However, since that incredible encounter, she could only think about Norse gods. She wanted to write something highlighting them, but until inspiration struck, Neila could only satisfy her thirst for Norse mythology with that series. Stepping into the living room, she suddenly spotted Loki standing at the table across the room, waiting.

"Good day, Neila," he greeted with a smile, scaring Neila half-dead with his appearance.

Neila jumped in her surprise, making everything on the tray clatter as she nearly dropped the whole thing. Loki stepped to her immediately, taking the tray as a precaution.

"Let me get that," he offered, still smiling. Not minding her upset state, he placed the tray on the table. Then, he stood with hands clasped behind his back, as if nothing particular was happening.

"DON'T EVER DO THAT AGAIN!" Neila cried out, finally finding her voice. Taking a few deeper breaths, she tried to calm down.

"I did not mean to startle you," Loki said almost apologetically. "Or bother you, if you're busy," he added, glancing at the still steaming lasagne.

"Oh, you're not bothering me," she replied with a wave of a hand.

"Please, continue, then," the Áss motioned at the table, earning a raised eyebrow as an answer. Even that simple gesture seemed so royal, as if he were graciously permitting her to dine in his presence.

Neila took a deep breath and stepped to the table by the window, overlooking the terrace.

"Then, don't mind if I do," she muttered with a small smile. "I'm kinda starving. Would you want some?" she offered, but got a shaking head as an answer.

"We generally avoid consuming things from lower-level worlds."

Puzzled, Neila sat down and started eating. Loki remained in the middle of the room, glancing around, as if measuring the place to himself.

Overall, it was a modest apartment, but Neila felt happy about it. Besides the medium-sized living room with a narrow terrace, only a tiny bedroom got place on top of the small bathroom and kitchen.

"It's probably nothing special compared to any higher-level apartment, but I like it," said Neila in between bites, answering to his inquiring glance.

"I'm sure," Loki said leisurely, turning to the bookshelf which was stuffed to the fullest. "You like to read, I see."

"Well, it's kind of an occupational hazard, since I'm a writer and all," she said.

"A good one, I'm sure."

Neila gave a somewhat cynical chuckle. Then, she thought it through while eating, eventually nodding. In truth, Neila believed this statement, if barely. After all, it was the reason she had changed her name to Neila.

At the beginning, she wrote under an alias. But about a year ago, she had enough of her given name and changed it to match the initials of her alias. The name Neila also belonged to her heroine, a mirror of herself in a different world.

"I can afford a place on my own, so yes, you might even say that."

"About what do you write?" Loki inquired further.

"Fantasy, what else?" she replied with a half-smile.

"Yes, of course. Your necklace and the Minoan labrys earrings should have made it obvious," he nodded, still looking over the books.

With his back to her, Loki missed her widened eyes in surprise. So far, only a few had caught the fact that Neila always wore a dragon medallion around her neck. Even less noted the Minoan labrys earrings, having no idea, what they were. Hence, a Norse deity mentioning a Cretan artefact struck her as peculiar.

"You know about Minoan culture?" Neila asked; her fork pausing midair for a second.

"Of course I do," replied Loki with a smile, settling down on the couch. "I have visited them, on several occasions. I've always found the Minoan people the most bearable of Ellas."

Neila just blinked, utterly stunned.

"How old are you?" she then asked, earning a somewhat disappointed glance.

"I'm not as ancient as you might think," he replied, irked. "The disconnected worlds experience time differently than the rest, that is all."

Noticing the excitement in Neila's eyes, Loki quickly continued before she swallowed the last bite.

"But, that is a conversation for another day," he said, obviously wanting to change the subject. When the tricolour eyes hardened, the Áss continued, "I am here, because I am in need of your help once more."

"Oh?" said Neila, now pouring tea into her mug.

"Indeed," he nodded, looking troubled. "Sadly, the ... How should I put it? Let us say, my *business partners* are still pursuing me. I know them well enough to say that they are angry now, in which case they need time to calm down and understand *my* perspective. In which time, I am best to avoid them. Since it's unlikely for them to come to Miðgarðr looking for me, I have decided that I will remain here."

"Say what now?" gasped Neila. "What the hell did you do?"

Loki seemed disappointed by the accusation; his voice turned tense when answering.

"As I mentioned before, it was a misunderstanding. We had an agreement, yet I have miscalculated the time I needed to deliver my part. That is all."

"Uh-huh," she nodded, sipping her tea. From her gaze, Neila was far from convinced. Which fact must have been obvious to Loki as well, because he continued, almost insulted.

"I must say, I do not appreciate to be treated as so," he said with a dangerous spark in his eyes.

"You're right, you're right," said Neila, holding a hand up defensively. "I'm sorry. It's just ... Well, it's difficult to imagine what a 'misunderstanding' would look like on a 'higher-level,' you know," she mused, making air quotes with a hand.

Loki rolled his eyes at this.

"If I am to stay here, you will have the chance to find out. However," he raised his voice, seeing Neila open her mouth to say something, "at the moment, I would like you to give me some guidelines about how to acquire what is necessary to live on today's Miðgarðr."

"Don't you know? I thought, a god knows much more than a mere human," she teased, although, when catching his sparking eyes, Neila quickly muttered an apology.

"I do not like to repeat myself, and I am not about to start this habit now," the Áss chided her. "I am aware of what you mean by 'god,' but if you ever encounter another higher-level person, they might not be as tolerant as I am. It *is* a great insult, after all. Forget that term and, if you must refer to us, do it by calling us a higher-level person."

"Got it, got it, I'm sorry," Neila mumbled into her mug, averting her gaze even after she finished her tea.

A momentary silence fell on the room, which Loki broke.

"Now, if you would be so kind and give me the information I requested."

"What do you have in mind, exactly?"

"Firstly, perhaps, what do I need to do to have a place to stay?"

Neila mused about it for a moment.

"Money?" she answered, looking unsure. "Money is everything. Dollars, specifically, if you plan to stay *here*. Then, you know, the usual, like a smartphone, laptop, or something of the sort," Neila mused aloud. "Oh, and papers, of course, for official identification, you know. You cannot have a bank account without any papers. So ..." she left the sentence unfinished, looking doubtful about Loki's capability to manage.

However, he just bobbed his head, as though all of these were most natural.

"Well, these should be easy enough," he muttered, thinking.

"Ya think?" asked Neila sarcastically.

"Humans are usually easy to deal with, so I would say so, yes," he said, disregarding her mockery. Before she could respond, he rose with the obvious intention of leaving.

"Wait!" Neila called out. "You cannot go outside, looking like this!" she said, gesturing at his outfit.

"What is wrong with my attire?" asked Loki, truly baffled. "It was never a problem beforehand."

"Well ..." Neila mumbled, glancing at him from tip to toe.

Where should I even start? she asked herself.

Truth be told, Loki looked magnificent. His demeanour radiated confidence, wearing that strange yet excellent overalls thing like a second skin. Perhaps it was, Neila would never be able to tell. The motives on his clothing looked unmistakably Nordic, but, perhaps, a tad too flashy with those metallic green shades. Despite Loki's impeccable taste, Neila doubted that anybody would take him seriously, looking like that.

Especially with that hair, she added. That anime style still looked marvellous, almost painfully perfect. However, to the average onlooker, Áss or no Áss, Loki would be taken as a wannabe dork, if not an actual crazy person.

A cough brought her back to the present. Loki was still waiting for an answer.

"Well, you look magnificent, of course. I truly like your style," she started with a smile. But then Neila bit her lower lip, signalling the following bad news. "However, nobody would take you seriously, especially with that anime hair and the way you talk."

"What is an 'anime hair?'" he asked, earning a dubious look.

"Really? THAT is your question?" she mocked. But, before he could say anything, she continued. "Never mind it. You just need to change. Get a nice suit, or something. I'd bet that it would look great on you."

"Would you escort me to a place where I could acquire one?"

"Absolutely not, I'm sorry," said Neila immediately. "I can barely deal with my own things; I cannot go to a fancy store to buy you stuff."

"Whatever is the matter?" Loki asked, catching her off guard with his genuine tone.

"I have social anxiety, a phobia, more like it. So I would really prefer, if you would leave me out of all this ... makeover," she said, dropping her gaze and blushing. "I'm happy to help, from *here*. But that's all."

Loki thought about this for a few moments, eyeing her so intensely, she started to fidget.

"Very well, I will not bother you with this, then," he said.

"It's no bother, it's just that ..." Neila stammered. "I just ... I really cannot ... I'm not good with other people, and I would die of embarrassment."

"I understand," he nodded. "Thank you for your help, and I will be back soon, I believe."

"Well, all right. Good luck," she said, but then quickly added, "but don't just pop-up anywhere out of thin air! People would not react to that very well, believe me. And you don't want THAT kind of attention."

"People would be just fine. *Humans* would not," he corrected her with a cynical half-smile, then disappeared, as if never existed.

Neila gave an agitated sigh.

"Now THIS is more like the Loki I've been expecting," she muttered under her breath, picking the tray up and heading for the kitchen. "I wonder, how he will get everything done, though."

Chapter 5

Neila stood before a display window, looking at the things inside without any real interest. Needing to calm down after a meeting, she walked around in the sunshine, window shopping. Sometimes she halted before one to look over some jewellery or something or other, never actually venturing inside any store. At the moment, there was no need for her to buy anything, or perhaps a salad and some other ingredients for her next meals.

Being outside among people would bother Neila greatly, if not for her noise-cancelling headphones. These truly were life-saving. Without them, the many noises overwhelmed her senses. Everything caught her attention—a car, music from a store, the closeness of other pedestrians as they walked by, the numerous conversations all around, the sweet and incredibly potent scents when walking by a cosmetic store, and so on. Not even a beautifully sunny day such as that afternoon could make Neila ease up. With darting eyes, she kept note of everything that happened all around.

The headphones helped her to remain focused and fairly calm. So now, looking at a particularly expensive pair of gold earrings, Neila could rethink everything that happened at the meeting. Did she say something silly? Did she make a fool of herself or embarrassed someone else by mistake? Was she clear enough for them to understand her side? Did SHE understand everything properly? What could they mean with that thing or the other?

The line of questions never seemed to cease.

"I thought, you couldn't get outside today, yet here you are," a voice suddenly broke into Neila's mind, making her jump and turn around frantically. Loki stood just behind her, smiling mischievously.

Neila took off her headphones.

"Gods, Loki! Are you trying to give me a heart attack?" she cried out, panting. Looking around to see how much attention they raised, Neila fiddled with her purse to put the headphones away.

"Apparently, you just wanted to avoid *my* company," he noted, watching her nervously darting eyes. "What brings you outside, then?"

"I had a meeting with my editor," she replied with an almost desperate voice. Neila only glanced at Loki briefly while speaking, looking mostly around and watching the pedestrians.

"Oh?"

"We have this deal, you see," Neila continued, gesticulating nervously. "Since she knows about my ..."—her voice dropped to a whisper, as though the matter was somewhat shameful—"*situation*, we never plan meetings. Whenever she wants to talk to me and has the time, she calls me and I cannot wiggle out of answering. So, here I am, getting a heart attack from you," Neila finished, but when looking at Loki, she halted and measured him from top to bottom. "You look different. What happened?"

The Áss almost blended in with the people on the street. The simple black trousers and the deep blue, long-sleeved shirt, paired with black shoes gave him a very simple yet elegant presence. Against the bright sunlight, he somehow got a very stylish pair of sunglasses. Even his hair looked more conventional, if still magnificent. Also, his skin seemed to have lost that strange glow or sparkle. A tasteful gold watch on his left wrist made his appearance whole.

Every piece of clothing was well made, from good materials, even Neila could see that. Overall, Loki appeared simple and tasteful, yet obviously luxurious.

"After I looked around, I've put together this outfit to blend in," he said so leisurely, as if this would be just another simple thing in his life. "However, since you're here anyway, would you accompany me for a late lunch?"

Neila raised both her eyebrows in surprise at this.

"I thought, you fancy-people try to avoid consuming anything on primitive worlds," she teased, earning a tiny huff that could have been a chuckle.

"Well, yes. But I need to get accustomed to it, don't I? So, would you?" he asked, motioning at the street.

"I'm not hungry, since I ate just a couple of hours ago. But you can go wherever you wish," she replied with a nervous smile, obviously trying to get out of the situation. However, Loki allowed her not.

"I am sure, there will be something you might enjoy, like tea? I've heard, there is a very nice café just around the corner."

Not even waiting for an answer, Loki started forwards, as though knowing that she would follow. Neila did so, but seemed less than happy about this whole situation. At the café, he let Neila choose a spot at one of the outside tables.

A waitress stepped to them right away, asking whether they needed the menu. However, she spoke only to Loki, sometimes almost giggling. Even after giving out the menus, she stayed close, always lurking around and trying to seem busy.

Neila watched the twenty-something woman dubiously. Currently, they sat in a fairly fancy café, with several good-looking business-men and -women everywhere. Regardless, nobody else made the waitress behave like a schoolgirl around her crush, only Loki.

"Is something the matter?" Loki asked. Even through the shades, his gaze remained intense.

"Oh, no," Neila replied, only pretending to read the menu. Seeing the steep prices made her stomach twist about payment. Being a 'successful writer' mostly meant that she could afford a low-middle-class lifestyle. Barely; and only thanks to her ability to plan a strict budget.

"Then what's wrong?" Loki asked further, putting the menu down.

"Oh, nothing. I just find it very interesting, how our waitress behaves like a fourteen-year-old girl around you, when there are several very good looking gentlemen all around, who would love to have the same attention from her, I'm sure," she said with a mocking smile, eyeing somebody at another table.

"It is a typical human reaction towards a higher-level person, especially us. This is why we need to shape-shift when dealing with them. Otherwise, they just gawk at us, as if we were some kind of spectacle, hearing only half of what we say, at best."

Loki seemed somewhat bothered by this fact, but not so much to be taken seriously. In a sense, he must have liked this 'effect,' otherwise he would not flash a charming smile at the waitress every time she passed by.

Neila rolled her eyes at this, asking for some kind of fancy-named black tea blend when they ordered.

"It's not just her, though. A lot of people watched you while we were walking here," she noted.

Just at the next table, she spotted a pair of men glancing at Loki with a mixture of confusion and awe, as though he were a celebrity. Seeing them, Neila gave a scoff.

"Even now, they just ... happen to give you attention."

"It is actually only a few," the Áss replied, flashing a half-smile at the pair of men. "Last time, around your fifteenth century or so, I could not walk anywhere in peace. Like moths to a flame," he mused. "Quite a lot has changed since then, and I don't mean the industrial revolution."

"How do you even know about that?" Neila asked, baffled. "Also, you've lost your accent and talk almost ... normally now. How?"

Loki gave a small laugh, then thanked the waitress as she brought their drinks. With flushed cheeks, she hurried away, looking everywhere but at him.

Neila just swayed her head, mumbling 'unbelievable' under her breath. Loki spoke further.

"Such things come easy to us. Learning a primitive language like anything on Miðgarðr takes almost no time. I've picked modern English up while I was waiting for somebody to finally hear me when I got injured."

Neila dropped her mouth.

"That is incredible!" she gasped. Then, another thought made her flash a confused frown. "Wait a minute. 'Waiting for somebody to hear me?' What do you mean by that? Wasn't there some old lady who scolded at you?"

Loki had just opened his mouth to answer when the waitress returned with his fresh salad.

"I didn't imagine you to be a vegetarian, though," teased Neila, measuring the fair amount of good-looking salad.

"I am not, but this was the only acceptable choice on their menu," replied the Áss, making Neila whisper another disbelieving wow under her breath.

While he ate, she sipped her tea silently. However, Loki never seemed to miss a glance or flinch. As the café filled, Neila started to get more and more agitated. It was late in the afternoon; a lot of people had just finished their day and wanted something to eat or drink before heading home.

Suddenly, Neila turned to him.

"How did you find me, by the way?"

Loki swallowed first, then used a napkin before answering.

"I didn't find you at your home, so I followed your essence here."

"My what?" she asked with widened eyes.

"Your essence," he echoed. "Would you like something else? A dessert, perhaps?"

"What is an 'essence?'" Neila wanted to know, not minding the questions.

"To put it simply, everything that you are. Your entire being."

"You mean, my soul?"

"No," he shook his head, then took another bite. Yet, since he talked only with a clear mouth, Neila got annoyed by the delay.

"An essence has a wider meaning. It is your thoughts, your feelings, your logic. Everything that makes you ... you. The patterns of your thoughts and feelings, the past and present, everything that you have lived through, wished for, or dreamed of. Are you sure, you don't want anything else?"

Neila just blinked, obviously puzzled.

"How can you feel something like that? Or, what does it feel like?"

"It's difficult to describe, to be honest," he replied, taking a sip from his water. "Perhaps, it's something like a breeze, when you feel the wind on your skin. Yet not just the physical reaction of your skin, but the sensation of your mind."

"Wow," Neila swayed her head. "I had no idea that a wind can cause a sensation in one's mind."

"Of course you had," argued Loki with a half-smile. When he continued, his tone and smile turned into a fairly cynical one. "Why do you think, you are 'overly sensitive' and need those headphones? Your whole mind buzzes just from sitting there. I know, I sense it."

That intense blue gaze now caught hers and did not let go, making Neila ashen. Then, his features became smooth once more as he returned to his salad.

"What?!" she burst out, earning a questioning look.

But, before she could say anything else, the waitress had returned, asking about whether they were satisfied with everything. Loki thanked her for the wonderful service and food, then asked for the check.

"Wait a minute," Neila stammered at this. "How the hell did you manage to get money so fast?"

The waitress approached again, babbling about something while Loki paid. Standing up, he motioned Neila to follow, and headed for the street again.

"You are not very focused, you know that, right?" he teased while walking. "Let's get you back home, so you can calm down and listen."

Without further ado, he grabbed her arm and made them both disappear into thin air. In the next moment, they stood on the tiny terrace of Neila's apartment. Loki merely passed through the door like before, then opened it from the inside.

"Welcome home," he motioned her inside with a half-smile, playing the host. But Neila did not move a muscle, just stared at him, completely stunned.

"What the ..." she exclaimed. "You can't just ...! What the hell?!"

Loki rolled his eyes then walked away and sat down on the couch. A moment later, Neila managed to find the strength to join him inside.

"Are you completely mad?!" she snapped. "You can't do stuff like that in the middle of the street! What if somebody saw us?!"

"Quite a few did, I would say," he said calmly. "Nobody cares, believe me."

"The hell they don't!" she argued further, becoming truly angry. "Perhaps they don't in some higher-level world, but here, humans are idiots! They DO care, believe me. Oh, gods, what the hell did you do ...?" she gasped, starting to pace around the room.

"Relax, please, everything will be fine," the Áss said leisurely.

"How could you possibly know?!" Neila cried out, turning to him, then inhaled deeply and massaged her forehead. "God or no god, you are an idiot to think that you can get away with such a thing! You HAVE TO stop, if you don't want to end up in a military lab somewhere!"

Neila truly looked panicky, so Loki intervened. Standing up, he grabbed Neila's arms to make her stand still. Wincing, Neila squirmed and tried to break free, yet did not seem to realise his touch too much.

Interesting, Loki thought, letting her go.

Only a few humans could bare the touch of an Áss; the difference between their levels being far too big. Without caution, the amount of energy an Ásgarðrian unconsciously channelled into a human could easily be lethal to the latter. Shape-shifting allowed them to avoid this issue, yet it also gave root to the many misconception about their kind.

On the other hand, Neila could handle his closeness almost effortlessly from the start. Oblivious to the situation, she broke his hold as a reflexive response to *any* touch. For whatever reason, the turmoil and imagined consequences of Loki's actions could drive Neila to panic, while she seemingly could not care less about standing right next to him.

To prevent Neila from reaching the breaking point, Loki grabbed her arm again and gently but firmly guided her to sit on the couch. A tiny jolt of his essence finally snapped her out of spiralling. Now, Neila glanced at him, ready to listen.

"I know, everything will be fine, because what makes humans drawn to us, also makes them disoriented," he explained calmly. "Even if a lot of people saw us disappear, afterwards, they would think it to be just a trick of their minds, blaming tiredness or something or other."

"You still need to stop doing that," Neila grunted, calmer now. "Sooner or later, your luck will run out. Just, be careful."

"I will be," he nodded.

Neila took a deep breath.

"And next time," she continued, "warn me or something, too!"

Loki nodded again, this time with a half-smile.

A momentary silence fell on the room, which Neila broke, inhaling deeply.

"Well, since I'm home, I will go change," she announced, standing up. Then, after a short evaluation, she added, "it might be a tad early, but I will take a shower as well."

"Go ahead," said Loki, but then his phone rang, so he answered.

Neila's eyes widened in surprised when hearing the foreign language.

"Was that ... Swedish, or something else Nordic?" she asked when the call was over.

"You have a good ear, yes. I have to go now, but will be back soon. Until then," he said as a goodbye, then vanished again.

"I'll never get used to that," Neila sighed, then shrugged and headed for the bathroom.

Chapter 6

Loki had spent three days to get everything in order. In that time, he forewent sleep to make phone calls, pay invoices, and give 'charity' to certain organisations, so he would have everything ready as soon as possible. When he finally made it back to Neila's, she almost dropped the teapot when spotting him in the living room.

"Can't you sense my arrival?" asked the Áss, puzzled.

"Do I look like I do?!" she snapped. "Why can't you use the door like a normal person?"

Crossing his arms, Loki slightly tilted his head.

"Why would the doorbell make any difference? You would jump just as much and would not want to even come to the door, let alone open it."

Neila's eyes widened at this, since it was an accurate description of the hypothetical situation. Loki knew that perfectly, since he had spent just enough time with her to understand her essence. A lot still hid in thick fog, though, which fact made her that much more interesting. Usually, humans were as easy to 'read' as opening a book. The few exceptions kept Loki's hope alive for Miðgarðr's returning to the connected worlds.

Even for Ásgarðr, a long time had passed since the disconnection of the third. Yet, the immense amount of unique energies it possessed remained, making Miðgarðr the most valuable in this regard inside the node. Wanting to harvest those energies was the main reason, a few sevenths tried to do something about the situation. Surely, the rewards would outweigh whatever complication it might cause, those few believed.

Therefore, Loki and the others visited Miðgarðr from time to time, trying to find the Missing Link, who would start the reconnection process. However, every such effort was in vain so far. No matter who tried, they all failed.

Well, not failed exactly, just left confusing knowledge behind, which the humans then twisted into those myths they are still so fond of, Loki thought bitterly.

"Hey!" Neila cried out, snapping her fingers before him. "Are you okay?"

"Yes, yes, I'm perfectly fine," stammered Loki. "Did you say something?"

"Not really, but you don't look so good. Are you sure, you're all right?"

Her genuine worry made Loki smile.

"Yes. I just haven't slept in the passing days, hence I'm tired."

"Well, next time, please leave a note or something before you disappear for days," she growled grumpily. "'See you soon' doesn't mean three days. I have better things to do than wait for you, you know. You always scare me to death when you just pop up out of nowhere! I don't know, how much longer I can take this," she swayed her head, then settled down on the couch, putting the pot on the little table beside it.

"I said, I'm sorry," replied the Áss almost apologetically, sitting down as well. "Just learn to sense my coming."

"Well, I'm learning not to have a heart attack, but one of these days …" she mocked, pulling her legs up to a sideways position.

Loki just rolled his eyes.

"What were you doing, anyway?" asked Neila, changing the subject.

"Everything that is necessary for a life here."

"Really?" she scoffed, dubious. "In four days, you have papers and all that?"

"Why is that so surprising?"

"It's not surprising, it's impossible," she mused aloud. "But, I wanted to ask before you disappeared: how on Earth did you get money only after a couple of hours? Not to mention shop for clothes, buy a phone, and only the gods know what else."

Loki opened his mouth, but she quickly continued.

"Higher-persons know what else … sorry, sorry," she babbled with a hand in the air. "It's an expression, I don't mean you, per se. You know that, right?"

"I do, but it is still offensive. Not unlike calling a woman a bitch, or something similar."

"Wait, are you saying that you guys are more powerful than a god?"

Loki took a deep breath at this, then closed his eyes for a little while as he continued.

"We're getting off-topic again. You were asking about my doings?" he changed the subject back, so Neila motioned him to continue. "To answer your inquiry about money, I sold a few things to some people. As it turns out, Ásgarðrian trinkets are very valuable, and they couldn't get their greedy hands on them soon enough."

"That's fine, but what about the authorities and banks? They can produce papers faster just because you flutter your eyelashes at them?"

"Something of the sort," he said with a well-yeah head bob. "Humans always did anything for something valuable. Just give them enough and they will bring down the Moon, if you want it."

"Yeah, easy for you to say," she muttered sarcastically.

"Didn't you sell the coin I left you?" Loki wanted to know now, almost sounding stunned.

"Why would I do that?" she asked with a frown. "I don't need it, I'm fine. My human-problem is not about money, you know that."

The Áss gave an all-right nod while she poured tea for herself.

"Truth be told, it's less about the money and more about my charming personality," he announced, earning a snort as an answer. This, however, made him raise a questioning eyebrow. "You disagree?"

"Oh, not at all," Neila muttered into her mug. "So, tell me this, then: why do you guys even come here, when Midgard is so low-level compared to you?"

"Because it still has the most energies of the seven realms that we know. They are incredibly valuable, and, according to our legends, even humans knew how to handle them at one point."

"Say what now?" she gasped, almost missing a gulp. "We had magic? What legends? What happened, then? When was this?" she bombarded him with questions.

"You know," he snorted, "for a composed writer, you are all over the place."

"Wow, that was modern."

Loki rolled his eyes in irritation, but then started to explain.

"According to Ásgarðrian history, when the node formed and joined the nine realms together, they all were connected. The one, who later became the highest, sorted the worlds and formed the order."

Neila listened with widened eyes, grabbing her mug like a child their toy.

"Over time, this hierarchy changed, developing our current one. The current first used to be the fourth; Miðgarðr used to be the sixth, just under Ásgarðr. We, as far as we know, were always the seventh. Then, the first and second broke off, and when it became the third, Miðgarðr did, too. Nobody knows with certainty, what had caused all of this, why it even happens, or how."

"Don't you have records of these times?" Neila cut in, still mesmerised.

"We do," Loki sighed. "But just a few and they only state the facts, not the reasons. Also, Miðgarðr's disconnection, so far the last, happened long ago. None of us, not even the oldest ones, remember the times when Miðgarðr was still attached to the rest. But the stories always say, those were the golden days. Everybody could visit without any kind of trouble and benefit from the abundance of energies there."

"So, what's stopping you from coming down here to have a little R&R?" asked Neila, puzzled.

"There is an unwritten rule among the higher levels, that one should not visit the disconnected worlds. We believe that an ascension or descension is a natural phenomenon, a part of the planet's and their inhabitants' life cycle. No higher-level person should mess with this natural order by trying to help or intervene. This is why we always must be careful when we visit."

"Well, we both know that you couldn't manage to keep it. So, who visited?" Neila wanted to know.

"I cannot speak for the other realms. From the seventh, most of the visitors were of the Æsir. The other nations are still not very interested in getting back a valuable energy source, it seems," Loki said, almost sounding sad.

"So, how do *you* want to reconnect Midgard?"

The Áss took a deep breath.

"I have … some ideas. But, in truth, I have no idea how humans should behave on a higher level. Based on what I've seen, I can't fathom, how they could ever hold a higher rank. What I see and experience now is just madness."

"No arguments from me there," Neila agreed grumpily. After a moment of silence, she asked, "so, what are the higher-level worlds? Who are the ninth ones? They must be very …" she halted, looking for the word. "I have no idea, what sort they might be. You are a … well, *that* word, in our eyes, so what über-powered creatures are at the top?"

Loki just blinked at first, trying to understand the question.

"Sadly, I cannot tell you much about the eighths and ninths. Nothing, more like it."

"How come? Are you not allowed to speak about them?"

"Nothing of the sort," he shook his head. "It is simply because we are not allowed there. Nobody can go to a higher level unless they earn it by finding the path. Accidents notwithstanding, of course. But, they might be as different to us, than I am to you."

"Really? Wow!" gasped Neila. "So what about the rest, then?"

"Well, from what I know about the sixth, there is quite a … jump, so to speak, between them and us. Óðinn always said, we are the gatekeepers between, and I quote, 'those who handle true power and the rest.'"

"Wow," she exhaled. "*You* can be condescending as well, and I imagined the Allfather to be even more so, but … Wow!"

"All right, we need to establish some ground rules," Loki announced, irritated. "Forget every name, word, or 'title' about us. If you would call Óðinn that …" he halted, looking for a good metaphor, but then just scratched his chin. "To be honest, I have no idea what would happen, but trust me, you most certainly don't want that kind trouble." After a moment, he added, "on the other hand, it might be fun to find out."

The mischievous light in his eyes made Neila wiggle uncomfortably, and she quickly changed the subject back.

"So, are Vanaheim, Jötunheim, and all the others I can't remember now, are these the worlds you are talking about?"

"What? No, of course not!" snapped the Áss. "This is one of the misunderstandings I cannot even begin to understand. These are simply various parts of Ásgarðr, our world, much like your continents and countries. Even the name 'giant' is idiotic. Do I look like a *giant* to you?"

Loki either started to lose his temper, or tiredness just got the best of him to talk in that manner. In any case, Neila's eyes widened, hearing his tone.

"Well, no," she admitted, dismissing the quite loud and enthusiastic 'thank you!' from him. "However, I have never seen a real giant either," she admitted, earning a dismissing wave from the other.

"Is Odin even the leader, then?" she wanted to know.

"Well, yes, he is. But how you humans describe our ... lives, or deeds, or even the relations ... Is simply and completely wrong!"

"I'm starting to take offence in how you put me together with 'these humans,'" Neila growled.

"Well, now you know, then, how it feels."

"I'm sorry, I just don't know," she apologised. "I mean, how could I?"

"Think, maybe?" he snapped, mocking. "Seriously, I have looked up these myths, and they are as confusing as nauseating. Especially the parts about me. Having spawn an eight-legged horse? *Spawn?!* I have never, ever turned into a mare!" he cried out, now sounding truly upset, which slowly turned into anger.

Loki's eyes sparked; the air around him seemed to boil, making Neila lean away as much as the couch allowed it.

"But even if I had, I would never, EVER, allow a STALLION to do anything to me! No higher-level would do anything like that to a lower-levelled creature, believe me! The sheer audacity! Just because you humans are incapable of envisioning anything else, THIS still takes the cake, as they say."

Suddenly, Loki jumped up, and started to pace around the little room. Apparently, they ventured into very dangerous waters. Neila even imagined seeing the air coiling up around Loki as he spoke further, sending those 'coils' away with his wide gesticulations. When one hit her, she felt, as if something would want to burst her from the inside.

"I, personally, have never, ever taken a wife, and NONE of us would engage in the colourful relations you idiots imagine. Why would we?! But this is nothing compared to any kind of ... spawn, as these myths might say. No Ásgarðrian has charmed any human woman, believe me. EVER! It's insanely insulting, you know. It is, as though YOU would visit the zoo, then get into a cage with any animal, bearing their offspring. It would not even work, we are too different! So infuriating!"

A stronger coil hit Neila now, making her feel burnt on that part. This was the moment, she decided to try to calm Loki down. Acting instinctively, Neila jumped up and stepped to him, grabbing his swinging hands, then held them in front of herself. Immediately, she felt like getting electrocuted—her mind buzzed like an overloaded circuit, and her body trembled from within, with vibrating bones.

Drawing a deep breath, Neila tried to get it under control and focus on Loki. Looking deeply into his eyes, Neila wanted to sound as calm as she could muster in the current situation.

"I understand, believe me, Loki, I do," she started, trying to grab his attention. "It is stupid, and incredibly primitive. I'm sorry to anger you, truly."

Something she said did the trick, because he halted, then closed his eyes to calm down. In a second, everything had returned to normal. Opening his eyes, he looked as composed as ever.

"I'm sorry, and thank you. I don't know, what came over me," he apologised, clasping her hands for just a moment, then let them go and stepped back.

"It's all right," Neila smiled. However, even after what had happened, she could not hold herself back from asking, "but, if all of this is wrong, where did the legends come from? Not even a human makes things up like a giant wolf or eight-legged horse."

A spark of anger flickered in his deep-blue eyes again, but vanished just as quickly.

"Well, yes. And I *might* even have had something to do with that," he admitted bitterly.

"How come?" asked Neila, sitting down on the couch.

"Well," he began, folding his arms while looking out the window. "I *did* save a few unfortunate creatures who were caught by a path and were brought to other realms."

"That can happen?" gasped Neila.

"Yes," Loki nodded. "In any given node, all worlds stay connected at all times, but these are small paths compared to what we call real Connections. These form naturally and are usually very difficult, if not impossible, to find, because of how weak they are. Also, they change position constantly. Sometimes, something or someone may venture into one by mistake, or caught by it when it forms, and is sent to another world."

"So, you're telling me now that all those mythical creatures actually exist?" Neila wanted to know. "There WERE griffins, dragons, and so on, here on Earth?"

"Yes and no," Loki replied. "Some are real, like griffins, some were just the active imagination of humans, who did not understand. These paths are dangerous, and don't work properly, so to speak. Therefore, accidents *can* occur, such as two horses merging together as they both were picked up at the same time."

Neila just blinked, confused. Seeing this, Loki settled down beside her again, explaining further.

"You see, such a connection can technically form between any two worlds. So, in theory, a human may wander directly into Ásgarðr. Well, this rare case happened with those creatures your myths lovingly call my offspring."

"Sooo, what happened, exactly?"

"I came across those poor things and healed them. Well, two of them, the ... what do you call it? That giant serpent?"

"Eh," Neila exhaled. "Don't know, sorry. I'm not good with names, especially not Nordic names."

"Well, doesn't matter. In any case, I couldn't separate the horses, so I rather created a functioning one than kill both. I did the same with the wolf. Then I sent them back to Miðgarðr. Somebody could have seen me with them during their release, I suppose, and then concocted those stories."

"What about the snake, then?"

"That was actually Þórr, not me."

"WHAT?!" Neila cried out. "But the myths say that it will kill Thor when Ragnarök comes. And, that they fought, and that Thor always tries to catch it from the seas, and—" she listed, but Loki cut in, holding a hand up.

"What did I just tell you about those myths? Þórr would do no such thing, believe me. He DID save a poor creature, just like I did, which, for some reason, grew bigger during the process. I'm not sure, why the wolf did the same," he mused upon this fact for a moment, then shrugged. "Anyway, he told us later that, when he wanted to release him back to a sea, it became violent for some reason, so something of a struggle happened there. Would that be enough for some colourful tale, I wonder?" he asked sarcastically, glancing at Neila expectedly, who just huffed as an answer, making him smile.

"All right," Neila said, thinking. "So, what about the part when Asgard is basically a flying disc city? Or about the Bifröst?"

"Ugh, how you say those names is nauseating," grimaced Loki.

"Well, sorry, I speak no Nordic language."

"Perhaps, you should. It bears the closest resemblance to our language, you know," he mentioned casually.

"We'll get back to that, but I want to know about the flying city part."

"Last question for now," said Loki, tired and rubbing his eyes. "Týr might manage to stay awake for five days, I cannot. I need rest."

"Fine. But just this one, please?" she begged with big puppy eyes.

"Ásgarðr is truly a flying city, hovering above the lands."

"Why?"

"Because our Bifröst generates incredible earthquakes, and this is the safest way to operate it," said the Áss with a huge inhale. "Now, will you let me rest?"

"Of course. I'll make up the couch for you," answered Neila with a smile.

Loki twisted his mouth, but said nothing.

Chapter 7

"Good morning, Sunshine!" Neila greeted Loki with a wide smile.

The Áss had just woken up, joining her at the table by the window.

"I must say," she continued cheerfully, "when you say you need sleep, you mean it. Not even a pack of dogs could wake you. I know, since one passed by."

Loki minded not the teasing, being lost in thought. Neila ate her breakfast in silence for a minute, eyeing the other inquiringly.

"Boy, you must be magic!" she jested, earning a questioning look. "Can anything flatten that hair? Or wrinkle your clothes?"

Since he still remained silent, Neila flashed a frown.

"Is something the matter?" she asked.

"No, nothing. I'm just not a morning person," he finally said, earning a smile.

"Well, do you want something to eat? I have a lot of teas as well."

"So I have noticed."

"So? What'll it be?"

"I think, I'll eat something later. I'm ought to go now anyway; I have some business to attend to."

"Don't you want to at least shower?" asked Neila dubiously. "Or to change?"

Loki rolled his eyes, then closed them for a moment. Suddenly, his clothes turned to different colours on their own. The Áss now wore light brown trousers with a long-sleeved black shirt. The shoes and watch stayed the same, as far as Neila could tell in her bafflement.

"Satisfied?" he asked, mocking. After Neila just made a not-bad head bob, he vanished.

"Well," she exhaled, rising to clear the table. "I just hope, he won't scare me to death when he appears again."

Fortune left her side, though. Loki returned that very day, and in an even worse circumstance than ever before.

Neila had a productive day behind her. Since the muse finally struck her, she spent the day working. After a satisfying amount of writing, Neila decided that she had earned a nice bath. It was Sunday as well, so a bath was perfect for washing her hair.

Despite the smallness of the apartment, it came with a comfortably big tub. Neila could submerge into the water quite nicely, letting go all the stress the last days had accumulated, completely forgetting about Loki and his ability to appear without the slightest warning.

Usually, Neila liked a little air bathing after a shower or bath, meaning that she remained naked. After drying her long brown hair, she put some lotion on, then headed back to the living room with the medium-sized towel in her hands. Stepping inside, Neila suddenly found herself in front of Loki, making her jump.

While trying to cover herself with the too-small towel, Neila turned deep red.

"WHAT THE HELL are you doing again?!" she cried out in a higher pitch than usual, obviously mortified. "Get out!"

"I don't understand," replied Loki, now looking at her, puzzled. That measuring gaze just made Neila turn even deeper red whilst slowly backing to the door.

"Out, until I am decent!" she snapped.

"Then do it quickly," said the Áss. Obviously unbothered by the situation, he stayed put.

"OUT!!!" Neila cried out, which finally did the trick.

Loki turned away, so Neila slipped into the adjacent room with the little dignity she still had left. The Áss remained in the living-room, though, talking to her through the walls.

"Get dressed quickly, please, I need you to come with me," he announced.

"What the hell for?!" she snapped while trying to find underwear. However, her hands shook so terribly, she dropped everything she tried to grab. "This is fucking humiliating!" she whispered. "How can I even look him in the eye after this?"

"The realtor finally called. He has found a few apartments for me, and I want you to come and see them."

"What?" she mumbled under her breath, still trying to calm herself down enough to be able to dress. "That doesn't make any fucking sense!"

Neila had managed to put on some outdoor clothes. The simple jeans and a long-sleeved black blouse made her comfortable enough once more. With her jacket, she should not even be cold.

Once finished, Neila stumbled back into the living room. Grabbing a pillow, she thudded down onto the couch, putting it in her lap. Looking everywhere but at Loki, she had just realised that she wore mismatched socks.

"Finally, you're dressed," said the Áss, turning to her again. "Come, we're already late. We'll need to meet him at one of the houses."

"What?!" she burst out, glancing at him. When their eyes met, however, she averted her gaze once again, blushing.

If Loki had sensed anything of the turmoil inside her, he showed or said nothing about it.

"Forget it," she announced, folding her arms before her breast defensively. "I'm not going anywhere!"

"But I require your assista—" he started, but Neila cut in.

"I don't care!" she cried out, obviously using anger to hide her embarrassment. "I'm not your secretary, or maid, or girlfriend! YOU want to live in this city, go find a place on your own! What do you need me for, anyway?"

"You have a good eye for these things."

"You've got to be kidding me!" Neila gasped. "Have you *seen* my apartment? What the hell says that I have any kind of sense for interior design?"

Loki remained silent for a moment, thinking through what he was about to say. He needed Neila, since *she* had to pick the apartment. However, this fact had to remain a secret until everything was properly set up.

Usually, convincing a human is easy, he thought, feeling unsure this time. With anybody else, it truly was effortless for him. However, that unfortunate mishap earlier set him back greatly. Anybody could have seen, how mortified Neila felt, and Loki actually sensed it. The air around her took on a pale, sick yellow shade.

"Let's make a deal," the Áss proposed, earning a cautious glance from her. "You will come with me now, and I will make the effort not to startle you anymore with my appearances."

Neila's eyes widened as she turned deep red once more.

"Fine!" she hissed in the end, jumping up and hurrying out.

"Marvellous!"

Neila gave an annoyed sigh while putting on shoes, then grabbed her purse, checking her papers and stuff. Loki then stepped to her, then with a touch on her arm he whooshed them away once again.

Neila blinked, finding herself on a hillside, only the gods knew where in the city, beside a modern and fancy looking house.

"I asked you to warn me before you do that!" she snapped, her heart racing. Yet, Loki emitted such calmness, it actually managed to soothe her and make her feel fairly safe.

Loki now altered his appearance to that of a 'normal human,' so nobody would notice the Áss he truly was. The shape-shifting happened in a literal blink of an eye, immediately returning to his original form when no other human was around them.

"This is the first one, on the very top," he motioned at the building.

Neila looked up, then around, measuring the landscape. Her lack of enthusiasm caught Loki's attention immediately.

"Oh, hello there!" an unknown voice broke the momentary silence, making them both turn to the newcomer.

A middle-aged man was heading for them in a sharp suit and inside a cloud of perfume. When he halted beside the companions, Neila visibly tried not to breathe very deeply. Not that the perfume smelt horrible, merely chokingly strong.

"David, it's good to see you again," Loki greeted him, yet neither of the men held out a hand for a shake.

"Welcome, welcome, what a lovely young lady companion we have here!" the realtor said too enthusiastically, holding out a hand for Neila, who took it with a nervous smile. That smile then turned into an almost frozen grimace when the man changed the handshake into an outdated kiss on the back of her hand.

Loki swayed his head slightly, seeing that the man remained oblivious to Neila's discomfort. With rising anxiety, she wanted nothing to do with the realtor altogether, yet he forced this type of closeness in the name of 'sophistication.'

"David Smith, at your service," the man introduced himself.

"Neila Saraven," she replied with a glued-on smile.

"What a perfectly unique name!" he said with too much fervency. "I'm sure, it belongs to an equally unique lady. Follow me, please, let me show you this marvellous home," the realtor said, obviously guiding the whole conversation as he pleased.

Now, David Smith gently ushered Neila forwards by putting a hand on her back. Immediately, she sped up just to get away from his touch. Loki followed, watching the man intently, who truly wanted to sweet-talk her with complete nonsense, probably thinking that the Lady of the House would have the final word in choosing a home for themselves.

This expectedness rendered Neila almost speechless. Feeling the pressure, she behaved skittish around the handsy realtor during the whole apartment hunting.

David Smith talked and talked, showing every 'gorgeous character' of every apartment he showcased.

"Wow, this guy just never shuts up!" Neila sighed in a brief pause when the realtor had to take a phone call. Who would call him at almost eight in the evening on a Sunday, remained a mystery, though.

Currently, Neila and Loki were sauntering in the living room of the third apartment. The first two flats made no impression on her whatever, so Loki graciously asked for more options. This one sparked a little interest in her eyes, but not much. The Áss truly hoped that one of the remaining two could be the winner. Not even Loki wanted to remain in the presence of the overzealous David Smith, who behaved like a know-it-all friend of theirs.

"Well, selling *is* his job," agreed the Áss, looking out the window. Just enough hills surrounded the peaceful city to make it appealing, with lots of parks and forests around.

"Less is more, in my opinion," she growled, measuring a very avant-garde bar next to her. "Both in words and in perfume."

Loki was just about to answer when the man returned to them.

"I am terribly sorry about this, Mr Leifsson," he said, grinning from ear to ear. "But, I pride myself in being there for all my clients, all day, every day. Whatever they need."

Neila rolled her eyes at this, but Loki just smiled leniently.

"It is quite all right. Now, I'm afraid, this one has missed the mark as well. Shall we go to the next one?" he said, turning the realtor's smile quite nervous.

"Yes, of course, follow me to my car, please," he babbled, heading for the door. Constantly, even during the drive, he gabbed further. "But, whatever the problem was with this apartment, I'm confident, the next one will make up for it. If not, then please, tell me a little bit more about your requirements, and I'll make sure, I find the perfect home for you," he babbled, only looking at the road half the time.

Neila exchanged a look with Loki on the back seat. When the realtor got occupied with his GPS, she turned to him.

"By the way, *Mr Leifsson*?" she raised a questioning eyebrow.

"Yes, I thought it was a nice play on words," he smiled, earning a confused glance.

"How come? Did you keep your name, by the way?"

"Of course I did. They shouldn't dare to question that. Regarding the surname, Leif, or rather, Leifr, is a perfectly acceptable name, meaning descendent, or heir."

"Sooo," Neila mused aloud, using air-quotes when required, "your 'last name' is son of the heir? An heir to the heir?"

"You take all the joy out of it," he sighed.

"What do you do on Asgard, by the way?" she asked, suspiciously narrowing her eyes.

"Lots of things. Apart from being a soldier, I mostly retain good relations between peoples and worlds."

"So, you're basically an ambassador of some sort?" Neila almost gasped.

"Well, it is much more complicated than that, but yes, you could say that."

"Huh," she huffed, surprised. "Not what I was expecting from the Lord of Chaos."

Loki was just about to answer when the car halted, signalling that they had arrived. Almost jumping out, the realtor hurried to Neila's side to open the door for her. His leg was caught in something, though, delaying him just enough for Loki to get there first. The man still managed to open the door before the Áss.

"Well, Mr Leifsson and Ms Saraven, get ready for your final destination," David Smith announced, as though everything happened according to script.

"Don't you have anything else, then?" Loki wanted to know, holding out a hand for Neila before the realtor. Annoyed by the shenanigans, she accepted.

"Oh, no, no, not what I meant at all," the man hurriedly answered. "I merely believe that THIS would satisfy all your needs. A huge living room with lots of natural light, four bedrooms, a modern kitchen ..."

Starting to feel overwhelmed, Neila's attention faded to the bare minimum. Tuning out the realtor, she distanced herself for a bit of solitude.

Admittedly, that apartment was *something*. Modern, yet not too edgy or shiny, or illogical. To Neila, at least. The kitchen truly was a marvel, and she dreamed of having a huge working platform like that. Loving to cook was not something one wanted to do in a teeny-tiny kitchen.

The apartment had an interesting layout, though, with two distinct sides, mirroring each other. Both had a huge bathroom with a tub and shower, and two bedrooms. The living room connected them seamlessly.

The view took Neila's breath away. Windows opened to every direction possible, huge ones at that, too, and there was an enormous balcony at the west side.

The only thing Neila disliked was the direct transition from the living room to the kitchen. But, given their sizes, it was a small price to pay for the overall gorgeous apartment. Neila did not even want to know, how much would the hundred and sixty square metres cost. Or, how Loki could accumulate so much in such a short time ...

"What do you think?" a question made her jump.

Loki was now standing beside her. Neila glanced at him, surprised that the realtor stayed away to give them some privacy.

"It's nice enough," she answered, brief. But her sparkling eyes told, *exactly* how much she loved the place. Which fact Loki noted as well.

"All right. Shall we go to the next one?" he asked.

"If you insist," she shrugged. "But I'm exhausted. This guy is too much after a certain point."

"You mean the first second, right?"

Neila gave a chuckle and a nod.

"I would really want to go home now. But, you can continue. You really don't need me for buying an apartment. I couldn't have been much help so far anyway."

"You've done what I required of you," Loki mumbled absent-mindedly, now trying to catch the attention of the realtor. The man hurried to them immediately, so the Áss saw nothing of Neila's questioning look.

"Is everything all right here?" asked David Smith, grinning.

"Yes, everything is perfectly fine," replied Loki with a lenient smile. "However, I'm afraid this was all the time we had today."

"Oh, I'm terribly sorry to hear that," the man responded with just enough genuine sadness. "If you give me more information, I can find more suitable apartments to show next time."

"It's perfectly all right," Loki continued with seemingly endless patience. "Now, if you'll excuse us, we should take our leave."

"Yes, yes, of course, I'll call for a taxi right away."

"No need for that, I've already done so."

"Well then," said the realtor, now a tad confused about how to proceed. "I'll escort you downstairs."

The three of them headed for the door. Outside, David Smith continued the charade of saying goodbye, making sure that Neila found everything satisfactory. Answering with mere half words, she looked more tormented by the minute. Still oblivious to every hint, David Smith lingered around her persistently. Since Neila occupied his full attention, he even missed to shake Loki's hand, as though it slipped his mind.

When the realtor finally drove away, Loki whooshed themselves home. After another quick shower, Neila headed for bed immediately.

Chapter 8

The next morning, Neila made breakfast while still being half-asleep. Rest eluded her, since she never liked going to bed so late and right after getting home from something. Therefore, grumpiness ruled her mood.

Sitting down at the table in the living room, she ate in silence, not sparing a glance at Loki on the couch. The Áss held some kind of e-book device, absorbed in his reading.

While nibbling, Neila wandered on her own path of thoughts. Not even the realisation of sitting there in the comfortably loose shorts and shirt bothered her in that moment. Normally, Neila would only appear in 'sleeping clothes' to her closest friends. Yet, for some reason, Loki's presence mattered not. Even if she blushed when the 'incident' of the previous day came to mind.

That accident would haunt her for a long time, Neila knew that much. But not because Loki had seen her undressed. Even without self-confidence, she realised by now that beauty was a relative term. According to various opinions, her body was very pleasant to look at. Sure, there was a bit of wobbly tummy, or some imperfection of her skin, but nothing too end-of-the-world type problem. Everything was normal, which was considered ugly in the intolerant human world.

Only one or two Pilates classes a week did not make anybody fit overnight. Especially, if they liked to eat whatever they desired, like Neila. The war between her and the couple of unwanted kilograms had lasted for some time now. But, this was perfectly fine in her eyes.

What hurt her was the fact that, despite many agreeing with her, nothing had changed in the general perspective. More and more people raised their voice in the name of body-positive thinking, but avoided to do the work, probably thinking that 'if someone else starts, I will too.' But this type of mentality helped neither the cause, nor anybody involved.

Neila simply despised any kind of make-up, which products were used as shields to hide behind. *If nobody can recognise you without make-up, you're doing something wrong, mate!* Neila thought grumpily. *Why not wear an actual mask, then?*

"What is wrong with feeling comfortable and looking good?" somebody asked Neila once during a discussion about make-up. Nothing, she answered, believing that if one wanted to paint themselves to feel happy, nobody should discourage them. Some created masterpieces on themselves that looked truly magnificent. *But that's art, then, and leave it at that,* she added in her head.

What nobody seemed to grasp that Neila's issue was with the 'urge' itself, which compelled people to use make-up to conceal imperfections. This socially accepted premise dictated that feeling bad for something completely natural must be the way to live.

Having to care for oneself should not mean hours before the mirror to achieve the 'perfect skin' or 'gorgeous hair,' Neila believed. She, too, used some products for her skin, but those were just washers or the occasional peeling mask. Perhaps a little eye cream could not hurt either.

However, Neila used these products to connect with her own body. When applying them, she would internally repeat 'I'm pampering myself, and that is a good thing' over and over again to recondition her mindset towards her body image. Part of her having no confidence came from the fact that Neila hated everything about how she looked. Growing up, every single outside influence suggested that one was just never enough, unless ...

Unless you literally break yourself to look 'acceptable,' Neila thought, grumpy. Taking a deep breath, she tried to break free from this endless misery. Sadly, not even a divine intervention could alter her self-perception, until SHE started to change.

In the next moment, Loki's question brought her back to the present.

"So, how was your night?" he asked, not even glancing up from reading.

"Chaotic," she growled with a mouth half full. "Even you were in it, and Fenrir, and a bunch of crystal octopuses."

The Áss raised a questioning eyebrow, but asked nothing further.

"Did *you* even sleep?" asked Neila, looking at the folded sheets on the couch.

"No."

"How come?"

"I usually rest in every two or three days; that is how time serves me well on Miðgarðr," Loki answered, still not glancing up from the book. It must have been something truly great.

"Can I ask about that now?" Neila inquired, just finishing the last of her cereal.

"Would this mean that you have finally decided on the order of your questions?" asked Loki, glancing at her briefly before returning to his reading.

"Can't you tell?" she teased.

"Of course, I can, but I wanted to hear it from you," Loki inhaled deeply. "In any case, what do you wish to know?"

"First of all, I still don't really understand this node thing, and how the realms are connected."

Loki glanced up, turning off the reader and put it down on the little table beside the couch.

"What don't you understand, exactly?" he asked with a strange glance. Somehow, he looked incredibly intense, though not dangerous.

"Well," Neila began, "I just don't understand, how it works. You have been calling the levels realms, planets, and worlds, and each mean a different thing. So ... what are they, then? Are they within the same universe, or this 'bubble' or whatever connects entirely different dimensions?"

Loki waited for Neila to finish her line of questioning. Even without feeling her essence, it would have been obvious that forming such deep-conscious thoughts into words was a difficult task. During this process, the meaning of the thoughts became lost while being 'translated' to words. Which fact could have caused problems for ordinary humans, but not for Loki.

When Neila had run out of breath and questions, Loki started the explanation.

"I used different terms, because they all are true. Every world is connected solely by the node, which allows said realms to communicate with each other, so to speak. As a whole, the nodes themselves could differ as well, containing just a few or many worlds. Nodes have no connections to one another, or if they do, we are unaware of it."

Neila just blinked, but Loki could tell, she was able to follow this so far.

"Within a node, as I previously mentioned, the worlds are interconnected by weaker paths. As far as I know, stronger connections could only form by the presence of a species that is capable of a higher thought process. Each world, or planet, has their own universe with solar systems, galaxies, and everything else.

"Since the node links specific worlds, their inhabitants tend to be similarly constructed creatures. What I mean by this is that, if you were to travel to the fourth, you would meet humanoids there as well. On others, the beings might have four arms or an exoskeleton, but you would still be able to identify a head, limbs, and so on. Regardless of their varied appearances, they're always capable of communicating in some way or other. This is because the worlds influence each other throughout the connections.

"For example, within a different node, should plants evolve to an intelligent level, there could be walking trees. No matter how many worlds are inside *that* node, they all would hold some kind of similar species to those trees. There might be walking fungi, or something entirely unknown to us, but fundamentally similar to each other."

Loki paused, seeing Neila's gaze becoming foggy as she slowly lost the thread.

"So, what you say is that, the nine worlds are basically similar to each other?" she asked.

"Yes."

"Can't I go to whichever with a spaceship?"

"No, because they are in separate realms, meaning different universes."

Neila blinked again, so Loki continued.

"Think of it as your dreams. Your mind is the node, and every single dream has their own universe, logic, pattern, and so on. They are connected through you, since they come from your mind.

However, they are also independent, and you wouldn't be able to go from one dream to another just by going in circles inside your mind."

"You mean some kind of dream within a dream?" she now asked, slowly looking lost.

"Not entirely, no."

"Oh. Uh-huh," Neila bobbed her head, trying to make heads or tails about this whole thing. "So, what would happen if I had a spaceship and started travelling?"

"You might stumble upon other nodes that connect different realms together, but in *this* universe, only one world exists from those. No matter how far you travel, you would never be able to find Ásgarðr, for example, just by flying around in a ship. As far as we know, that is."

"Uh-huh," she bobbed her head again, then started to massage her forehead. "This is too heavy stuff for a morning," she groaned, sounding overwhelmed.

Neila tried her best to find the meaning and logic in the heard information. Feeling the pattern, a deeper level of her mind understood, she was fairly sure about that. But the 'surface' part, the one that controlled her waken, normal self, needed more time to digest.

"So, how does the Bifröst work, then?" she asked. "Where can you go through that?"

"You are talking about two different concepts, although, through no fault of your own. Originally, we call the steady Connections between realms Bifröst. In our current hierarchy, Ásgarðr became a sort of peace-keeper force for reasons only Óðinn knows, needing a faster travelling system, so to speak. Therefore, we've managed to create a device that could send us directly to a world, not through the stop at the fifth, like normally. This, for better or worse, we also call Bifröst."

"So, the movies were right about *something*? Go figure," Neila snickered.

"I'm not sure whether this is good or bad, or that I should be concerned about these movies you keep mentioning," the Áss mumbled.

"You should probably avoid them," she advised. "So, where can your Bifröst go, then?"

"To any lower-levelled world inside our own node, and a little bit outside of it. We know about other nodes nearby, but don't really mind them, to be honest. Everything anybody would ever need is right here, in our own node. No need for us to go meddling with others."

"Wait, you mean *other* other worlds inside a node?" Neila asked, starting to get really lost.

Loki sighed, pondering about how to clarify.

"Let's just stay on Miðgarðr for the time being. You know about your own solar system and galaxy, correct?"

Neila nodded.

"And, you also know that there are other solar systems, and other galaxies. Some hold intelligent life forms, as you call them, some not. Still correct?"

Another nod, so he continued.

"Now, since there is life in a neighbouring solar system to this one, it is part of *this* universe. And since this universe is connected to Ásgarðr's through the node, we could go to *that* planet through our Bifröst. This is still simple, right?"

"Define simple, but yeah," she said with a hint of cynicism.

"Now, let's say that, in another neighbouring solar system, there is a planet where the walking trees live, which planet is also part of a node. The trees would be able to go to another realm, like I can to the sixth or here. But, *we* would not be able to follow the tree through our Bifröst. We could only follow, if we would join the tree on its home world, then walk through one of *their* connections with it. It's quite simple, really."

"Sure," Neila agreed. "If you learn about this stuff since the moment you were born. My brain literally hurts!"

"At least you can understand it now. Look what happened when I tried to mention the other realms to your ancestors, they mistook my metaphor for a literal tree."

Neila gave a huff and a half-smile.

"Will you ever be able to let that go?" she teased.

"Not in the foreseeable future, no," he admitted with a shrug. "We put real work into our teachings, it is not a good feeling, seeing how distorted they got."

"Yeah ... This reminds me, how old are you again?" asked Neila with a mischievous smile. "I must say, you really look good for a couple of thousand years."

Loki flashed a disapproving glance at her.

"The higher you are in rank, the longer you live, since you know more and more about how things work. Regardless, I am *not* thousands of years old, as your myths would suggest."

"You mentioned something about time before. How does it work, then?"

"Are you sure, you are ready for another lesson?" asked the Áss dubiously. When she just nodded, saying 'what could happen,' he gave a sigh, but continued. "Time is the same for every planet inside the node. This means, if there is morning on the fourth, there is morning on the fifth as well, and so on. The disconnected worlds, however, don't follow this rule."

"How come?"

"I am not entirely sure, and I wouldn't talk about what I don't know. But, risking the danger of being misunderstood again, I will use a metaphor."

Loki fell silent for a moment, deep in thought.

"Take your time, I'll make some tea and change," Neila cut in, earning an eye roll and a mutter about 'being all over the place again.'

Until Neila had returned, Loki continued reading.

"What are you reading, by the way?" she asked, thudding down beside him on the couch. But before she could catch anything on the screen, he turned the device off.

"It is unimportant at the moment. Are you comfortable enough?" he asked, eyeing her inquiringly.

"Perfectly," she answered with a half-smile. The teapot and her mug was in arm's length on the dining table next to the couch. Neila now used the folded sheets as a pillow to the armrest, so she could put her legs up and still face Loki comfortably.

"So, imagine one of those big black records."

"A vinyl?"

"Indeed. Now, you are aware that, if you pick a point close to the middle, and another at the edge in the same line, they travel different distances in the same time as the record spins. To simply put it, the outside point is faster than the inside one."

"Obviously."

"Now, imagine that the record broke, therefore a ring in the middle is separated from the rest of the record. If you spin the record, the middle part may go faster or slower compared to the outside ring. Correct?"

"I'm a visual type, so I think I get what you mean, yes."

"The rings still might spin together, if friction forces them to. But, most of the times, the outside ring spins at a different speed than the inside. Simple enough, I'd say."

Neila nodded, although, a spark of fear flickered in her gaze of what might come next.

"Now, imagine that the record is not about distance, but time. So, the two identified points experience the passing of time when the record spins. Can you imagine this?"

Neila just blinked, and Loki could feel her mind buzzing to figure this out. She understood and saw the pattern, just needed some time to actually comprehend.

"Now, if the record is whole, everything is perfectly fine, wouldn't you say? The same time of day would be everywhere in a line. However, if the middle is broken, the inside ring experiences time differently. This is what had happened when a realm got disconnected from the rest. They are spinning much faster at the moment."

"Oh, dear gods," Neila exhaled, but then corrected herself almost immediately. "Sorry, oh dear higher-levels. This is ... Heavy."

"Well, yes. And it was even more difficult for somebody in the ancient Ellas to understand. That is why we are not really allowed to intervene with lower-levels."

"Sooo, why are you telling me all this, then? Aren't you breaking some important rule?" she asked, pouring tea for herself.

"Not exactly," Loki started. "You see, telling somebody something 'superior' is not the problem. I could teach you advanced maths, for instance, that none of your scientists have seen before. You could even recite it by heart, if you wish. Just using something and understanding its true meaning are two, very different things. Helping in the latter is forbidden, the former problem has never been truly regulated by any kind of rule."

"But you are now breaking the latter, aren't you?" asked Neila. "With me, I mean. You're basically spoon-feeding me by answering everything, aren't you?"

"As I see it, I am merely answering questions," replied Loki mysteriously. A strange spark flickered in his eyes now, suddenly changing his whole appearance into a dangerous one. "If you don't understand the answer, I cannot help you with that now, can I? I can only show some tools, but *you* have to figure out on your own, how to use them."

"That is a *very* fine line," muttered Neila, grim.

"Indeed," he admitted. "A grey area, at best."

"I would hate it, if you would get into trouble because of me," she admitted. "Why are you doing this? Is the punishment so mild that it's worth it?"

"The consequences of breaking a rule like that would be anything but mild," he said, suddenly turning incredibly solemn, his gaze distant.

Seeing his change of mood, Neila was about to ask, but then let the matter slip. Finally, she started to understand, how Loki could have got such a controversial, mostly negative, reputation.

If he would try this with a normal person, they would surely go crazy, Neila thought with a grimace. What could have been so valuable that he and some others would risk so much to obtain? *He mentioned something about energies,* she recalled while sipping her tea. *What kind could they be, I wonder? Could they be truly* that *important?*

Loki seemed to be deep in thought, and Neila wanted not to disturb him. Thus, she sipped her tea in silence, trying to digest the incredible information she had just heard. Working the deeper levels of her mind, Neila would sort things out fairly soon. Getting that understanding to the 'surface' afterwards, however, was the truly tricky part.

Both of them seemed comfortable enough in the forming silence, so neither broke it. Neila finished her tea soon, while Loki's gaze almost pierced the distance. Glancing at him, she now suddenly got the feeling that he was dealing with 'out of this world stuff.'

Before Neila could ask anything, Loki turned to her. The sudden movement made her jump, earning a confused frown from him. The Áss then let the matter go.

"I must leave now," Loki announced, standing up. While he spoke, his clothes changed back to its original attire. "I've finally got word, so I must hurry. I will probably be away for a few days."

Loki nodded in farewell then disappeared, as if never existed.

Neila gave a hopeless sigh, then tried to move on. She had her own problems to sort out, starting with her newest book, which the editor loved a little bit too much. Apparently, Norse mythology had a come-back in books as well nowadays. However, as good the idea seemed at first, Neila now felt uncertain about the theme.

What would Loki think about this? she asked herself, glancing around purposelessly. Somehow, it did not seem likely that he would take it lightly, if she 'blabbed' about everything without restraint. Writing, however, was Neila's coping mechanism in dealing with serious matters. And getting to know an actual god certainly qualified as such.

Neila's heart felt heavy. Not wanting to be disrespectful, she needed another approach to her story. But what could she come up with in so little time? The truth was always what she wrote.

Well, MY truth, anyway, Neila thought bitterly. *Just use your imagination,* she suggested to herself. *You're a writer, it is what you do. All you have to do is think of a different plot. That's all. A romance, perhaps?*

Neila gave a huge sigh, dismissing the idea immediately. Somehow, she could not picture Loki in any kind of romantic scenario. Also, she was not a romance writer, by any means, and she was not about to start now.

The desire of not wanting to disrespect a higher-level person made Neila incredibly anxious. In truth, she still could not believe that all of this had happened to *her*. Stumbling upon something 'cool' was one thing, but for that the 'cool thing' to remain in her life was another.

The possibilities seemed endless, and Neila wanted to seize this opportunity for as long as Loki allowed. No price seemed too high for her to give this situation up. At least, not yet.

Chapter 9

Loki glanced around in the peaceful landscape. The grassland stretched comfortably inside a ring of mountains; the Sun shone brightly on the clear blue sky. Yet, an ice-cold wind rendered the area rather unpleasant.

Loki cared not for the inhospitable environment. He, himself, rather liked the cold, barely feeling its bite thanks to his abilities and technology. Looking around, he tried to find the spectacle the connection was. It was a natural one, therefore much smaller and far more unstable than a Bifröst.

Usually, a realm was connected to two or perhaps three others at any given time, without any particular order or reason as of to which ones. Theoretically, Miðgarðr could have been directly connected to Ásgarðr right now. But not even the Æsir had the capability to search a planet over and over again to look for such a tiny thing compared to the vastness of a world. Hence, when one found a raw connection, they took it then and there. Fortunately, the energies that made up the path revealed the planets it connected.

On the other hand, travelling through these paths was always a gamble and incredibly dangerous, even for those equipped with the technology or abilities to compensate the risks. This was one of the reasons, higher-levels avoided visiting the disconnected worlds.

However, Loki had little choice in the matter. It was kind of a miracle in the first place, that a connection just happened to be close by.

Let's hope that this would be one of those cases when they miss my arrival until I can get to the Bifröst, Loki thought with a grimace.

At the moment, his biggest issue with the fifth was that they had the technology to track essences. And since they had several meetings with Loki beforehand, his essence was well known amidst their ranks. Meaning, nine out of ten times, the fifths would be able to track his travel and get to the entry point in time to catch him.

Technically speaking, Loki could have been found easily by them, even on a disconnected world. The technological level of the fifth realm was incredibly advanced. Only their strict policy of never to intervene with other realms kept them from actually hunting Loki down. Which position might change, depending on how angry they got as time passed.

I would really want to avoid hurting them just because of a simple misunderstanding, Loki thought with another grimace, looking into the distance. Despite being one of the best fighters, he had never before taken a life. Not even in self-defence, and he was not about to start now. At the same time, sacrificing his life was not very appealing to him either.

Starting to feel the pressure inside, Loki took a deep breath and got back to the present. Nothing would be solved, if he just stood there like a statue. Loki had to make this right, so continued looking for the connection.

However, the pathway seemed to be amiss. Neither Loki's visor, nor his mental abilities could find any trace of it, which could mean only one thing.

"Of course, it had to disappear when I needed it," Loki growled, thinking about the next step.

Natural connections formed and shattered all the time, it was the order of things. Some lasted only for a couple of days, others might persist for cycles. Usually, Loki could estimate the lifespan of a connection, yet it was more of a bet than a fact.

Activating the visor once again, he increased its sensitivity to its limit, then added his own abilities to scan as much territory as possible. Despite preferring his own natural skills for doings things, Loki fused himself with a lot of technology. Unlike most Ásgarðrians, the Æsir preferred mixing tech with innate abilities to extremities. And Loki was not even the most 'zealous' in this regard.

Luck smiled at him this time—he managed to locate another connection soon, teleporting there immediately. *Riding on a planet's own energies is always fun,* he thought, feeling the nice tingling inside.

The found connection seemed to be a small one, only going to the fourth realm. To the naked eye, it looked, as if hot air would stream upwards, like a strange thin tornado. Humans would not even spot it, lacking the sensitivity to do so.

The fragile thing streamed upwards, sometimes twitching or twisting. It was an old one, at the brink of collapse. Dangerous and risky would not even begin to describe such a spectacle. However, since it was better than nothing, Loki hesitated not to enter.

Usually, travelling through a normal, stable Connection like a Bifröst was nearly instantaneous. One simply stepped inside the massive 'tube,' then walked out on a different realm.

A wild one behaved differently. Governed solely by the Laws of Nature, using them required an innate understanding of these forces. Pure Chaos lived inside such a path, which is exactly why Loki had a fondness for them. Inside, he needed to create his own order to move whilst battling with the natural wilderness of energies.

Arriving on the fourth realm, all Loki had to do was go to the Bifröst. Even from that distance, he could sense the connection and teleported himself right beside it.

Nobody paid his arrival any attention. The Bifröst was situated in a populated area on each realm, where all kinds could mingle. Not even the appearance of a seventh felt too out of the ordinary.

The Áss glanced up at the massive connection, beholding the true form of the swirling energies. Those below the sixth could only perceive and measure the effects of the Bifröst. Like a black hole, it folded everything around itself, creating something akin to an event horizon.

Loki stepped inside without a second to waste. However, the moment he emerged, a shot struck his left shoulder, making him cry out. Loki immediately jumped, using the enhanced abilities of his boots. Shots darted by from everywhere, missing him by a thread.

The Áss assessed the situation in a fraction of a second. Apart from the attackers, the huge square around the Bifröst stood empty. Meaning no collateral damage, at least. Through his visor, Loki could see the positions of fifths, allowing him to zigzag and avoid any other shots. Seeing this, the fire ceased.

Loki now halted. Standing tall, he eyed the leader of the fifths, who moved closer with weapon aiming at him.

The approaching creature could have been described as a giant. Twice as tall as Loki himself, with four arms and two sturdy legs, the figure slowly approached. Confidence radiated from him, despite facing a seventh.

Only an Ásgarðrian could kill them with ease, anybody else would have had an incredibly tough time doing the same. That grey skin was harder than rock, and despite their size, these creatures moved with astonishing agility. All this, paired with their advanced technology, left them to be one of the least killable things inside the node. Fortunately, they were peaceful and kept to themselves. Only when provoked, they used force to deal with a situation.

Loki glanced at the gun calmly, dismissing the pain from his bleeding shoulder. They were obviously waiting for him, knowing that only that fraction of second when he stepped out would be the sole opportunity for a strike. In that position, even Týr would have been vulnerable.

"You must let me pass," Loki broke the heavy silence. "I cannot keep my part of the bargain, if you won't let me back to Ásgarðr."

The creature gave a snort. With a mere thought, he activated a machine. Hearing the buzz in the air, Loki glanced behind him just in time to see a huge iris closing on the Bifröst, sealing it shut. Nobody was allowed to go anywhere, apparently. Only here, could such a technology exist.

Every single Connection ran through the fifth realm, serving as a central junction within the node. Utilizing this unique position to the fullest, they operated a wide-ranging trading hub. Despite never mingling with others, they actually liked visitors coming to *them*. Given their sophisticated tech, the fifths possessed all kinds of valuables and trinkets, for anybody. All the visitors needed to do was learn their impossible speech well enough to understand it, since no fifth would speak any other language.

On the other hand, not even Loki could pronounce anything in the fifth's native tongue. Thus, he spoke in the language of the fourth when dealing with them, while they answered in their own.

"Fill your side of the deal, or you are going to be imprisoned," said the creature, aiming his gun at Loki again. Despite using only a few words, they made themselves perfectly clear at all times.

"I cannot without going back to Ásgarðr," Loki replied, thinking.

"You are bleeding," a voice now said in Loki's head, making him grimace.

"Thank you for noticing," he answered in his mind sarcastically.

Lovely, the Áss thought, even more agitated. *Just what I needed, an android in my head.* Despite the other being connected to him, Loki knew that Heimdallr could not 'hear' a thought from a deeper level of the mind.

Hearing Heimdallr chuckle did not lighten Loki's mood. The fifth's raspy voice brought him back to the conversation.

"We kept our side; you haven't. The time has passed; you are now accountable for breaking your given word. Surrender peacefully or suffer the consequences!"

"They get right to the point, don't they? Lovely people," continued Heimdallr.

A momentary silence fell on the square, in which Heimdallr chatted further, as though nothing particular was happening.

"What will you do now, I wonder?" the Lookout asked Loki.

"Well, I could ask you to bring me home by the Bifröst, for one," the Áss answered, tense.

"I would love to," replied Heimdallr. *"But I'm prohibited to, unless—"* he continued, but Loki interrupted, finishing the sentence impatiently.

"Unless we are on an official business, I'm aware of the rules."

Loki took a huge breath, irritated. No matter how much he worked, Óðinn had never seemed to acknowledge any of it as an 'official business.' Although, since the interesting and not less frightening happenings on Ásgarðr, even Loki understood. Ever since the strange attacks had started a few cycles back, not many mingled on other realms.

"If you refuse to help, can you, at least, watch some other realm?" Loki snapped, now pressing his nose bridge, pondering.

"At the moment, nothing remotely interesting is happening anywhere else."

Loki gave an annoyed sigh. Pain flooded his mind, turning his awareness to his still bleeding shoulder. However, he could do little to nothing about that now. The fifth realm had barely any energies for mental abilities. Unfortunately, Loki had nothing for healing in his suit.

"Technically, I have *advised* against sending the piece to Ásgarðr, until I could speak to Freyja. It is not my fault that you heeded not my word."

An irritated grunt was the answer, followed by a warning shot beside Loki's head, who did not even flinch.

The Áss needed a solution to the situation, and fast. He really, really did not want to hurt the others because of a simple misunderstanding.

The creature continued, relentless as ever.

"We kept our part. Ásgarðr answers not to our calls. You remain, then they will."

"It is not as simple as that, and you know it," argued Loki. "They need *my* word as well. You cannot deal with Freyja directly. How much time do you wish to waste with trying to imprison me? Just allow me to go back and everything will be fine."

Even though the creature had to know that Loki was telling the truth, he apparently just could not or would not understand.

"We need her NOW! You promised and broke the deal. By law, you are bound to go to prison, so others would need to come," the other stated.

Nobody, especially not an Ásgarðrian, should flee from justice, therefore, the Áss should allow himself to be locked up.

Loki understood their position. The fifth turned desperate, and with good reason. Which is why, Loki wanted to help them in the first place. *What THEY need to comprehend is that I'm the only one who have every information to get Ásgarðr actually involved,* the Áss thought, feeling stuck between a rock and a hard place. Hence, he must go and explain everything to Óðinn and Freyja. In person.

"Back to Miðgarðr, then?" Heimdallr suggested in Loki's head, breaking his train of thought.

"I hate this place," the Áss thought, grumpy because of the waste of time. Yet again, he needed to flee, only because some literally rock-headed creatures could not see past their rigid laws.

The moment he activated his visor, the fifths started shooting again. However, Loki dodged everything, halting behind a creature to seek refuge while trying to find a natural connection to anywhere, preferably to Miðgarðr. Moving in unison with the fifth, Loki remained behind him, so the others would not shoot either.

After a few moments of this dance, Loki spotted a natural connection just outside the city. Leaping towards it, he left the creatures behind. Not even slowing down, he dived into the tube without a second thought.

After a rough travel, Loki landed in water. Salt stung his wound instantly, making him hiss in pain while floating on the surface of the ocean. But, at least, he had managed to get back to Miðgarðr.

The rich energies all around almost made his mind buzz in ecstasy. With their help, the Áss healed his wound, then teleported to the little terrace of Neila's home. Surrounded by bushes for privacy, nobody saw him appearing.

"Well, this went well," Loki mumbled, agitated while stepping to the door.

However, the incredibly dark energies leaking from inside snapped him back to the present, wary. Stepping through the door, Loki glanced around, measuring. Neila sat on the couch, huddling under a blanket, almost becoming one with it. Having her headphones on, she realised his presence not, seemingly resting with closed eyes. But that darkness lazily oozing around her told the truth.

Loki could have touched that abysmal aura, it was so thick. Like a living black fog with a mind of its own, it lingered in the air, spawning tendrils all around. Some of these headed downwards, inside the floor and earth underneath, others netted the walls or the furniture.

Neila, herself, looked asleep and dreaming—sometimes taking a shaky, deep breath, she shook her head, or frowned, as though arguing. Or, she merely exhaled long, like in acceptance of a thought or something or other. However she reacted to the scenery inside her head, it resonated in the pitch-black aura as well. It trembled as she inhaled, or a tendril twitched when she frowned.

Loki stood in place, surprised by the situation. Only once before, he had sensed something like this, and it ended in the saddest way possible.

As though realising his presence, one of the tendrils now headed for Loki through the air. Holding out a hand, he allowed it to connect with him. Immediately, the blackness retracted, and Neila opened her eyes.

"Oh, hi," she said huskily, sitting up and putting the headphones down. "How was your mission?" she asked, apathetic.

Neila had obviously fallen into a depressed state; the black tendrils still squirming. Despite seeing the heavy energies all around, Loki could not really do anything.

"As well as expected," he answered, musing. "What's the matter?"

"Nothing," she shrugged, but her quivering lower lip betrayed this statement. "Everything."

Measuring the emitted aura, the Áss mused about what to do. When their eyes met, she dropped her gaze immediately.

"I'm fine, you don't have to stay here," Neila mumbled. "Go, have fun, or something. I'll be fine in a couple of days."

Loki doubted this, but argued not.

"Have you eaten anything?" he enquired, already knowing the answer.

Since she replied only with a shrug, he took out his phone.

"I'm going to order a pizza. You like those, correct?" he said, already tipping the phone.

"I'm not hungry," Neila muttered, staring out the window with an empty gaze.

"Of course you are. And I'm going to make some tea."

"I'm not thirsty either."

"Then you won't have to drink," he agreed with a half-smile and headed for the kitchen. There, Loki mused about how one could have fallen from a fairly stable state to *that* deep in only a day.

Chapter 10

Loki placed the teapot on the little table beside the couch for Neila, who followed his every move with an empty gaze. The Darkness still surrounded her like a fog, stretching its tendrils in every direction. It shrank compared to what greeted Loki, but still ruled her mind unopposed.

The Áss felt the anguish inside her soul, yet was powerless to do anything about it. Not because of the lack of knowledge, but rather that it was forbidden.

Neila probably was aware of this, too, if not of the rule itself. Only she had the power to eliminate her own darkness, facing Fear, Anxiety, Sadness, Anger, Doubt, and all the other Demons that existed in her soul. They all were there for a reason and played a crucial part in her own development.

However, knowing this made none of it easier, by any means.

Loki settled down on the sofa at Neila's feet.

"Would you be interested in a story?" the Áss asked, earning only a sad look and a shrug. "Then, let me tell you my favourite tale about how our node was created."

A flicker of interest ignited in the tricolour eyes. A couple of dark tendrils pulled back and even the rest fidgeted less afterwards.

"Long ago, there was only one planet. Incredible creatures lived there, using powers far beyond our imagination, like shape-shifting into elements with ease," he started, sometimes gesticulating to help the story come alive.

Even if Neila sensed nothing of the shifting of energies by his movements, she could most certainly feel *something* of it. The dark tendrils slowly pulled back, one by one, while Loki spoke.

"Male, female, energy, or something else; they could transform into anything they desired. Into gods, even," he added with a half-smile, earning an almost-could-be-a-chuckle huff from Neila. "They lived in a perfect world, in peace with everything and everybody. They also understood how the universe worked, wielding the ability to create gates, or, rather, rifts to other realms."

All but one tendril disappeared by now; the Darkness ever so slowly shrank and faded. Neila listened, eager to hear more, yet the Demons still held her tight. A sole tendril remained on the back of the couch, faintly pulsating with her breath. Loki shifted position slightly, resting his right arm on the backrest just next to the tendril. Sensing his closeness, it wriggled closer and closer to his fingers, then attached itself to his palm.

The Áss talked further, keeping an eye on the tendril at all times.

"Because they lived in isolation for so long, they longed for companionship. Hence, one of them set out for the quest of finding another world akin to their own. It was an incredible task to take on, and required an even greater will and patience to see it through.

"For nine hundred full cycles of their planet around their star, he had found nothing. Rift after rift, he looked for kindred spirits, but had found only stars and empty planets. It truly seemed to be a hopeless effort, yet he never gave up. Then, on the ninetieth day of the nine hundredth cycle, he had finally made contact."

Neila now gave a tiny gasp, listening further, completely captivated. Night fell on the lands outside, unnoticed by the two of them. Loki talked with a smile, mostly because Neila had finally started to get over the Darkness. The howling Demons slowly quieted down in her soul; the black tendril that was still attached to him faded away. When the aura disappeared completely, Neila suddenly sat up and poured a mug of tea for herself. Sipping it quietly, she listened with sparkling eyes.

"Naturally, everybody rejoiced. Finding a kindred spirit could be an incredible feeling, even for a mighty race such as theirs. It was such a wondrous moment that the seeker actually started to cry. His tears brought his essence with them to the new world, forming the very first Bifröst. This world, was Ásgarðr."

"Really?" Neila gasped.

"According to the story, yes," Loki smiled. "After the first contact, these creatures continued to find more to share their joy with. In every nine hundredth cycle, they could add another world to their known circle. In the end, they had stopped looking for more after eight new worlds. This is how our node became to have nine realms, all connected by the joyful tears of the First Ones."

"Who were these beings? Is this really true? Did it truly happen this way?" Neila wanted to know.

"They are the inhabitants of the ninth realm. As for whether it's true or not, until they come down and tell us what had happened exactly, it *might* be even true."

"So, you have your own legends and myths, too, just like us!" she said, now enthusiastic.

Loki gave a little laugh.

"Yes and no," he smiled. "These are mere stories, coming from the imagination of a writer or poet. They *imagined* what *could have* happened and how, then wrote them down, not unlike your books."

"But you *do* know about your exact evolution of your kind, don't you?" she wanted to know.

"Almost, I would say. Some things still await for proof, but otherwise, we are aware."

"Do you know anything about humans, perhaps?"

"Sadly, that I'm not allowed to say."

"Aw," Neila grimaced. "What about how the realms got their ranks? If you have never met somebody from the eighth or ninth, how do you even know your own rank?"

"Well, they've told us," Loki admitted, his expression turned troubled. Either he was not allowed to say more, or just did not find the proper words. "Sort of. It is ... difficult to explain, to be honest. We just ... know ... All I can say for certain that anything can travel through a Bifröst, even thoughts and feelings. Therefore, whenever there is a change, they inform us."

"Really? That's it? Wow," she bobbed her head, baffled. "What else can a Bifröst do?"

"Well, it is not that it can 'do' anything. A Bifröst only allows travelling. However, anything can travel: a person, an item, or even a certain thought or feeling."

"And how does this work, exactly? I mean, is it a 'fix' route like a highway, linking the realms together, or every realm has that many Bifrösts, or what?"

Loki flashed a measuring glance at her.

"Are you sure, you want to hear about how the Bifröst work? It is not at all interesting, believe me."

"Maybe to a person accustomed to travelling through them," she argued, then shrugged and dropped the subject. "But, whatever. Tell me stories about the others, then. How is Baldur, for instance?"

"How should he be?" asked Loki, surprised.

"Well ..." she trailed off, obviously not wanting to actually mention the human myths. Catching this meaning, Loki rolled his eyes.

"Please don't tell me that you want to hear about that mistletoe incident."

Neila gave an apologetic smile and shrug, making him sigh.

Well, at least she's got out of the Darkness, Loki thought, yet her current enthusiasm baffled him. Never before was anybody *this* interested in actually getting to know them. Usually, humans just wanted to hear exciting stories about gods and monsters, afterwards distorting those tales to match *their* way of thinking. Or worse, they sought powers for serving *their* interests.

"You don't have to answer, if you don't want to," she said, bringing Loki back to the present.

"I am aware," he nodded. "It is just baffling, how these things changed, you know. Although, sometimes decades, or even hundreds of years had passed between our visits. But still ..."

"Yeah, how does this time-thing work again?" Neila asked. "In the disconnected worlds, I mean. And, I would really want to know, how old you are." When Loki flashed a disapproving glance, she quickly added, "only to have a reference, nothing more. It doesn't really mean anything to me either way."

"How old do I look to you?" he then asked instead of answering. Neila now measured his features inquiringly.

"Thirty-eight? Forty? But, you could easily pass as thirty-five. So that's good news for you," she noted with just a hint of mocking.

"I believe you," said Loki plainly. "I don't quite grasp, why knowing my ... 'age' ... would tell you anything. As I've mentioned before, time passes differently on the disconnected worlds. Most often, they are spinning faster. But it varies greatly. Here, a full day on Ásgarðr could mean anything from a day to even a year. Not to mention that a 'year's time' still can differ on every realm."

Seeing her disappointed grimace, Loki gave a sigh.

"However, if you cannot live without the information, I have lived three hundred and seventy-nine cycles on Ásgarðr."

"How many could that be in Earth-years?"

Loki took a deep breath, falling silent for a moment.

"If I can calculate correctly, four hundred and sixty-seven, give or take."

Neila's jaw dropped.

"The more abilities you discover, the longer you can live, even as a mere human," Loki said, looking at her too seriously. "As I've mentioned this before. Just try to connect to my essence, so you can feel my arrival sooner, among other things. It only takes practice."

"Yeah, sure, *after* you've figured out what to do," Neila grimaced. "I don't truly understand what an essence is, let alone feel it."

Suddenly, the Darkness reclaimed her mind again, casting a gloom over her mood.

Regardless of Neila's attempts to understand things in general or specifically about herself, Doubt always challenged everything. Never could be silenced, the questions emerged without an end. Neila struggled greatly to believe in herself, because Doubt hovered over her, whispering 'What if the others are right?'

The constant 'what if'-s rendered her life unbearable. Nothing was certain. Ever. Peace seemed unachievable, even for just a moment. With Fear on its side, Doubt grew stronger and stronger by the moment.

"It's easy to believe that you are special. Deal with the fact that you're nothing; a speck, an insignificant thing nobody cares about," the Demons taunted, nearly crushing Neila's soul.

Just thinking about how powerless she truly was made her sink into the Darkness once more. *'All you have to do is,' he said,* Neila thought, feeling the tears well up. *Yeah, right. I can do NOTHING, and have ZERO ideas about how I should even try. I'm a useless piece of shit.*

A gentle grip on her hand brought Neila back to the present. Glancing up, she even imagined to see some kind of black fog disappearing from her vision. Suddenly, Neila felt nauseated; her bones vibrating, and she believed to feel the immense amount of energy that was now flooding her system through Loki's hand.

Neila could not recall, when he moved closer to her. The Áss's presence was so overbearing that it made even breathing difficult. Regardless, that gentle touch felt incredibly good, Neila even considered sliding closer to him. The mere fact that she knew that Loki actually understood ... That he *felt* what she did ... That was more comforting than anything else in her life.

Therefore, reluctant to pull away, Neila clenched her jaw and tried to just 'roll with it.' Fighting the happenings probably would accomplish nothing, since the Áss was incredibly powerful compared to her. Thus, Neila tried to let that power flow through her.

Neila closed her eyes for a moment, wanting to relax as much as possible. Her mind literally buzzed now, as if she were about to faint. The dizziness appeared so suddenly, it caught Neila completely off guard. Her entire body vibrated strangely, giving the impression of falling apart. At the same time, Neila's mind almost felt to fly away. Almost, since *something* held it back, like an anchor. Living in that incredible moment, she tried to 'yank' on that chain to break free, yet nothing happened.

Before Neila could think of anything else, everything had returned to normal. In a literal blink of an eye, all strangeness ceased. Gasping for air, she opened her eyes, looking around.

Loki crouched beside her, now offering a glass of water. Confused, Neila tried to take it, yet her muscles wanted not to contract.

"That's enough for now," Loki announced, earning a puzzled glance from Neila. Seeing this, he continued with a smile, "but next time, try not to draw so much from me."

"What?" she panted, stunned, almost dropping the glass. Her hands just refused to work, forcing her to hold the half-full glass in her lap.

"Essentially, you were trying to drain my powers. You didn't even realise? Interesting ..." he mused aloud, looking at the still baffled Neila inquiringly. His heavy gaze made her uncomfortable, though, so she dropped her head.

"I'm ... sorry?" she mumbled, trying to drink a little bit more.

Neila's essence showed great strain, almost to the brink of collapse. Yet, she managed, much to Loki's surprise.

Normally, humans unconsciously avoided venturing too close to an Áss. It was a game of finding the balance—as much as they were drawn to their personality, their power repelled them just as much.

Occasionally, someone appeared, who could at least tolerate them. Miðgarðr used to be the sixth, just under Ásgarðr, meaning that humans possessed great powers at one point or other. To Loki's knowledge, only a catastrophic event could have caused a species to rapidly lose such a position. As a result, Miðgarðr had dropped to the fifth then fourth, where it remained until the third realm eventually 'usurped' that position.

On the other hand, not even Ásgarðr possessed too many records of these happenings. Ever since the Disconnection, Miðgarðr was only referred to as the third, leaving Loki in confusion about what had actually happened and how. Everything had occurred so long ago, the facts turned into opinions, then faded to speculations.

Loki was no scholar whatever, and liked action more than sitting around, researching. Yet, he did his fair share of reading up on history, since he set himself on trying to reconnect Miðgarðr. Especially, when people like Neila could walk on the third. Whatever befell on humans, some of the lineage remained. At least, Loki interpreted it this way.

In any case, Neila now seemed to be a promising candidate to be the Missing Link. *If she can get over the Darkness, that is,* the Áss thought bitterly.

A worried question brought him back to the present.

"Are you all right?" Neila asked, looking at him. "I didn't ... hurt you, or?"

"Oh, no, nothing of the sort," he replied with a smile. *Typical human ego,* he mused. *After finally doing something, they think that it is actually something.*

Glancing at her again, he finally realised how exhausted she became.

"Let's put you into bed, you'll need rest now," he said, standing up.

Holding out a hand, he offered assistance, waiting for her decision with sparkling eyes. Neila glanced at his hand, thinking of taking it. However, she seemed to understand the seriousness of the situation, and she might not want to immerse in it further just yet.

Closing her eyes, Neila clenched her jaw as she accepted his hand. Despite wincing under his touch, she seemed to be able to handle it. Regardless, when standing up, she suddenly collapsed, forcing Loki to catch her.

Not wanting to make the situation even worse, he quickly carried her to the bed, laying her down gently.

"Well," he muttered aloud while tucking Neila in. "At least it was a first step."

Chapter 11

Neila sat at the table, nibbling on her cereal and mulling over what had happened yesterday. Waking up quite late, she decided to have another 'breakfast for lunch' day. Loki was absent, so she had the time to analyse the happenings.

At first, she found it exhilarating that she *did* something magic-like. Having no idea how, though, repeating it remained doubtful. Anxiety plagued her mind; and with Fear at its side, they rendered Neila useless. Regardless, she now had tangible proof of such things *were* possible.

Truth be told, Neila had always liked to believe, even toyed with the thought, that she might possess 'powers.' But without confirmation, it was just a theory. Every supposed 'ability' could be dismissed as a mere coincidence, or explained as 'it's just how life is.'

Excitement now managed to make Neila feel almost good. Perhaps, she was not so insignificant as she had believed. *Still terribly small, but a little bit bigger now,* Neila thought with a smile. Then, Doubt made its entrance, plunging her mind into a whirlpool of torment once again.

Even if she possessed some form of power, what if she were unable to use it again? Loki would be disappointed, although, Neila doubted that he cared too much in the first place. Why would he?

Yeah, like an Áss would babysit an idiot like you, Neila thought bitterly. *Even if you had powers your whole life, you're just too stupid to figure them out. So why would anything change now, just because he's here? Be real, you're still nothing!*

Tears started to gather, stinging her eyes.

"UGH!" she moaned, agitated. "What did I dohohooo ...?" she whined, now dropping her head on the hard table, softly thumping it a few times.

The chime of her phone made her jerk her head up. Not having the mood for leaving the apartment, she hoped that it was not her editor. Neila's eyes widened upon seeing a message from a contact named 'Loki.' Apparently, he added his number without the thought of asking her.

Neila just blinked, feeling a tad violated. Brushing the feeling aside, she suddenly found it odd, why he chose to message instead of just popping up as before. Not that she minded, though. According to the message, Loki had some 'issues to address,' so he likely would not return home for a couple of days.

As nice this note was from him, Neila felt confused. After last night, she felt nothing but relief about not having to deal with Loki. Needing a little bit of time to digest and put the happenings in perspective, Neila wanted peace and quiet. At the same time, she found it equally peculiar and flattering that Loki now left messages. The fact that he actually listened and tried to act according to her requests showed kindness and caring.

Loki's a nice person, isn't he? Neila thought, musing. A refreshing change, indeed, from the kinds of human relations she had throughout life.

In any case, Neila now could think on her own terms. Although, these thoughts mostly revolved around her upcoming work during the next few days.

Maintaining focus proved challenging when Loki *did* appear from time to time for whatever reasons. Never staying for too long, his visits suggested more boredom with his 'issues' than anything else.

Yet, Loki clearly wished to share some of these experiences. Neila listened and responded as any friend would, not really minding the breaks from her work. How an Áss faced mundane problems proved to be very inspiring for her writing, so she found herself genuinely interested in his challenges.

Neila sometimes wondered, where and how Loki had spent the nights away. However he did it, the Áss had become acquainted with a vast array of individuals. Mostly rich ones at those, too. Some were 'mildly interesting,' as he put it, others 'just bearable.'

Also, Loki had purchased that last apartment they visited together. However, the interior designer proved to be a difficult woman. Despite the clear instructions, she often opted for a different direction.

"I am aware that humans hear only half of what one might say, but I made myself clear," said Loki at one time, annoyed.

"Why don't you fire her, then?" asked Neila.

"Because she is the best, and it took me quite the effort to convince her to take on this project at such short notice."

"Is she immune to your charms?" she teased.

"Of course not," Loki scoffed. "But some grow even more wary when around us, hence they behave so hard-headedly like never before. In any case, her work thus far has been good enough. She just struggles to grasp the difference between Nordic and Celtic sometimes."

"The horror!" Neila gasped with faked terror, then smiled at his disapproving glance.

As the week passed, apart from these little breaks, Neila spent her time working. Friday, though, brought a very upsetting message.

"A house-warming party?" Neila read the message out loud. "How the heck did he manage everything in just a few days?" she asked, baffled. Then, dismissing the matter, she typed a reply. "No ... can't ... do ... sorry ... But ... have ... fun ... at ... your ... party ..."

Immediately after hitting 'Send,' she grimaced, concerned that she might have come across rude. Anxiety rose its head, yet she tried to let it go. Neila now hoped that Loki would not simply appear unannounced, trying to persuade her in person. If anybody, then the Áss should understand.

The answer proved Neila right.

"'I'm sorry to hear that,'" she read aloud again, commenting on the messages as they arrived. "I'd bet you are. 'You'll be missed.' Yeah right, I can imagine. 'If you change your mind, it starts at 8PM.' I won't but thank you. I don't even know, where— Oh, never mind, he's just sent the address."

Neila gave a huge sigh. *What a perfect answer!* she cried out in her mind. No guy would ever construct such a terrific response. Loki had not just said the perfect things, but in the right order, leaving the overall decision to her. Also, even she could not twist this, thinking that he tried to manipulate or emotionally blackmail her. Neila just *knew*, he wrote and meant exactly what he intended.

"Disgusting!" Neila growled with a grimace, staring at the messages. "So perfectly disgusting! UGH!"

Neila felt torn; she really, really did not want to go. Engaging in a conversation was a terrifying thing for her. Humans seldom listened; and if one made a less-than-perfect first impression, no path remained for redemption. Also, they monopolised conversations with monologues, minding not if the other did not even listen. Until they got the occasional uh-huh-s, yeah-s, or any other of the meaningless 'positive' responses, they talked further like they had a gun held to their heads.

Neila harboured little to no interest in others' lives. *Plus, it would be an absolute posh fest,* she though grumpily, of which lifestyle she had no knowledge whatever. Eventually, she was bound to say something awkward.

On top of everything else, Neila lacked any suitable attire for such a party.

"All right, maybe we can find a compromise," Neila mumbled, thinking. "If Loki meant what he wrote, and why wouldn't he, he wants *me* there. But he did not specify, when."

The loophole felt appealing enough to take it. In a couple of hours, she would be in and out, without meeting any of the actual guests. Therefore, Neila started to get ready. It was already half past four in the afternoon, and the road should take her around forty to fifty minutes. However, while in the shower, another problem emerged—the house-warming gift.

"What could I bring for an Áss, who already has everything?" she pondered aloud whilst drying herself.

In the end, Neila decided that a gift was unnecessary. First of all, Loki clearly had enough money from selling his 'Ásgarðrian trinkets.' Given his likeness to luxury, a 'fine' bottle of wine would be unaffordable to Neila. Not to mention that her knowledge in drinks was far from an expert's. Just because something was expensive, it did not mean of a better quality. Not even a plant seemed logical, knowing about the interior designer.

On the other hand, in theory, her mere presence should suffice. Or, so he said.

While getting dressed, Neila had just realised that she actually trusted Loki. This thought, however, sent shivers down her spine.

"Trusting the Father of Lies ..." she mumbled, combing her hair in front of the mirror. "What could go wrong ...?"

Immediately, Neila reminded herself, how insulted and hurt Loki was upon hearing these ... 'accusations.' Never acting against her, he had never given her no cause to doubt him. Every motion, every micro-expression, and his tone suggested truth. Even if Loki *were* representing Chaos, as Neila believed, his intentions appeared genuine. In his presence, Neila remained calm. She felt safe.

Venturing outside was still a challenge due to all the noise and people. Hence, Neila went nowhere without her noise-cancelling headphones. On the bright side, the public transportation system in her city was superb, enabling her to reach even a remote location fairly fast. Neila still had to walk uphill for around fifteen minutes to get to Loki's house. After finally arriving, she remained outside for a little bit to catch her breath.

Just when Neila turned to get to the entrance of the house, she found herself in front of Loki.

"Welcome," he greeted her warmly, dismissing her startled squeal. "I'm glad you came," he continued, motioning her inside.

Entering the apartment, Neila gasped openly, looking around with widened eyes.

"This is ..." she whispered. "Unbelievable!"

"You think so?" Loki said somewhat critically. "It will do, I guess. It was an impossible deadline," he shrugged, earning an are-you-serious look from Neila.

The entire apartment could have featured as a showcase for 'Norse style' in a designer magazine. Not too much, yet just enough symbols could be found everywhere. Nothing looked out of date or rustic, but rather modern and incredibly sophisticated, infused with the ancient magnificence of Norse culture. The high-class technology everywhere only seemed to emphasise the simpleness of the displayed artefacts scattered around in the apartment. Even a few plants could find space for themselves in a corner or two, further brightening the flat.

"Are these real?" Neila gasped, stepping to what seemed to be a gorgeous necklace proudly sparkling inside a glass box.

"Of course they are," snorted Loki. "That was a gift from the sixth."

"Why did they give you a *necklace*?" she inquired.

"Well, it was meant for Angrboða, with whom I worked on that particular case. However, this is not truly to her liking, so she passed it to me. Later, I hid this with the other items on Miðgarðr. I had a hunch, they might prove useful one day."

Neila raised a questioning eyebrow.

"Did nobody ask, how you've just appeared from nowhere with such artefacts? Without a paper trail?"

"Of course they did. But I could change their minds about asking questions," he gave a cynical half-smile. "As it turned out, they would rather *have* said trinkets than dig around their origins."

"Pun intended?" Neila asked with a smile.

"In any case," he continued, "their primary concern was agreeing on a price. Apparently, they are literally priceless here."

"Is it wise, then, displaying them inside your apartment like this?"

Before Loki could answer, the main door slammed open as a middle-aged woman rushed inside, bearing what appeared to be a huge silver tree adorned with gems. Without a spare glance at Neila, she placed the object on the table in the living room, just in front of the electric hearth. Then, she gingerly adjusted it to look perfect.

"This is the last one, Mr Leifsson, I promise, but I just could not let this slip when I saw it at an auction. It looks magnificent, doesn't it?" the woman said, gazing at the centrepiece with clasped hands.

"It is nice, but didn't I tell you: no tree symbols?" asked Loki, earning a horrified look from the interior designer, and a puzzled one from Neila.

"But ..." she stammered, looking unsure. "Mr Leifsson, I can assure you that this IS the final piece! It brings everything together perfectly."

"And I believe you, but I must ask you to remove that ... *thing* ... at once!" demanded the Áss with such an intense glance, it made the poor woman tremble.

"Thing ...?" she echoed faintly, getting pale, yet unable to turn away from his glare. Apparently, the woman could not decide, whether she should be insulted, mortified, or angry. "It is such a gorgeous piece, made by—" she started again, but Loki cut in. Though his voice remained steady and his tone unchanged, the Áss sounded incredibly tense.

"I'm sure, that it is, but I have no need for such a thing."

Neila glanced at him, then at the almost trembling woman. Curiosity shone in her eyes as she stood beside him calmly, seemingly unaffected by Loki's mood.

"But ... But it's the last piece," the woman whispered, still mustering enough courage to argue, even though she looked so scared, as if she were held at gunpoint.

Loki exhaled, agitated, while pushing on his nose bridge.

Unbelievable, these humans are. Incapable of understanding a thing, he thought. *Why must they always know better?* he asked himself, trying to calm down. That poor woman looked terrified enough just from catching a hint of his powers, and he needed to pull himself together.

Taking a deep breath, he now rather glanced at Neila beside him. Interestingly enough, she appeared to be perfectly calm, despite standing so close. His powers intensified when getting emotional, even when 'wearing' a human form. Neila must have felt it, too. Yet, she seemed rather amused by the situation than anything else. From her look, she understood his anger perfectly.

"Well, you'll have to find the last piece at another time, since THAT will not remain in in this apartment," Loki announced, agitated. As he calmed down, the woman seemed to find her voice once more.

"But, why not?" the interior designer asked, measuring the centrepiece. "It complements the Nordic theme perfectly."

Loki took a sharp breath, closing his eyes in frustration. Those strange anger coils appeared around him once again. Neila glanced at the woman, who still fixated on the piece, mumbling about its perfection and how she could not understand. Even when looking at Loki, the designer did not seem to spot anything out of the ordinary.

"Even if that were true," the Áss said with restrained anger, earning a disapproving glance from the woman. *She* obviously did not find his questioning tone appropriate. "Should anything similar appear here, I will make sure that you will never find work in the industry again. Do I make myself clear now?" he glared at the woman with furious eyes.

The designer turned ashen as she dropped her mouth open. With trembling hands, she picked the piece up, nearly dropping it, then hurried away.

Loki took another deep breath. Few things bothered him in general, but sheer idiocy was intolerable. Being primitive was one thing. The complete lack of listening or comprehension skills was another.

"Are you okay?" Neila asked, concerned. So, he forced a smile.

"Perfectly," he said, although, from her look, she could not have been fooled that easily. Thus, he tried to change the subject. "Would you fancy a drink? Champagne, perhaps?"

"No, thank you. I don't like champagne," Neila declined, now wandering to another artefact, a few coins this time.

Loki glanced at her inquiringly, trying to figure out her preference while walking to the bar cabinet beside the kitchen.

"How about a spritz veneziano, then?" the Áss suggested.

"I don't know what that is, to be honest," replied Neila, sauntering to the kitchen isle and taking a seat on a bar stool. Watching Loki making the cocktails himself, she raised a questioning eyebrow. "Is there anything you cannot do?" Neila asked with a half-smile.

"I don't know," he answered, placing the drinks on the counter before sitting beside her. The moment the designer left the apartment, he reverted to his 'true form.'

"Wow, talk about humble," Neila teased, raising her glass for a toast. "Skal," she said, looking into Loki's eyes.

"Skál," he replied.

"Hmm," her eyes widened. "Very nice, I must say. Dangerous, though."

"Why would it be dangerous?"

"Because this is the sort of drink that one just drinks and then gets hammered without even noticing," replied Neila, sipping the cocktail, then turned with her chair to look around in the living room. "You truly have a magnificent apartment."

"It will do for the time being," he answered, earning a dubious glance.

"Still, aren't you worried about somebody stealing those artefacts?"

"Not at all," he replied, bored. "Nobody would dare to break in *here*, believe me."

A dangerous spark in his eyes showed this statement to be absolutely true. Nevertheless, Neila felt it to be arrogant. But then again, if anybody, Loki would know how to protect his valuables without relying solely on an alarm system.

They sat in silence for a moment, savouring their drinks and wandering on their paths of thoughts. That is, until Loki rose, heading for the door.

"My apologies," he said, assuming his human appearance. "I must let the caterers inside."

"What ca—" Neila started, but got interrupted by the beep of the intercom system. "Wow, he's good," she muttered, watching Loki opening the door for them.

Clearly, the Áss constantly monitored the perimeter. Probably not a single car or pedestrian would miss his attention. Watching the caterers arranging everything in the kitchen reminded Neila that, perhaps, it was time to go.

Finish the drink first, though, don't be rude, Neila thought, moving to the sofa, not to be in the way for the servers. Loki joined him shortly, occasionally answering their questions.

"It will be a fancy party," Neila said, fidgeting with her glass as a sign of anxiety. Also, she often checked her watch when thinking that Loki would not see it, contemplating the right moment to leave.

"Not in the slightest," he gave a sigh. "But, it'll have to do."

"So, about that necklace," she changed the subject. "It seems Asian, and I found that very interesting."

"That is because it is form the sixth, who mostly visited the Asian parts of Miðgarðr."

Neila now widened her eyes, then glanced at the busy caterers nervously.

"I know, I asked this already, but is it wise to speak about such things so freely?" she lowered her voice, earning a huff and a half-smile.

"They won't mind, believe me. Those three are incredibly weak in mind, probably would not even remember this event in detail, just that it happened. I could show myself fully and they still wouldn't put two and two together."

"I find this unbelievable, but all right."

"Some react this way," Loki now shrugged. Then he added, insulted, "probably these types were the same sort, who then talked about trees connecting the realms and me spawning an eight-legged horse."

"Didn't Odin have a horse like that?"

"Oh, it's the same horse, still alive and well," the Áss nodded. "*I* allowed that poor creature back to its natural habitat, but then *he* came and took it as a pet."

"Well, given that pets live longer than their wild counterparts, perhaps it was not that bad of a decision," she mused, but when he flashed a disapproving glance at her, she quickly sipped the cocktail again.

Abruptly, Loki's phone rang. From that moment on, he became occupied with several more calls and messages, leaving Neila alone with her thoughts on the sofa. When finishing her drink, she stood up and turned to the Áss, who was taking a call by the window. When spotting her, he quickly ended the conversation.

"Please, stay for the party," Loki said before Neila could open her mouth. "I would like you to meet some people."

"You clearly don't know what social anxiety means, then," she scoffed. "In any case, you have a lovely apartment. I'll see you around, then?"

Loki measured her, thinking how to persuade her to stay. In the end, he gave a sigh.

"All right, if you must go, then go," he yielded, sounding sad. "I simply would have loved to have a person here, with whom I could have a normal conversation. This 'party' is more about business than about anything else and I wouldn't mind your insights, to be honest."

"Really?" she asked, sceptical. "You can literally read people's souls, and you want *my* opinion?"

"Believe it or not, a lot has changed since the last time I was here," explained Loki. "Yes, I am that much more powerful, I still can make mistakes. The difference is just too big, hence it's always good to have a buffer, so to speak," he shrugged.

Neila narrowed her eyes at this, trying to figure out whether any of this was true or not. After all, the Æsir were not all-knowing beings; sometimes one just could not see the forest from the tree.

"Even if I would consider this," she mused. "I have nothing to wear, and I cannot appear like this," she motioned at her jeans and shirt.

"I had a hunch that you might bring this up, so I took the liberty of selecting something for you," said Loki, gesturing Neila to follow him to his room.

Inside, Neila spotted an outfit that was laid out on the bed. It was a plain beige pantsuit, paired with a black, probably silk shirt. On the floor stood a pair of elegant black shoes.

"How did you …?" Neila mumbled, completely stunned. The simple elegance emitted by the ensemble took her breath away. Despite being so modest, the material and style made the clothes truly high-class.

"It was no trouble," Loki smiled. "Now, I leave you to change."

Neila had no time to argue or even react. Numb from bafflement, she changed. Everything fitted her to perfection, including the shoes, and were incredibly comfortable. Even the around five centimetres heels felt bearable. Neila could never pull off a true high-heel thing.

Neila watched herself in the big mirror at a corner, her heart pounding. *How could I agree?* her mind screamed. *Let's just go before it's too late.*

Before panic could take over, Loki returned.

"Now, the finishing touch," he said with an almost sparkling gaze.

In his palm lay a beautiful necklace with an Asian-styled dragon medallion. The incredible details made Neila freeze in awe. The dragon almost seemed to be alive.

"That is …" she whispered. "Incredible!"

"I'm glad you like it," the Áss said, still smiling. "It was also a gift from the sixth. Since I don't use such items, I thought it would fit you well. May I?" he asked, obviously meaning whether he could put it on her.

In her stunned state, Neila could only muster a nod. With a fluttering heart, she detached her own necklace and put it away in her purse. Then, she stood still while Loki stepped right behind her to attach the new one.

Neila's whole body trembled, suddenly feeling Time to halt. Her throbbing heart felt, as if it wanted to break out from her chest. Despite the fact that Loki tried to avoid making a direct contact with her, his hand still brushed against her skin.

Neila would not want to think about how much Loki could sense of the tornado of feelings that ruled her soul. The situation itself was an incredibly intimate one; and normally she would have never got herself into something like this.

In truth, Neila treated Loki differently, never having a romantic thought about him so far. Now, however, it suddenly struck her, *how handsome* Loki truly was, making her very uncomfortable overall.

Oh, those eyes ...! Neila lamented internally, then mentally shook her head. *It's just his powers, you know that,* she thought, but something from deep down objected.

The only consolation she had was the fact that falling in love was out of the question. Neila never had crushes on anybody. Physical attraction was one thing, but that on its own never gave a reason for her to try to get close to anybody. On the contrary.

In truth, Neila had never tried to get serious with anybody on her own. If the situation presented itself, she might not refuse an attractive man, but she never anticipated it to happen. For better or worse, Neila was painfully aware of how she looked—nothing like a 'beauty' who would grab anybody's attention when entering a room. Therefore, she always treated men according to this knowledge. *Why try when nothing would happen, and you can only get hurt? It's not worth the trouble,* she believed.

A tingle on her skin brought her back to the painful present. Loki still stood behind her; mere seconds had passed. Yet those few moments caused more pain than anything for a long time now.

After the necklace was secured, Neila stepped away from him immediately, trying to calm down. In that moment, she could only curse human physiology and primitiveness. Everything was about sex with humans, and sadly, *some* biological 'urges' proved to be impossible to shed.

"Is everything all right?" asked Loki, making her blush deeply and avert her gaze.

"Of course not," she mumbled, using anger to mask everything else. "I have no idea, why I am even considering this in the first place."

"Because you are a kind person and I am in need of your help."

Neila gave a snort and an eye roll at this.

"Yeah," she mocked. "Yet, I have the feeling that I will regret this rather sooner than later."

Before the Áss could respond, the intercom buzzed, signalling the arrival of the first guests.

Neila remained in the room for a few more moments, trying to pull herself together. At least, the upcoming party filled her with so much anxiety, she almost could forget about that 'moment' with Loki. *It was nothing like that, and you know it!* she chided herself. *This is not a fairy-tale or a romcom movie. Keep it together and stay in reality-land!*

However, Neila just could not shake the feeling that staying was a dreadful mistake.

Chapter 12

"I knew, this was a bad idea," Neila mumbled into the darkness.

Currently, she stood on the huge balcony, leaning on the rails. After an hour of sauntering around in the apartment and trying to avoid any kind of conversation, she sought sanctuary outside. Despite the cool night, she had enough drinks not to feel it.

Since the arrival of the first guests, Loki had said nothing to her, dealing with business opportunities and whatnot. Neila lingered around for a while, but nobody really minded her and she did not try to mingle. Since Anxiety hindered her ability to interact with people, she rather stayed in the background, observing. Until she decided that a little air would do her good. The balcony was packed with smokers and people in general, it still felt better than the crowd inside.

Turning, Neila spotted Loki in a group of five, having a serious debate, it seemed. Many stood around them, listening and exchanging a word or two in the background. As the centre of the party, all eyes hung on Loki. Since the Áss showed no intent of including Neila, she was thinking about sneaking away and go home.

"Is this spot taken?" a voice startled Neila back to the present.

A handsome man in a suit stood beside her, now waiting for an answer.

"No, no, I'm sorry, I was just lost in thought," she stammered quickly.

"I've noticed," the man gave a charming smile, pulling out a vape from his inside packet of the suit jacket.

Neila shifted from one leg to the other, thinking about what to say, if anything. But the man solved the problem himself, holding out a hand while introducing himself.

"I'm sorry for my poor manners, my name is Richard White. I'm Mr Leifsson's bank liaison."

"Neila Saraven, nice to meet you," she took his hand.

Hating handshakes altogether, Neila got a pleasant surprise. His grasp was firm yet not too strong, and he released her hand after one quick shake. Afterwards, she mused upon the fact that why such a person was there in the first place.

"Well, not the reaction I was anticipating," he said now, looking at her inquiringly.

"Oh?" said Neila, confused. Only after the other gave a disbelieving scoff and flashed a smile, it finally made sense to her. Her realisation must have shown in her eyes as well, since he gave another chuckle.

"Well, it's quite refreshing, I might say. My name did not do me any favours, as you can imagine," he smiled further.

Neila raised a questioning eyebrow. The fact that this was considered an actual conversational topic filled her with sadness. Richard was a man with coloured skin, and with a surname like White, she could easily imagine those 'difficult times' he mentioned.

Come to think of it, though, this whole party is incredibly diverse, the thought now flashed through Neila's mind. Given her social anxiety, *everybody* made her uncomfortable, race notwithstanding. But now, she suddenly realised the variety of different peoples present. Blacks, Asians, Indians, mixed together with only a few Caucasians, lingered everywhere. Women and men alike; young, middle aged, or older. Apparently, Loki cared not about appearances and social expectations.

Richard drew a few puffs from the vape before breaking the momentary silence between them.

"So, how do you know Mr Leifsson?" he asked, obviously trying to place her in this whole charade.

"I'm ... uh ..." Neila started, but her words trailed off. Unsure, she flashed a nervous smile.

"It's fine, none of my business," he smiled as well, exhaling a huge cloud. "What do you do, then?"

"I'm a writer."

"In earnest?" he echoed, now looking interested. "Anything I might've read?"

Neila measured him with an incredibly piercing look, then dropped her gaze.

"I highly doubt that," she said, almost shyly.

At this, the banker flashed a confused frown, unable to put together that reflexive stare with the honest tone. In the end, he took it as a jest rather than an insult.

"I might've deserved that look," he said with a half-smile, taking another puff from the vape before putting it away whilst exhaling. "The word 'liaison' doesn't make me look good, does it?"

"I have nothing against liaisons," she said, picking up the friendly teasing. "Although, I have never met one in person before."

"Well, I've never met a writer either," he shrugged, then followed Neila's glance into the living room, where Loki was still having the discussion. "Good looking man, isn't he?" Richard now added, earning a confused frown from her.

"I guess," she shrugged. "But I was just wondering, what would be able to flatten that anime hair."

Immediately, Neila bit her lower lip, regretting that she ever opened her mouth. However, hearing the delighted chuckle, she glanced at him questioningly.

"I know, right?" Richard said, almost laughing. "It should be purple or green, and he would be a perfect character."

"You know animes?" Neila now asked, baffled.

"Well, to be honest, I prefer mangas over animes. I am fluent in Japanese, and I have quite a collection, too," he bragged. Seeing her widened eyes, he added with a playful tease, "not so dull now, huh?"

Neila blushed, sipping from her drink.

"*Gomen, gomen,*" she apologised, smiling. "But you have to give it to me, *that* is not something one could expect from a person such as yourself."

"Myself, as in ...?" he asked now, leaving the sentence open.

"As in a bank liaison," Neila finished with a playful smile.

Richard gave a little laugh.

"Well, I wouldn't have thought you being a writer either, sooo, call it even?" he proposed a 'truce.' Neila nodded, still smiling while sipping her drink. Seeing this, he continued with the common topic they have found. "So, you know animes?"

"Oh, compared to you, I just dabble, I'm sure."

The conversation finally took off between them, leaving even Neila to ease up. They talked about the Japanese culture, of which Richard truly knew a lot. When Neila pointed this out, he almost shyly admitted that he lived there for almost five years during his youth.

They even concocted a story about Loki, imagining him as an anime character. They shared a laugh about some development or other, playfully teasing the Áss just enough to have themselves a good time while remaining respectful. Without telling anything specific, Richard admitted that Loki could behave a tad … firm, when it came to the schedule and the amount of work he demanded.

When their fun came to a natural halting point, Neila suddenly shivered from the cold. Having the same drink since stepping outside, slowly every drop of alcohol started to disappear from her system, leaving her shudder.

"Well, this was fun," she said, turning to Richard. "But I think I'm going to go home now. Enjoy the rest of your evening."

With this, Neila headed back inside. Keeping her head low, she avoided everybody while slipping in to Loki's room. There, she quickly changed back, leaving the outfit on the bed with the necklace nicely laid on top. Unsure about whether this was the right thing to do, she then decided to deal with the issue later. At the moment, she just wanted to get out of there.

Given the late hour and free drinks, nobody paid her any attention. Neila could slip out without anybody noticing. On the street, she took a deep breath, then tried to fish out her headphones from the purse.

"Great minds think alike, it seems," Richard suddenly said behind her, making her jump. "I'm sorry, I didn't mean to scare you," he held both hands up apologetically, stepping back to look anything but threatening.

"It's all right," she said, smiling nervously and having no idea about how to proceed in a situation such as this.

"You've changed," he noticed, looking at her from tip to toe.

"Well, no matter how much I like fancy clothes, that was not really my style, you know," Neila muttered, blushing in embarrassment.

"Do you need a lift? We could share a taxi," Richard offered.

"No, thank you, I'm okay."

"Do you have a car?"

"No, but I prefer to walk anyway. Well, good night," Neila said, nervous and trying not to think about how rude she must have sounded. However, she wanted to get away from this situation already. His call made her halt, though.

"Wait a minute, please. I just wanted to say that I had a really wonderful time," he started, sounding genuine enough. "Maybe, we could do it again? Continue our little Adventures of Loki ... over dinner?"

Neila had to gather every strength she had left not to gasp openly. Sure, they had a nice time, but she would never ever anticipate a man such as Richard to ask her out for a date. Especially not after seeing her dressed in 'normal clothes.'

"Erm ... Sure, why not?" she flashed a nervous smile.

"You don't seem too excited about the prospect," Richard observed and raised a questioning eyebrow.

"I'm just tired, I'm sorry," she quickly corrected herself, trying her best to sell the act. "That would be lovely, yes."

"Then, if you give me your phone number, I can call you?"

"Erm ... sure, all right. Give me your phone and I'll type it in," she said, then took his when Richard handed it to her. When she gave it back, she added, "but, rather message me. I don't answer calls."

"Oh?" he asked, holding the phone in a hand. "Why not?"

"It's a long story, involving social anxiety and such," she averted. "Well, enjoy the rest of your night."

Neila turned around and hurried for the train station, but then her phone suddenly started to vibrate. Fishing it out, she saw an unknown number.

"Just checking, sorry!" Richard shouted after her, then he waved goodbye and got into the arriving taxi.

Utterly stunned, Neila watched the taxi drive by with the widely smiling Richard.

"What the ..." Neila muttered, frozen in place.

Then, she put on her headphones and started a soothing playlist to calm her nerves. Fortunately, her journey home was completely uneventful. After a fairly long shower, Neila curled up under the blanket in her bed, trying to sleep. Despite the eventful night, she managed to fall asleep almost instantly.

Chapter 13

Loki watched Neila on the balcony while keeping track of his discussion. If it were possible, he would gladly have joined her outside. However, the people he was currently speaking with were all crucial to his plan. They all agreed to meet up next Monday to finalise everything, which was more than Loki could have wanted.

In exchange, the Áss had to give them enough attention to feel important. Despite the short amount of time he had spent on Miðgarðr, he had gained a fairly significant reputation in certain circles. With a flourishing social media presence, these people were drawn to the envisioned opportunities he represented like moths to a bright light. At the moment, however, this was also more bothersome than advantageous.

Despite finding another special human capable of taking Loki's hand, it started to backfire. *The more the merrier,* he thought, keeping the overall goal in mind. Richard finding Neila was not the least surprising. However, seeing *her* enjoying his company somehow felt like a knife in Loki's back. While smiling and laughing when needed, Loki found the emotion of jealousy interesting. It was the very first time for him, and could not quite grasp its nature.

Feeling obliged to do *something* about the situation, he then spotted Neila sneaking away, leaving. *Without a goodbye, even,* the Áss mused, which hurt him more. A moment later, Richard entered the living-room, heading straight for Loki.

"Thank you for the invite, it was a wonderful party," he said, holding out a hand for a shake.

Loki found this remarkable. Taking his hand firmly, he watched the other's features for any reaction. Richard did flinch, but his smile remained just the same.

"It is a lovely home, and I wish you all the best with it," said the liaison, now jerking his hand away a tad too frantically.

Seeing this, Loki could not withhold a smile.

"Thank you for coming. See you on Monday, then?" the Áss asked. Richard merely nodded, then said goodbye and hurried away.

Loki followed his movement with his mind, knowing that Richard wanted to catch up to Neila. The urge to intervene popped up stronger this time, yet he stayed put, only watching.

You see her distress, yet cannot stay away, can you, human? Loki thought, knowing perfectly, what was happening outside. Then, he took a deep breath. *No wonder ... You could teach each other a few things. So, perhaps, it's for the best.*

For the remainder of the night, Loki was musing about the significance of this connection between Neila and Richard. In truth, they both could prove valuable resources for him. In theory, two could potentially start the process, like the forming of a snowflake.

After everybody had left, Loki threw himself down on the sofa with a drink in his hand.

"Unbelievable," he muttered to the ceiling. "Not even a battle is this exhausting."

Just as Loki was thinking about taking a relaxing bath before turning in, he got the faint sensation of a message. With closed eyes, he used his deeper part of consciousness to understand it.

Only Heimdallr was able to send such a message to the disconnected worlds without physically being there. The android had been created by a lot of people and was crafted entirely from technology. Unlike any other robot, he possessed a consciousness, as Heimdallr liked to call it; was alive and had abilities, just like any other Ásgarðrian. Better abilities, even, allowing him to function as the protector of Ásgarðr itself—the Lookout.

On the other hand, despite all the efforts since then, Ásgarðr had yet to create another android like him. They could make robots, clever ones at those, too. Even some child-like AIs could be 'birthed,' useful for several things overall. But nothing remotely close to Heimdallr's level had emerged.

Loki disliked him.

Heimdallr had no essence whatsoever, which made the Áss distrustful. Also, he understood little about the android overall. *Perhaps, there is a natural connection from Miðgarðr directly to Ásgarðr,* Loki now mused, thinking about how the Lookout could have sent the message.

In any case, Heimdallr said that Loki was needed back on Ásgarðr. Freyja was open to talk to him, finally, which was more than he could have ever hoped.

Time truly was of the essence now.

Without a second thought, Loki teleported to the connection again that led to the fourth.

Let's see, whether this would be the time ... the Áss thought, taking a huge breath and jumping into the connection. Travelling through the fourth posed no problem whatever, but when coming out from the Bifröst on the fifth, Loki felt a sharp pain in his right leg.

No luck whatever, he thought bitterly, jumping away immediately. Hiding behind a huge building, Loki heard the machine sealing the Bifröst once again.

"Well, this is starting to get repetitive and boring," the Áss growled aloud, scanning the perimeter through his visor. Several fifths lurked around, all with weapons aimed at him.

"It's nice that you came right after I have sent the message," Heimdallr's voice broke into his mind, making Loki grunt again.

"Can you just shut up and bring me back directly?" the Áss snapped, having had enough of this charade. Since his presence was detected by the fifths, no other options remained but to return to Miðgarðr once again.

"You could also look for a direct connection either from Miðgarðr or from the fourth, you know," Heimdallr suggested in his head, obviously hearing Loki's thoughts.

"Yes," he agreed. *"But if I had that much time, the fifth would be less pissed."*

"I resent your tone, my friend. But I'll try to help, if I can."

Loki grunted again, now leaping forwards to avoid a few shots. Heading for the same connection as last time, he got back to Miðgarðr without any more trouble.

Plunging into the ocean, the Áss felt the salt sting his wound, again. Floating on his back, Loki glanced at the dark blue sky, full of stars. After healing himself, he remained there for a little while, enjoying the silence and the rhythm of the water. It was the closest to true Peace on Miðgarðr.

Taking a deep breath, Loki composed himself. Heimdallr only tried to help, he knew that as well. The situation frustrated him, not the android. It was just unbelievable, how and why the fifths could be so stubborn. On any given realm, visitors were bound by the rules of that world. Even Ásgarðrians must oblige.

However, since Loki had become a fugitive, the fifths wanted to catch him at any cost. *Literally,* Loki thought bitterly. *They'd rather go extinct than to let me pass and have Ásgarðr's help.*

For having such aid, one from the seventh had to arrange it personally. It also had to be for a very, very good reason, like an outside attack. In this, even a serious disease that could make the fifth go extinct, mattered little. It was the nature of things. Sometimes life emerged, at other times, it ceased. If it were to happen on Ásgarðr, nobody should help them, even if they were capable.

On the other hand, Loki had enough evidence to think that this *was* an attack instead of a natural sickness. This is why he promised Freyja's help.

Not to mention that, Loki pondered, *who would take the place of the fifths as the overseers of the junction? The fourths are still far from that level; the sixths are not interested. No outsiders had earned the right, so ... what other option remains, then?*

Loki merely wanted to deal with one serious change at a time, if possible. Hence, he meddled. Even if such actions were frowned upon on Ásgarðr.

Since nothing would change, if he remained in the middle of the ocean, Loki headed back to his apartment. Looking for a clock to see how much time had passed, he grimaced to find that it was the middle of the night, on Sunday.

"No luck at all," he growled, pouring himself a glass of water. At least, the water tasted quite rich, thanks to the surrounding mountain springs. Then, he decided to rest, needing all of his energies to convince Neila for what he wanted of her.

Stepping inside the bedroom, Loki flashed a frown at spotting the clothes and necklace on the bed. Anger bubbled up, but he let it go at once. Since he understood her reasoning perfectly, there was no use getting upset about it. After a little rest, he could assess the situation with clarity.

Loki woke around noon, chiding himself for not rising sooner. This way, he would only have a short time to fetch Neila. Which fact could work in his favour or go horribly wrong.

"Well, let's see, which it will be," he muttered, disappearing.

When he next looked around, Loki stood on Neila's terrace. In the living-room, he saw her on the sofa, watching something on the TV while eating. When spotting him, she immediately put down the tray and turned off the show.

The Áss walked into the room, as if there were no door. After greeting him, she asked whether it is all right if she finished the last bites of the meal. Loki just gave a wave of hand as he took a seat beside her. Then, he pulled out something from his pocket, putting it down on the sofa. Neila inhaled sharply upon seeing the gorgeous necklace that she wore at the party.

"I thought, you'd like this, that is why I wanted you to have it. As a gift," Loki broke the silence, sounding hurt. Apparently, Æsir could or chose not to hide their emotions.

"I'm sorry," Neila said, putting the tray down on the floor. Then, she poured tea for herself. "It's just so gorgeous. I don't deserve such a ... treasure."

"I think, you do. Isn't that enough?" he asked, still sounding hurt.

The way she averted her gaze while sipping her tea answered—it was not. Confidence needed to stem from within. Until *she* believed, nothing Loki could say would make a difference. Perhaps, if he were steadfast enough, she would start to believe.

"Well, I would like you to have it. It suits you," Loki smiled. Neila glanced at the necklace with sparkling eyes, showing how much she loved the jewellery.

"Are you sure?" she asked, taking it to her hand.

"Yes."

"Well ... thank you," Neila finally accepted, still unsure. Swiftly, she took off her own and put the new one on. "Is this white gold, by the way?"

"No. I believe, you call the material iridium."

Neila gasped.

"This must be worth a fortune! I cannot wear something like that in the open!"

"Why not? Would anybody be able to tell the difference?"

Neila blinked, confused. The Áss had a point. Sipping her tea, she unconsciously fidgeted with the medallion.

"In any case, I would like you to accompany me for a meeting this afternoon."

"Why?" she jerked her head at him. "Also, in what language? I've heard you speak at least five different ones. How many do you speak, by the way?"

"In English, of course. And, a few hundred, give or take."

Neila's eyes widened at this again, but then she gave a not-bad grimace.

"So, why should I go?" she inquired.

"Because you need to sign a few papers."

"For what purpose?" she wanted to know. Fear sparkled in her eyes.

"I will tell you everything, but try to remain calm, please," Loki began, making Neila even more confused and scared. "Overall, this was a surprise for you."

The Áss halted for a moment, probably thinking through again what to say.

"The apartment I purchased, is for you. It is on your name, as well as a bank account with some funds. I need you this afternoon to sign the necessary papers to make this legal and official. I've arranged for everybody to be there, in a conference room at the bank. Originally, I wanted you at the party to get to know the people, who would manage your assets and so on. So you wouldn't be too anxious today."

As he spoke, Neila turned paler and paler; her eyes widened, and seemingly she forgot to breathe. Completely frozen, she was rendered speechless. Loki watched her, worried.

"Are you all right?" he asked, just to make her respond anything. Neila's whole essence was in turmoil, reflecting the tempest inside her soul.

"What?!" she exclaimed. "NO!"

Jumping up, Neila now started to pace around the room, panicky.

"How?" she managed the question. "Or, rather, why?"

Loki gave a soothing smile, emitting nothing but calmness.

"I owe my life to you. So, it seemed only fair to return the favour, that is all."

"What?!" she burst out, still walking to and fro. "I did no such thing!"

"Of course you did."

"No I didn't!" Neila argued, looking more and more in despair. "You said it yourself: you would've been fine without my help. So, don't try to bend the truth."

"Believe me when I say, I wouldn't have asked for help, were it not necessary," said Loki, still with a soothing tone. "Yes, I might have prevailed on my own, but it would have taken far longer. Everything would have turned out differently. In my eyes, that is saving my life."

Halting, Neila glanced at him disbelievingly. Then, as if something had just popped to mind, she posed a question.

"How much money, exactly?" she asked, looking frightened of the answer.

"Not much. A hundred million dollars, give or take."

"A hundred million ..." Neila whispered, getting ashen once again. This, however, gave Panic the strength to take over.

Feeling faint, Neila stumbled to the sofa, thudding down. Despite being wide awake, she saw almost nothing of the surroundings. No matter how fast she gasped for air, the feeling of drowning grew stronger.

Neila remembered clutching her chest while desperately trying to breathe. Inside, the thoughts and feelings rampaged freely and without any restrain, overwhelming her system.

Then, a gong went off in her mind; its tone wiping everything away.

Neila opened her eyes, once again comprehending surroundings. The tempest inside ceased; her mind cleared in an instant. Taking a huge breath, she glanced at Loki beside her.

Seeing her clear look, the Áss pulled back his hand. Neila flashed a frown, thinking that *he* must have had something to do with her sudden calmness.

Before she could ask anything, Loki broke the silence.

"If you've managed to calm down, please get ready. We need to go now."

Neila's essence flickered at this again, making Loki raise an eyebrow.

"Why are you doing this?" she asked, looking and sounding serene.

"I've told you."

"No," she shook her head. "There is something more. And I want to know."

Suddenly, that tricolour gaze felt heavier than ever before.

"Everything, I've told you, is true," said Loki; a strange light in his gaze. "You've helped me a great deal, whether you accept this fact or not. I cannot do much in return, but I can do this. So why not?"

Neila narrowed her eyes at this, looking even more fierce than before.

"However," continued the Áss, feeling the piercing gaze on himself. "I will not deny that I have my plans with you. You need to evolve, and for that, you'll need a calm environment. Hence the amount and extent of my gifts."

Interestingly enough, Neila had seemed to accept the answer. Getting something for 'free' signalled danger to humans. But, if there were a barter involved, suddenly everything became acceptable.

Loki found this notion rather appalling. However, since he got what he wanted, it also seemed a small price to pay. Now, all Loki had to do was nudge Neila in the right direction.

Starting with attending the meeting that afternoon.

Chapter 14

Neila lay back down, stretching comfortably on the huge sofa. Looking at the ceiling, she inspected the ornaments, thinking about the decorator's intent. They were intriguing enough to make the top of the room interesting by complementing and, at the same time, concealing the lamps.

The centre of the living room was the sunken part around the modest-sized electric hearth. The set of sofa and armchairs filled that square-shaped space. Above the hearth, a cleverly disguised cabinet hid the TV.

Initially, Neila found the layout of the apartment a tad too modern, yet it also caught her imagination. Seeing the work of the designer, she completely fell in love with it. After moving in, she could fully occupy herself with glancing around and admiring everything.

"Ah, I won't leave the apartment for at least two weeks!" she exclaimed, stretching once more.

"What about the dinner plans we've talked about, then?" asked Loki, making Neila sit up abruptly.

Until then, the Áss was taking a bath, despite the early hour in the morning. Neila enjoyed her 'freedom' in the living room, slowly getting used to the new environment. Glancing at Loki now made her eyes widen, then she averted her gaze while turning deep red. Loki wore absolutely nothing at the moment, clearly feeling comfortable enough to do so.

"Is something the matter?" he asked, sauntering to the kitchen counter where a bowl of strawberries awaited. Picking the bowl up, he walked to the sofa while nibbling a berry.

"No, not at all," she said, still blushed but she managed to control her tone. "This is your home as well, I'd want you to feel ... free," she said, now with a restrained smile.

Abruptly, her phone gave a chime on the coffee table, signalling an incoming message. Neila did not reach for it, giving all her attention to the Áss.

"So, what about our dinner plans?" he repeated, taking another bite.

Neila just shrugged.

"You have to give me time. I barely survived that whole shenanigan with the meetings, then the moving, the attorney, my 'assistant,' and all that."

"You handled all the meetings very well, in my opinion," Loki argued, sitting on top of the sofa backrest, looking over the strawberries to decide which one to pick.

"It wasn't all me, and you know that," Neila shook her head. "If you weren't there, I would have actually run off."

"That is untrue. You've managed quite well without my help or assistance," he said, glancing at her for a brisk moment before biting into another strawberry.

"What about that gong before?" asked Neila, confused. "YOU touched me, YOU did that. Or?"

The memory of Loki revealing his plans of giving her this apartment with an insanely generous bank account lived crystal clear in her head. This sudden change of unbelievable series of events pushed Neila into pure Panic. But just before it could consume her, there was a sound of a gong or bell. The single-note tone wiped away everything in an instant, leaving only Calmness behind.

"I just showed the way. *A* way. *You* have learnt to use it," Loki answered. Seemingly, the fruits occupied his full attention, but the strange light in his eyes told otherwise.

Neila decided to let this slide and not ask too many questions. Another chime of her phone broke the moment anyway. Then another, and another, showing that somebody truly wanted her attention.

"Who is that?" Loki wanted to know, glancing at the phone. If he tried to behave leisurely about how much it bothered him, he managed poorly.

"Richard, probably," Neila said, still not picking up the phone.

"Since when are you so familiar with him?" asked Loki with a faint frown, halting with eating.

"Since that abysmal party you dragged me to," she answered, raising an eyebrow. "He ... actually messaged me the morning after, and since then we are on talking grounds."

Loki gave a grimace, obviously not liking the prospect.

"What's the matter with it?" she asked, seeing his discontent. "He WAS a big help during the meetings as well. He's a liaison after all. He helped me a great deal by lining up those people one by one, so I only had to deal with one at a time. Plus, he helped me moving. AND he knew the 'correct people,' so I could donate everything I didn't need anymore. Wow, I cannot believe that all this happened in just two weeks!" she mused aloud, baffled.

"Why did he get involved? That is what the assistant is for," grunted Loki.

"Honestly, I keep forgetting about her, since I am not an 'important person,' who would actually need a gofer, you know," replied Neila, sounding strained. "And, he *offered* to help without me asking or hinting at anything. I don't even have a driver's license, you know." Seeing how he just clenched his jaw, Neila added, "Richard is just being nice. Or, he wants some of the money that badly," she shrugged, earning a confused frown. "But, I don't really understand your dislike, since YOU were nowhere to be found, and YOU hired him in the first place. Where *did* you disappear to, by the way?"

"I was looking for a direct connection to Ásgarðr," Loki growled, rolling his eyes. Then, he picked another berry and bit in it. Immediately, his features smoothened out, enjoying the taste.

"Are those *that* good?" asked Neila.

"Well, I have never had strawberries before, and I find them extraordinary," he replied, finishing the piece.

"Really?" she asked with a disbelieving smile. "But you've travelled around on Midgard, how could you miss something as ordinary as this?"

"You have travelled a little yourself," replied Loki. "Have you tried *everything* where you had your vacations?"

Neila gave a well-yeah grimace. Another chime came, so she picked the phone up, quickly looking over the messages.

"Don't worry," she said, feeling Loki's piercing gaze on herself. "I'm fairly convinced that he's only doing this because of the money. He knew the whole thing from the beginning, right?"

"Yes, and untrue."

"Yeah, sure," she snorted, starting to type a reply. "Will you leave me some, or you want the whole bowl?" Neila asked, not even glancing at the berries.

At this, Loki simply chose a piece and offered it to her mouth. Biting it, she took the fruit without halting with typing or even looking up.

"You know what could make them better?" mused Loki aloud. "Chocolate."

Neila glanced up at him disbelievingly, trying to withhold the chuckle until she could swallow the bite properly.

"You want chocolate-covered strawberries?" she echoed, now with a shaking tone of restrained laughter.

"Yes," the Áss answered, oblivious to her mirth while choosing another berry for himself. "I might even get some," he said. Hearing the laughter, he gave a questioning look at her. "Did I say something funny?"

"Oh, nooohooo," Neila replied while biting her lips not to laugh aloud. Glancing at the naked Áss again, his confused look merely fuelled her mirth further. "Never mind it," she said with a higher pitch, still struggling to remain somewhat composed. "If you want chocolate-covered strawberries, then you can have chocolate-covered ... ahem ... strawberries. Naked ..."

Just as Loki opened his mouth to ask, she jumped up and walked to the kitchen; her shoulders still shaking with restrained laughter. While Neila made tea, Loki nibbled on the remaining strawberries, musing.

Truth be told, he anticipated more difficulties from Neila during the whole apartment change. Given her initial reaction to the news, he was prepared to intervene when necessary. Even if that would push him dangerously close to breaking the rules. However, Neila adapted astonishingly fast.

The ancient blood runs strong within her. I just hope, she can learn to harness it properly, Loki thought, biting into another strawberry. Right after showing her a method, she adopted it instantly. *Butchering it, more like,* the Áss admitted, still feeling overall pleased with her. Loki heard every such 'tone' whenever she used one.

Abruptly, a buzzing sensation interrupted his musing, making

Loki rise, alert. Neila glanced at him questioningly while putting her tea down on the coffee table.

"Are you decent enough?" Loki suddenly turned to her, earning a widened pair of eyes as a reply. After a moment, though, she nodded, unsure. "Good. We have company," he announced; his usual attire materialising once again.

Neila's eyes widened even more, seeing his clothes manifest from thin air. Like ice crystallising on a surface, the usual metallic-green outfit grew. It took only a second or two for it to appear in its entirety.

"Company?" echoed Neila, watching Loki step closer to the window. "Who?"

"Týr."

"Tii—" she echoed but before she could even finish his name, a man appeared in the living room.

Neila gasped at him openly. Týr, the God of War himself, the strongest of the Æsir, according to human mythology. However, he looked nothing like she or any 'portrait' imagined him to be.

Týr was a tall, tall man, around two metres, Neila guessed. Yet, instead of bulky and full of muscles, he looked rather lean. Still broad-shouldered and well trained, his every movement seemed more elegant and swift than merely powerful. His attire mirrored Loki's, only in shades of grey, resembling steel and coal.

While Loki kept a mid-long, incredible hairstyle, Týr opted for a simple short Mohawk, complemented by gorgeously maintained, stylish short beard. Now, Týr smiled warmly at Loki while they greeted each other by firmly grabbing the other's lower arm.

Unconsciously, Neila stepped closer to them.

"It's good to *sjá pér gott*, Loki," said Týr, patting Loki's shoulder a few times.

Neila almost dropped her mouth open, seeing that perfect smile. Paired with his indigo eyes and that enchanting deep voice, she felt the need to obey his every wish just because he asked. Not even a scar running through his left eye could mar Týr's perfection.

Then, he glanced at Neila, who seemed to pause with breathing and just stared into that indigo gaze.

"*Sæl!*" greeted Týr with a charming smile, measuring Neila from top to bottom. Then, he flashed a look at Loki, who replied with a twitch of his mouth.

"Hi," whispered Neila, still merely glaring into his eyes. Then, as if waking from a charm, she blinked in confusion and broke the eye contact herself. Afterwards, she looked around somewhat normally, if anxious.

Seeing this, Týr held out an arm to her, with a smaller smile this time; anticipation sparkling in his eyes. Neila welcomed this a tad unsure, but then started the motion as well. At this, Loki stepped between them, grabbing both of their arms.

"It is too dangerous," he said to Neila, who flashed a questioning look.

"Now, now, Loki, don't be *rudda*," said Týr, in almost perfect English, albeit heavily accented. Yet, even that seemed to disappear by the moment, leaving Neila even more baffled.

"What's the problem?" Neila inquired, seemingly not feeling Loki's touch anymore. Which fact, of course, both Æsir noticed.

"He is the strongest of the Æsir," explained Loki, still holding them.

"I know," she said. "But, would it not be beneficial for me to know the difference, then? You wanted me to learn, did you not?"

Loki narrowed his eyes at the mocking tone, but Týr just flashed a smile again.

"She's a warrior, let her learn, then," he said, earning another disapproving glance from Loki.

"One touch of his can kill you," Loki continued to Neila.

"That's fine with me," she replied without hesitation.

The Æsir exchanged a look.

"Come now, my friend, you know I will be gentle," said Týr with a half-smile.

Seeing this, Loki just inhaled deeply and stepped back with his hands held in the air.

"It seems, nothing I say matters, so do as you wish," he growled, hurt.

Hearing this, Neila flashed a confused frown. Feeling somewhat regretful, she had just started to rethink this whole thing, when Týr grabbed her arm with a firm motion.

Neila felt as though literally struck by lightning or got a severe electric shock. Despite never experiencing such a thing, she imagined it just like this.

Suddenly, her whole body exploded from the inside, as it felt. Every single nerve lit up, sending an enormous amount of signals everywhere, flooding her every system with the myriad of information. She even imagined to 'fly' backwards, as though pushed back by the electric shock, landing on her back. Or, perhaps, that really happened, she had no true idea.

Although wide awake and staring at the ceiling, Neila somehow perceived at least three other realities or timelines simultaneously. Every single happening, a heartbeat or a breath seemed to happen incredibly slowly, taking up an eternity.

In the next moment, she saw Loki leaning over her. Neila comprehended his presence, anticipating his words and even had at least three complete conversations with him inside her mind. Týr mentioned something as well in the background, in Norse, as it sounded. Yet, Neila understood, or thought she did, or, perhaps, she would have understood in the future.

Time just seemed to behave very strangely, showing past, present, and future at the same time, in variations.

"Next time, perhaps you'll heed my words," Loki said for the fourth time, it felt to Neila.

While constantly having multiple trains of thought simultaneously, she also pierced inside her own soul, hearing her own subconscious. Several layers of that, in fact, all talking differently and in various ways to her mind.

Completely out of space and time, Neila barely registered when Loki gently lifted and then laid her down on the sofa.

"Well, she took it remarkably well, I would say," noted Týr, clasping his hands behind his back. Looking calmly at Loki, he dismissed the other's warning gaze.

"You could have used less power," he growled, stepping to the other.

"I knew, she could handle it, and she wanted to learn," answered Týr soothingly. When he saw the other open his mouth to argue, he quickly continued. "However, this is not why I am here. So please, tell me about the situation with the fifths."

Loki seemed to consider continuing to lecture Týr; his essence flickering with different patterns. Not many were allowed to see such a subtle thing. Even on Ásgarðr, they restrained what they showed from their essence. Some things were obvious or were not considered worth hiding. But others, like certain thought patterns or emotions, were only meant for a close friend, family member, or mate.

In the end, Loki decided that it was not worth the trouble. Time was of the essence, although, Neila's fairly quick recovery must have added to his decision. Sitting up, she now poured tea in her favourite mug. Still looking confused and not truly in the present, Neila glanced towards them several times, listening.

Feeling this, Loki continued in Old Norse.

"So, this is the help Heimdallr has promised?" he started, earning a playful bow from Týr.

"He also managed to convince Freyja to listen to you," said the other with a half-smile. "With the help of Baldr, of course."

Thinking, Loki started to walk to and fro between the sofa and Týr.

"How did you come here?" he then asked, halting.

"Same as you. Óðinn would not allow me to use the Bifröst for something like this. So, through the fifth, then that rogue connection to Miðgarðr," answered Týr. "But the fifths concern me. They surrounded me immediately, and, despite not using force, they firmly urged me to stay and listen. I almost accidentally broke one's chest when he did not let me pass. Very strange, indeed."

"That is because they need our help," answered Loki, deep in thought. "They are all but gone. From what I know, only the city around the Bifröst remained somewhat populated, everything else died out."

"Need I remind you," Týr said, "that we can only intervene in the case of a direct attack?"

"Yes, but I have proof that this IS an attack."

Týr's gaze darkened, drawing even Neila's attention, feeling the sudden change in the mood. The air in the living room seemed to freeze.

"You know that I cannot consider you as my friend when ruling in such a matter," rumbled Týr solemnly.

"I know. And I wouldn't ask for anything else than justice," nodded Loki.

Týr was the Lawmaker of Ásgarðr, representing Fairness and Justice. While Óðinn decided most of the things, Týr could overrule him, if he saw fit. As the strongest of the Æsir, his job also entailed leading the armies of Ásgarðr during war or a defence.

Loki knew, after only a few visits to Miðgarðr, Týr quickly became the most popular deity amidst many. While never breaking a rule, he, too, knew how to walk on the line. In fact, Loki himself had learnt a lot from him in this regard during their youth. Týr was the one, who first introduced him to Miðgarðr and the energies there.

"Speak, then," said the Lawmaker.

"The infection of the Bifröst and what decimates the fifths, is the same virus," Loki began, getting straight to the point.

Týr's expression darkened, yet remained calm.

"What proof do you have of this?" he wanted to know.

"We both saw the thing when the Dvergar found it in the Bifröst. Then, if you recall, you sent me to obtain the needed meteorite, should the fifths have it. The moment I've stepped out of the Bifröst, they approached me, telling me about this sickness. Naturally, I remained neutral in the matter, but their words prompted me to look into it. Firstly, they said that they sent word to Ásgarðr, yet no reply came."

Týr flashed a frown at the news.

Despite never intervening unless there was an attack, Ásgarðr would *always* reply to a call. Mostly to remind the other party of this rule, but still would send some word.

Seeing the darkened indigo gaze, Loki nodded, continuing.

"Perhaps, what had disabled our Bifröst, might have impacted the other one as well. Alas, I had no time to investigate that particular matter. In any case," he took a deep breath, "while I was waiting for the ship with the meteorite to arrive, I mingled, as usual, to keep up good relations."

Týr scoffed at this, knowing well what this meant when it came to Loki.

"No, it was nothing like that this time," Loki growled, eyeing the other knowingly. "The few survivors told me, how the illness emerged abruptly, virtually overnight. Right when we had to disable our Bifröst, it started to spread in a pace nobody has seen before, and, without fail, killing all who had contracted it. The fifths could do *nothing*, which is why they turned desperate enough to call upon us."

The Lawmaker still remained silent; his gaze turned even darker. Loki spoke further.

"Neither of us believes in coincidences. Everything seems just too well coordinated. It was fortunate that I went there at all, before the fifths got annihilated."

"Given everything, I believe that goes beyond mere chance," Týr murmured, deep in thought. Loki turned grimmer at the prospect. If somebody was able to manipulate the happenings so precisely, they truly faced a formidable threat.

The Lawmaker took a deep breath.

"These reasons may be sufficient enough for us to help the fifths. Do you have evidence of who could be behind this onslaught?"

"I suspect that outside world, neighbouring the fifths. I've looked into the fifth's security systems, and there were sightings of those creatures, lurking around. Somehow they obtained higher technology, because some of those readings were inconclusive."

"I presume, during your surveillance happened the 'misunderstanding' that led to your current situation," noted Týr with a knowing glance.

Many on Ásgarðr knew that Loki's so-called diplomatic travels often led to trouble. The Áss's occasional misjudgements regarding how the lower-levels would react to certain situations resulted in issues. In such cases, Týr bore the responsibility to mitigate the mood, often punishing Loki in the process. He, of course, had never escaped judgement, but there was nothing that could keep him away from creating chaos.

Regardless, nobody doubted his noble intentions. More often than not, Loki *did* gather valuable information, technology, or insights that greatly benefitted Ásgarðr.

Loki rolled his eyes at the tone.

"I explicitly told them to give the piece to *me*," he growled. "They listened not, too eager, or panical, or fearful to do so. The next thing I knew was that the iris had been shut on the Bifröst, and they were firing at me with all they've got, demanding the arrival of *her*."

"Mm-hmm," Týr raised a questioning eyebrow, but returned to the more pressing issue. "Still, we have not enough against that world. Even if it suits their style. They are still outsiders to our node, we can't simply go there to investigate. Given the ongoing war between them and the fifths, that is."

"I know," Loki sighed. "We need further proof of their involvement. But the fact that ... *somebody* was able to infest our node with such a virus worries me greatly."

"Agreed," nodded Týr. "Also, they must know that this can be interpreted as an act of war, in which case we would certainly get involved. They must have prepared for that possibility."

Loki nodded, concerned.

"This is why I would want you to talk to that woman to help the fifths. We simply cannot allow *those creatures* to take over the fifth."

"As much as I would want to help with Freyja, I cannot," Týr shook his head. "She is prepared to talk, but only to *you*."

"Even after I've told you this?"

"She was adamant about this. She also said that you have to 'beg like you have never begged before,' if you want her to consider listening to you."

"I hate that woman!" hissed Loki angrily. The coils of power appeared around him again.

Meanwhile, Neila only watched the Æsir from the background. Feeling the seriousness of the atmosphere, she stayed as invisible as possible, quietly sipping her tea. However, seeing those anger coils appear around Loki, Neila rose a bit, probably thinking of calming him down. Then, she slid back with a confused look.

Týr watched her in the background during their conversation, and obviously Loki did as well. Both felt her desire to understand the situation, yet she refrained from interruption.

"Needless to say, the feeling is mutual. You have to get back as soon as possible," Týr noted, earning a scoff.

"I've tried, but the fifths won't let me pass! And I cannot get lucky enough for them to miss my arrival!" Loki cried out, then paused to compose himself. "Can you help me scout for a direct connection to Ásgarðr?"

"That could take a lot of time, even for us."

"I might have no other choice, since Heimdallr won't help, and neither will you, apparently."

"You know our rules. I cannot intervene like that."

Loki just took a deep breath in agitation.

"How long are you planning to stay?" he then asked the Lawmaker.

"Since Miðgarðr is currently faster, I might look around for a wee bit. I haven't been here for a long time now, and I'm curious," Týr answered, easing up and glancing around.

Despite his eyes looking elsewhere, his focus remained on the watching Neila. Which fact was clear to Loki as well, who flashed a confused frown.

"I'll stay until you try again," Týr declared, turning away and started to saunter around. If he were bothered by the artefacts, he showed it not.

"You mustn't do anything to her!" Loki announced tensely, it made even the Lawmaker glance back.

Týr eyed the almost flaming essence of Loki, undisturbed.

"You cannot have any relations with her," he said so calm, it literally choked those flames.

"I ... I know that!" replied Loki a tad too fast and in a higher pitch than normal, then closed his eyes, drawing a deep breath. "*I know*, believe me, I know. I have other plans with her, to be honest."

"Uh-huh," agreed Týr, sounding all but convinced. His gaze became so heavy, even Loki avoided it for a few moments.

"Well," Loki then cleared his throat. "Take care until I get back."

Týr nodded, so Loki disappeared without another word.

Chapter 15

Neila straightened up when seeing Loki disappear without a word to her. With her still buzzing mind, she somehow was not bothered by it. Týr turned to her, stepping to the sofa.

"How are you feeling?" he asked with a knowing smile.

"I'll live," Neila answered, her tongue feeling awkward and uncooperative. With a still vibrating body, her mind felt equally sluggish and racing. Despite understanding everything perfectly, her reactions remained slow, as though dulled by strong painkillers.

"All I know is that I need another tea," she sighed, standing up. Mentally, she asked Týr whether he wanted some, but the words did not leave her mouth just yet.

"Yes, that would be lovely," answered the Áss nonetheless, making her turn back, baffled.

"Are you telepathic as well?"

"No," he smiled. "Your essence is just easy to read."

Neila raised a questioning eyebrow, pondering whether she should feel insulted. In the meantime, she filled the kettle and cleaned her teapot.

"Wouldn't you like something else? Like a beer, or something?" she broke the momentary silence.

Týr, in a literal blink of an eye, appeared at the kitchen isle, sitting down on a stool. Neila mouthed a wow at this, yet she seemed unsurprised. Apparently, her threshold was so high at the moment, such acts could not trigger bafflement anymore.

"No, I actually prefer tea over anything else," replied the Lawmaker, earning a well-all-right grimace.

"Not what I expected from the God of War," she chuckled, then hurriedly corrected herself, "oh, sorry, from the 'Higher-Level Person of War.' I have excellent teas, though. Do you have a preference?"

"Whatever you see best is perfect. And I don't mind being called a god."

"How come? Loki has a ferocious opinion about this."

"Indeed, he does," he chuckled. "Though we both understand why lower-levels call us that, I can ... erm ... step over it. He cannot."

"That sensitive, huh?" Neila mused as she poured water on their teas. "Oh, this reminds me, could you teach me how to pronounce your names properly?" she asked, earning an interested glance. "I don't speak any kind of Nordic language, and Loki already said my accent is horrid. I would like to at least try, you know."

Týr gave another chuckle, hearing her honest worry about this.

"I can, but it doesn't really matter, you know. These are not our true names."

"Oh?"

"We always adapt to the peoples we encounter, hence our names change," said Týr with a tone that showed, he deliberately left the answer so vague.

A spark in the tricolour gaze showed that Neila understood this intention, raising Týr's interest.

"What did Loki tell you?" he asked inquiringly. His firm indigo gaze grabbed hers and did not let go.

The Áss felt her immediate reaction—she tried to 'raise a shield,' so to speak. Of course, he used only a hint of his powers, careful not to overwhelm her. Regardless, the intensity of her reaction surprised him. Somehow, Neila not only broke the connection, but adapted to Týr's level, becoming immune to his natural 'charms' on humans.

Was Loki truly right? he wondered. *Could this truly be the ancient blood we were looking for? Could we use her? There must be others as well.*

"Ask him yourself!" Neila cried out, backing to the fridge in fear. Yet, her gaze almost sparked with anger, understanding his intentions. "And you better not use such force on me again!"

"Just out of curiosity, or what?" asked Týr with an amused smile whilst stirring his tea with the ball infuser. Then, he put it on the little plate Neila placed there for that very purpose.

"Then, I would ..."—she tried to think on her foot—"I would ask you to leave!"

Angry, Neila grabbed her pot and mug, storming over to the sofa.

"No, you would not," smiled Týr, sounding, as if reciting one of the Laws of the Universe.

"No, I would not ..." she growled, thudding down, pouting. "Still, it's unfair. I wouldn't lie to you either way, you must know that."

Suddenly, the Lawmaker appeared beside the sofa, sitting down on the other end as far from her as possible.

"My apologies, you are right."

In the momentary silence, Týr observed her slowly waving essence while she wandered on her path of thought. In the end, Neila broke the silence.

"I assume, you cannot talk about how things work 'up there,' but can you tell stories about you and the others?" she asked. "You know, to clarify mythology with facts."

"I would assume yes. What do you have in mind?"

"For starters, you."

"What about me?"

"Well, there are several possibilities about your connection to Odin, for instance. Are you his son? His father? Brother?"

Týr raised a questioning eyebrow, but started to talk.

"I don't know, why this matters; or how this even came to be part of Miðgarðr's stories about us. Truthfully, I, personally, have no blood relation to Óðinn. I am even older than he, and trained him and Loki back in our youth."

"Really?" she gasped. "Wait, *you* trained Loki ...?"

"Yes. Although, both of them are only a few cycles younger than I. Normally that would mean nothing, but I always was the best fighter, advancing faster than anybody else. We spent much time together, back in those days. Visited Miðgarðr together, and so on," Týr explained, sounding almost nostalgic. "But then, Óðinn and we have fallen out. He was always a ... how do you say it? Alone wolf?"

"It's lone wolf. But, really? How come?"

"Well, he had different interests. For example, despite being a decent fighter himself, he was more invested in the mechanics and tactics in the background. In truth, when I say decent, I mean mediocre, at best. On the other hand, his uncanny plans were, and still are, unmatched. He understands patterns like nobody else."

"Huh," Neila scoffed, interested. "Is it true, then, that he sacrificed his eye for knowledge?"

"Yes, but not in the way you might think. He's lost it in a foolish accident whilst investigating something or other. I can't recall now; it was a long time ago. What's baffling in this story that he refused to have a bionic replacement, choosing an eyepatch instead. He's peculiar like that."

"How can he be a ruler, then?" asked Neila, pouring tea for herself. Despite having drunk half a litre already, she still felt parched.

"Because he is incredibly smart. And, because I didn't want to, when they offered me the position."

"Huh, interesting. What about the ravens and wolves he keeps?"

"Don't, just don't," growled Týr at this. "You have no idea, how much trouble those animals cause sometimes. Essentially, Óðinn does nothing else than sits in his hall, surrounded by those *things* he collects as pets, doing only he knows what. He's weird, I tell you."

Neila's eyes widened, surprised not only by Týr's words but his friendly tone, too. Sipping his tea, he spoke further, sounding as though relieved for the possibility to 'just complain.'

"Wait, so he DOES have a hall? Valhalla EXISTS?!" she burst out, stunned.

"Valhǫll?" echoed Týr, looking puzzled. "I'd need to look into those myths, wouldn't I?"

"I don't know," mused Neila, unsure. "Loki got truly angry about them, and that was scary enough. I wouldn't want to see what the strongest Áss is like when angry."

Týr gave a half-smile at this.

"In any case, tell me about Valhǫll, then," he said.

Neila gathered her thoughts.

"Well, in a nutshell, it is said that Odin, with the help of the Valkyries, collects the souls of the fallen warriors, who die well in battle. Half are taken to Freyja's hall, the rest sits in Valhalla with Odin and Thor, drinking mead, fighting, and laughing happily, all day, every day. Until Ragnarök comes, when the doors open and Odin rides to war alongside these warriors."

Týr finished his tea, looking almost astonished at the tale.

"It seems that Þórr had quite the imagination during his visits to Miðgarðr," he mused aloud.

"What do you mean?" asked Neila, not pressing further about Valhǫll. Just like Loki, Týr would only answer what he saw fit. If he steered the conversation in another direction, she ought to accept.

"Loki was a frequent visitor on Miðgarðr, but Þórr had practically lived here for a time. He is still a young man, and thrived on the attention humans gave him."

"How come Odin didn't say anything about it? Or you, for that matter. Wouldn't this go against your laws?"

"Not particularly, no," Týr shook his head. "Visiting a lower realm was never forbidden. And, Óðinn could not care less, believe me. He probably has no idea, what Þórr or any other offspring of his is doing. Why would he?"

"Excuse me?" burst out from Neila, baffled. "Why wouldn't he? They are his sons, aren't they? Frigg would surely say something to him, if nobody else."

"Who is … Frigg?" asked the Lawmaker, making Neila drop her mouth.

"Odin's wife! Mother of Baldur, and some others whose name I cannot remember. Although, Thor is from somebody else. Sorry, I'm bad with names. But how can YOU not know this?"

"Oh, I know her, yes. I just did not realise her Miðgarðrian name. I am not fully aware of Þórr's doings, apparently. I need to have a talk with him," the Lawmaker muttered.

"So, care to enlighten me, then?"

"First of all, Óðinn has no wife; never wanted to choose anybody. Nor did he desire offspring. The fact that he has any children at all is due to those women *choosing* to carry his offspring, with the full knowledge that he wouldn't be involved. Apart from his animals, Óðinn is only interested in gaining knowledge. If anybody, Loki and I are fathers to Þórr, since we train him to become an Áss."

Neila listened with widened eyes and mouth agape. But this last sentence jerked her mind out of this stunned state.

"Wait, you and Loki? Fathers *together*? So you two are …?" she asked, leaving the question open.

Even if Týr would not have understood her implication, her essence was 'talkative' enough.

"I forgot that everything is about sex with you humans," growled Týr. "You need to put such labels on things, when you just simply don't understand."

Neila blushed, acknowledging the truth in his statement. Seeing this, he took a deep breath and explained.

"Þórr is still a young man, only on the verge of manhood. He is not even an Áss yet; his training is incomplete. Since he showed his potential early, he has been placed under my care. And since Loki is closest to me, we give guidance to Þórr, together. In this sense, we are his fathers."

"But, if he's just a teenager, how can we know him as ... well, as a great warrior, with a beard and all that?" asked now Neila, then something else came to mind. "Wait a moment, how does Odin look, then? Is he truly a bearded, elderly man with a hat?"

"Because of his youth, Þórr still has more vanity than desirable. I assume, he takes that form for humans, imagining himself as an adult and 'great warrior,' as you said. Apparently, he then wanders on Miðgarðr, entertaining humans with his tales. Óðinn, on the other hand, had an accident, of which I cannot speak further. As a result, he now looks far older than he truly is."

"Huh," Neila scoffed with a half-smile. "Honestly, I'm surprised that he doesn't lose his hammer more often."

"Lose it?" echoed Týr, too serious. "Losing such a weapon is impossible. Though, I cannot fathom his fascination with war hammers. Like father, like son, I suppose."

"Is that why he has a chariot, pulled by two giant goats?" asked Neila, cheerfully mocking.

Týr just rolled his eyes at this, taking a huge breath.

"Oh, yes, the goats ... We have nothing alike on Ásgarðr, you know. But he loves goats! I can't grasp their appeal."

"In earnest?" laughed Neila. "I like feta just as much as the next man, but this sounds serious!" Then, she added with a sudden realisation. "Oh, but this explains so much! The mead in Valhalla, comes from a goat as well!"

Týr looked at her with a mixture of surprise and disgust.

"I have nothing against any kind of animal, but this is just ..." he shook his head. "Perhaps, Þórr would have been a better fit as a storyteller," he muttered, thinking.

"Well, he certainly has the imagination for it," chuckled Neila. "So, the *story* part of the mythology comes from Thor, apparently. While the closer-to-reality knowledge comes from Loki, I'd imagine."

"What knowledge?"

"You know, the nine realms, the Bifröst, and from what I can understand, that your technology is built by dwarves, and so on. What I don't understand now is the prophecy of Ragnarök."

"Should I even ask ...?" Týr sighed haggardly.

"Well," Neila began, unsure. "It is essentially the end of Asgard and Midgard; the end of all Worlds. It starts years before the actual war, even, with unnaturally cold winters and earthquakes and all that. Then, it's the war between the Aesir and ... well, almost everybody else. It basically starts with Baldur's death, after which the Vanir declare war against the Aesir. Although, some say that *that* war is just the kindling for Ragnarök," she explained. "In any case, the wolves that chase the Sun and the Moon finally catch them. Fenrir breaks free from his invisible chains, and swallows Odin whole as revenge. He then is killed by ... One of the sons of Odin. Vidar, perhaps?

"Meanwhile, the giant serpent, whose name I always forget, kills Thor with its venom, but not before Thor manages to slay it in return. The giants, led by Loki, invade, too. You, in fact, battle the giant hound, or wolf, that guards Hel. You slay it, but die from the wounds. The giant, Surt, sets Asgard and everybody in his way ablaze with his flaming sword. Also, Loki and Heimdall kill each other. Technically speaking, this whole thing is a war between the Aesir and Loki, leading his 'spawns,' Hel, his giants, and the dead from Helheim. Destroying everything during. I think, this is all I can recall at the moment."

Týr just blinked, astonished.

"Excuse me?!" he then erupted with a wave of anger, making Neila freeze in her seat.

Immediately, he restrained his emotions. When next speaking, his voice sounded only a tad tenser than before, although, his gaze still shot sparks.

"Who is responsible for this ... prophecy?"

"I don't know, honest," replied Neila, still looking upset. "It's just a myth."

"Well," Týr closed his eyes, taking a huge breath. "Given the human belief that the parts of Ásgarðr constitute the nine realms, it is safe to say that this ... story, is nothing more than a tall tale to scare humans into submission."

A moment of silence fell on the room, which, then, Neila broke. "So, none of it is true, right?" she asked.

Glancing at her, the Lawmaker could see her doubts. Myths, apparently, *could* come alive, Loki and Týr proved that much. Therefore, she truly feared the End of the Worlds.

What baffled Týr, however, was the fact that Neila's fear was not of Death itself, or of dying brutally. Instead, her essence revealed that she was rather afraid *for them.*

For Loki, to be exact, the Áss thought, interested. Despite after only a brief acquaintance, the two of them had obviously formed an attachment to one another. A deep one at that, too, which might prove to be problematic in the future. But for now, it seemed wise to console her in this matter.

"No. Loki would never do such a thing. Nor would Fenrir, since he lives with Óðinn, much just like the serpent and all those animals you mentioned. And believe me, no Jǫtunn would attack the rest of Ásgarðr. The Æsir is the military force of the seventh, protecting *all* inhabitants of our planet. In fact, most of us come from Jǫtunheimr, like Loki. Or me, for that matter."

"Really?" asked Neila, relieved.

"Yes, truly," smiled Týr. "Ásgarðr has never had an internal war like that in our history. I honestly have no idea, how such a tale could be born," he shook his head, looking more troubled than anything else. But, noticing that Neila picked up on this, he changed the subject again. "Perhaps, a happier story might ease your mind."

"It might," agreed Neila mischievously smiling. "But it has to be a good one."

"I'm sure, you have several in mind already."

"Just a couple," she grinned. "The one about a giant stealing Mjölnir, with Loki actually playing a positive character. And the one about Fenrir biting off your hand."

"I *ought to* have a word with Þórr after this," growled Týr, slowly swaying his head disapprovingly. "Nobody has ever stolen an Æsir weapon, believe me. It would be as possible as stealing an arm. In reality, it was a training exercise. Æsir don't lie; I cannot fathom, why Þórr would fabricate such a tale. How does the story go, exactly?"

"Huh," exhaled Neila, trying to remember. "There was a giant, who stole the hammer, and demanded Freyja as his bride in return. In the end, Loki tricked the giant and got Mjölnir back without Freyja marrying him."

"Exquisite," said Týr cynically. "Everything truly is about women and sex here."

Neila gave a well-yeah head bob, followed by an apologetic smile. The Lawmaker, continued, calmer now.

"That Jǫtunn was Loki, and as I said, it was part of Þórr's training. Mjǫllnir ... No, I cannot say that name seriously. So ... the hammer ... was not stolen, but *given* to Loki by Þórr himself, since it was the point of this exercise. The youngling had to retrieve the weapon using his wit and skills."

"Then, how did Loki return it, becoming the hero of the story, for once?"

"Because Þórr failed. Miserably, I might add. But, in all honestly, that was the first more serious training session he endured. He has improved greatly, since."

"So he managed to get the hammer back?"

"Oh, no," Týr smiled. "Loki is one of the best, Þórr has little to no chance in outsmarting him."

"All right, this will take some getting used to," mused Neila, then she hurriedly excused herself to go to the bathroom. After returning, she continued, "so, what about Fenrir?"

"I believe, that story might also be Þórr's doing. You are aware that Loki saved the wolf, correct?"

Neila nodded, but her gaze showed that the question piqued her interest. Týr had no true idea about their previous conversations, yet he posed this, as if the answer were obvious.

"For some reason, that animal had been enlarged by the process. Loki tried to return it to its natural habitat. However, due to its size, it no longer fit. Therefore, we had to retrieve it. Óðinn, Þórr, Loki, and I came to get it. We brought special chains as well, just in case, but of course, wanted to avoid any violence. Óðinn has a way with animals, yet he couldn't make headway with this one for some reason. At least, not at first.

"Thus, we needed to use the chains to restrain the wolf. Which turned out to be incredibly difficult, because we did not want to harm it. Eventually, the wolf became aggressive, and tried to bite us. Because I didn't want anybody to actually get hurt, I let him grab my right arm, so the others could chain him. However, with a sudden move, the wolf managed to break off my arm."

Neila gave a sympathy gasp at this.

"Didn't it hurt?" she asked. "Is he truly *that* big?"

"It hurt, but it was just a bionic arm, so easily replaceable. And yes, immense, with fangs the size of my hand. In any case, that gave the wolf something to do while we brought him back."

"Bionic arm?"

"Yes. I have lost my arm when I was not much older than Þórr is now. I had planned to replace it with a better one anyway, so it all worked out just swell," he smiled.

Neila blinked, baffled.

"How *did* you lose your arm, then?"

"That is not a story to tell."

"How come?"

"Because it would entail information, you shouldn't acquire," said Týr with a strange light in his eyes. "Ásgarðr has never had internal wars, but this doesn't mean, we have never fought anybody else. Let's leave it at that, please."

Neila flashed a fair-enough glance.

A momentary silence fell on them, which Týr broke.

"Care for a walk? I would like to look around."

"What if Loki returns? Shouldn't we wait for him here?"

"Miðgarðr is fast, compared to the other realms. We have time; days, maybe even weeks, before his return."

"Really?" she exclaimed. "Well, in that case, I'd be happy to show you around, if you'd like. Just, let me change, and we can go."

Chapter 16

Týr walked silently, looking around sometimes amused, in others rather sad. Occasionally asking questions, he showed interest in a lot of things Neila found ordinary. They spent the afternoon in the centre of the town, enjoying a lunch before continuing their walk. After a while, Neila asked for a break because she still felt parched. Since the 'accident' of touching the Áss, her thirst felt unquenchable. Therefore, they found a café.

"Are you comfortable enough?" Týr asked almost kindly.

"As much as I can be among humans, yes," Neila muttered, not even looking at the other.

Given how people reacted to Loki, Neila was prepared for a lot of attention. Yet, none came, interestingly enough. Seemingly nobody noticed the Lawmaker, raising Neila's interest in the matter.

If nothing else, a tall, good-looking man like that would turn a few heads. Not even the scar through his eye could lessen his handsomeness. Especially with that Mohawk, which was not a usual hairstyle for a man in an expensive suit. Týr chose an outfit after looking through Loki's wardrobe, changing his own appearance with a thought. Since he took a shape of an ordinary man, his skin lost that characteristic glow.

Now musing about why the skin of the Æsir glowed, Neila tried to keep the billowing mass out from her mind. Something in the back of her mind whispered, that light was their power, perhaps literally leaking through their skin. Neila noticed before that Týr's appearance changed slightly, according to his mood. The more emotional he got, the more he 'glowed.'

"Ask, if you want," Týr broke the silence, making Neila blush and drop her gaze. She might have stared at him the whole time whilst thinking.

"I was just wondering about that ... erm ... how should I put it?" she mused, now glancing at the neighbouring table, where a group of twenty-somethings sat down. "That glow you all emit."

"Glow?"

"Uh ... yes. I cannot really describe it otherwise."

The Lawmaker mused upon it for a moment while eyeing her inquiringly, 'reading' her essence to find out more.

"You are correct in your conclusion," he said in the end with a small smile, earning a confused frown, which then turned into a oh-really-wow look.

The waiter now arrived at their table, asking for their order. Neila asked for two pots of tea, earning a questioning look from the man, yet he complied.

"Why did he look at me, as if I were alone?" asked Neila.

"Because I make them avert their attention, hence they cannot perceive me."

"Huh?"

"I believe, you've witnessed what happens with ordinary people when around Loki. And, if he wants to blend in, he needs to shape-shift. I must take even more drastic measures to remain unnoticed. Otherwise, my presence would surely cause serious disturbance."

"But everybody behaves, as if you don't even exist."

"They cannot see me, in a manner of speaking. They can sense me being here, thus they would not walk into me, for instance. But to engage with me, one must 'acknowledge' my presence, if you know what I mean. I take *this* away."

"So how can I ... uh ... see you, then?" asked Neila, puzzled.

"Because it doesn't work on you," said Týr with a charming smile. "Not anymore, it seems."

Before Neila could ask anything more, the waiter arrived, putting the little kettles down with the accompanying cups.

Týr watched Neila pour the tea for both of them. From her lingering essence, she was lost in thought. Not wanting to disturb her, the Lawmaker glanced around, measuring the unending mass on the streets.

So sad, what they have become, thought the Áss. *It is difficult to believe that they were once the sixth. So much is here, and none can use it.*

Then, a sudden shift in the air drew his attention back to Neila, whose essence started to form thorns. With eyes darting around, Anxiety rose inside her. Also, her breathing started to become shallower and faster.

"What is the matter?" asked Týr. Nothing remotely dangerous was lurking around, he would know otherwise.

"I don't know, I just … suddenly feel very anxious. Do you think, something has happened to Loki?" she asked, worried.

"Loki can take care of himself, you needn't worry," answered the Lawmaker.

Naturally, he should know, if Loki got into trouble. Regardless, the possibility existed that his senses somehow got shadowed. *I am not all-knowing, after all,* Týr mused, looking at Neila.

If she felt something, perhaps it was time for them to go to her apartment. There, Týr could regain his form and watch more carefully.

"We should leave as soon as you finish," he said, earning an almost fearful gaze. Seeing how upset Neila got, he continued soothingly. "There is no need for you to get upset. He will be perfectly fine."

"Can't *you* feel, if something went wrong?" she inquired.

"If this were a connected world, I would, without a doubt. But Miðgarðr is different, and it is possible that something slips by me with all these energies around."

Somehow, this did not seem to console her. Neila gave a disappointed grimace, then hurriedly finished her tea. Týr did the same while Neila paid, then he motioned them to take a silent little side street. Nobody was around them for the time being, so he gingerly touched Neila's arm to teleport them home.

In the apartment, Neila fell to her knees, hugging herself and shaking vigorously.

"I'm sorry; I tried to be as gentle as I could," apologised Týr, taking back his original form and stepping away from her. Alas, he would not be able to do anything more for her.

"It's fine," answered Neila hoarsely, slowly standing up, but still winced from time to time, as though getting shocked. "I wouldn't have minded a warning, though."

Týr smiled and shrugged apologetically, sauntering to the artefacts. Looking over them one by one, he sometimes gave a scoff or a disapproving shake of head.

Abruptly, he halted, focusing on something intently while glaring into the distance. Feeling the sudden change of his mood, Neila glanced at him. When Týr shook his head again with an agitated sigh, she flashed a frown. Neila was about to ask, when Loki materialised in the living room and immediately dropped to his knees.

"What the ..." gasped Neila, turning pale.

The Áss had a large spike sticking out of his chest. Now, he faintly glanced up at Týr, who looked quite unaffected by this.

"No luck?" he noted, walking to the other.

"It appears not," agreed Loki weakly, sitting back on his heels. "I would require your assistance, if you would be so kind."

Neila, too, rushed to his side, deathly pale, glaring at the spike. Blood dripped from the wound, and Loki truly seemed to be losing the battle this time.

"I've told you several times to fuse yourself with healing technology," said Týr, still looking calm as ever.

With a hand, he grabbed the spike and concentrated. A certain pattern lit up on his lower arm, glowing silver, making Neila drop her mouth open. Then, the glow seemed to 'infect' the spike, growing on it like ice on a leaf. The metallic object had not merely pierced into Loki's shoulder, but melded with his skin and muscles.

Loki grunted and hissed in pain while Týr worked. The bluish light from him netted the spike completely, heading deeper and farther into the muscles.

"Could you hurry a little bit?" asked Loki now with a painful tone. "A tendril is getting dangerously close to my heart."

"What?!" whispered Neila at this, but the Æsir paid her no mind.

"I'm trying to work as painlessly as possible," answered Týr calmly.

"Just do it, please, I would not want to know, what this thing can do when reaching my heart."

"As you wish."

Týr's whole outfit lit up, making Loki cry out in pain. The otherwise gorgeous motive on the Lawmaker shone strongly, getting deeply into Loki's body, netting his whole chest. Some 'tendrils' even went up his neck under his skin.

With a swift, strong motion, Týr pulled the spike out. Loki cried out again, collapsing onto his hands as blood poured from the wound. The Lawmaker knelt down beside him, helping him sit upright again. Placing a hand on his bleeding chest, Týr healed the other.

Neila watched the happenings utterly stunned, with hands clasped over her mouth to silence herself from crying out. After finishing, the Lawmaker powered down his suit and stood up, measuring the strange spike in his hand. Blood still dripped from the remaining tendrils.

"What happened?" asked Týr.

Loki inhaled deeply, then he cleaned his outfit with a thought.

"This is something new, as you can see, made especially for our kind, I'd say," he said, folding his arms. "Every time, they shot me with something new, but this was the first, I couldn't heal or get rid of it on my own."

"You could have, had you heeded my advice," argued Týr. "This is nothing new, just a modification of an earlier design," he noted, then the motives on his lower arm lit up again, disintegrating the spike in a blink of an eye.

"Easy for you to say," growled Loki, rubbing his shoulder. "You are more tech inside than flesh. I don't need that kind of trouble, thank you."

"It is no trouble at all," answered the Lawmaker, clasping his hands behind his back. "And I merely suggest to upgrade your healing abilities. Why face such disadvantage, I ask now, given that they've managed to shoot you at least once every time?"

"Yeah, don't remind me," sighed Loki. "They're running out of places to shoot me."

During their conversation, Neila just stood in her place, completely frozen. Glaring at the bloody floor, she pondered on how to clean that up. Blood was a tricky thing, getting it out from anything was a difficult job and needed special detergents.

In a momentary silence in the others' conversation, she faintly cut in.

"Could you help me clean this up?" she asked. "I wouldn't want the housekeeper to see this, and I had to throw everything out last time you bled over my couch."

Loki had just opened his mouth to answer, but Týr now turned to her, looking incredibly intense.

"You got in contact with Æsir blood?" he asked with a terrifying tone.

Suddenly, the air in the room turned cold as ice. Týr's whole appearance radiated incredible power. Neila even imagined him turning into a giant, growing until his head brushed the ceiling. He now glowed with incredible light, hurting the eyes.

Neila could not feel anything else than pure Fear. Trembling, she backed to a wall.

Loki jumped before her defensively, looking into Týr's eyes.

"How could you be so careless?!" Týr boomed to Loki in a voice that seemed to shake even the walls.

Neila collapsed to the ground with a miserable whimper, putting her hands over her ears. But nothing could keep *that* voice out, as if Týr spoke directly inside her brain.

"Calm down," said Loki, holding out a hand at Týr soothingly. Even he winced, though, when that sparking indigo gaze fell on him.

In the next moment, Týr seemed to shrink back. Regardless, when speaking, his voice held incredible strength. Paired with pure Wrath, his essence still threatened to wipe everything away.

Shaking, Neila managed to glance up from behind Loki, too afraid to move. Even if she wanted to, it was doubtful that she could muster enough strength to flee.

"Is ... it ... true?" Týr asked with controlled anger in his voice.

"Yes," admitted Loki, dropping his gaze for a moment. "But I've disabled the nanocytes inside her stream. There is nothing to worry about."

The Lawmaker inhaled deeply.

"This changes nothing!" he thundered. "It is forbidden for a lower-level to possess any kind of Ásgarðrian technology!"

"She's blameless!"

"Irrelevant!" snapped the Lawmaker so coldly, it rendered even Loki speechless.

Yet, Loki somehow had found the strength to cut in before Týr could continue.

"As I said, I've disabled all of them, so nothing can happen. However, this might be the proof we were looking for! No ordinary human would be able to have them, not even inoperative. In the big picture—"

"Irrelevant," echoed the Lawmaker, still sounding angry.

"I know, I know," agreed Loki. "Look, you can punish me however you see fit. You know, I won't escape anything."

"Oh, I intend to, worry not about that!" hissed Týr.

"AFTER we've helped the fifths," announced Loki firmly. "In this moment, nothing is more important than that. If I am right and this IS an attack, we have to act now! Help me find the direct connection to Ásgarðr; help me talk to her. Afterwards, you can do whatever you wish with me. Deal?"

Týr narrowed his eyes, thinking through the offer. Since the atmosphere seemed to thaw, Neila shakily stood up with the help of the wall. Panting, she still looked trembling and worried, but her fear seemed to be under control now.

Týr glanced at Neila, then back to Loki.

"This is not over," the Lawmaker growled, inhaling deeply. "But the happenings on the fifth *are* more urgent. Since you cannot get back on your own, I will assist you. Time is of the essence. Let us go."

With a small bow of his head, Loki dropped his gaze in agreement and said nothing else. Týr also nodded, then ordered Loki to clean up his own blood, muttering about 'causing enough trouble already.' Afterwards, both of them disappeared without further ado, leaving the completely aghast Neila alone.

Chapter 17

Neila leant against the wall, feeling that she could collapse at any moment. Utterly stunned, she glared at the empty space where the Æsir stood just a second ago. Despite the fact that they spoke English, nothing made sense to her.

Shuddering, Neila decided to sit down. With wobbly knees, she managed to reach the sofa, where she huddled up with a few pillows, staring into the distance. Rocking herself, she tried to decipher the happenings.

In truth, she could not grasp why she still felt in shock. Yes, facing the strongest Áss when angry was not something she wanted to experience ever again. Her heart still throbbed, and she breathed too fast for normal. But on the inside, Neila felt calm. Somehow, her mind detached itself from her body, finding sanctuary somewhere far, far away. Now, when it finally returned, Neila could examine what had happened. If only her body could catch up to this.

However, sitting there 'in shock' helped nobody, least of all her. Therefore, after a couple of minutes, Neila forced herself to stand and do some simple tasks. While making tea, her growling stomach suddenly reminded her that a bite or two would not hurt either.

After successfully managing these, Neila decided to dine in front of the TV, watching some movie for the hundredth time. Then, she changed into her comfortable pyjamas, despite the early hours and the fact that she wanted not to sleep. Feeling too rattled to truly rest, she just sat in the dark, glancing outside at the landscapes and musing about the happenings.

Neila had learnt a long time ago that giving herself time to work through issues was the best way. There was no use for distractions;

only immersing herself in the feelings and thoughts allowed her to move forwards.

Therefore, Neila did just that. Not even the only-two-hour sleep could ruin her next day. In truth, she could not sleep because of worrying *for* Loki and Týr. Hoping that they could find a connection to Ásgarðr and do whatever they needed, she also feared that she might never see Loki again. Which thought filled her with sadness.

Too aware of this very real possibility, Grief seized her soul, refusing to let go. Neila walked through the day with a foggy mind and a heavy heart. Only time could ease her pain, she knew that. It did not make it any easier, though.

After the third of such sorrowful days, Neila walked to the kitchen with a huge sigh. While preparing her breakfast cereal, she growled at the happy weather. The Sun was shining like it ought to; the sky stretched clear, with only a few puffs of clouds in it.

"Disgusting," rumbled Neila gloomily, wishing for rain and darkness.

Sitting down in front of the TV once more, she deliberately avoided anything that reminded her of Norse mythology. Which was more difficult than she anticipated. Yet, somehow she managed to find a series that could occupy her mind. Neila even changed into comfortable indoor clothes between two episodes, sliding back to the sofa, now perfectly cosy.

After a few more hours of meaningless time-cheating activities, she was just about to prepare lunch when her senses suddenly went haywire. A freezing chill run down her spine, making her spin around. When spotting the stranger, Neila froze, watching and waiting for the intruder to do something other than looking around.

"Oh, hello!" said the newcomer cheerfully, catching Neila's eyes.

"Unbelievable!" whispered Neila in return, making the other tilt her head questioningly. "A *kitsune* ..."

"Oh, so you know my kind by that name. How lovely!" said the other, still joyful.

This is unbelievable! Neila's mind screamed. *I can't believe that there is a living fox spirit in my home!*

The kitsune glanced around interested, it seemed. Her nine tails waved slowly in the air, or they formed one huge tail together, depending on her mood. Now, she sniffed the air, despite having no true fox-like nose. Measuring, her golden gaze with vertical pupils looked around, with fox-ears prickling to every noise. The traditional Japanese kimono looked incredible on her.

"Oh, wait, I know that!" she now cried out happily, then skipped to an artefact. "You are so lucky to have this!" she turned to Neila, who got over her shock by that time.

"You're from the sixth, right?" Neila asked, recalling Loki's explanations.

"At your service," she answered, playfully waving with a slender hand; her fingers ending in claws instead of nails.

Neila blinked, unsure about what to feel right now. Despite intruding, the kitsune looked more benevolent than dangerous.

"Care for some tea?" Neila asked in the end, confused.

"Oh, how lovely, thank you!" said the kitsune. "I must say, I didn't anticipate such hospitality from a human. But, we have a little time before we have to go, so yes."

"Go? Where?"

"To the fifth, of course, where else?" answered the kitsune, yet a strange light sparkled in her eyes.

Seeing Neila's confused frown, she turned to her with folded arms; her tails swaying near the ground.

"You don't know, do you?" she asked, although, it sounded more like an announcement.

"No. Do you have a preference?" asked Neila, playing further the perfect host as a coping mechanism to the surprise visit.

"Oh, whatever you see best is fine," the kitsune waved dismissively. "But, where are my manners. My name is Kasumi. It is lovely to meet you, Neila!"

"You know me?" she asked, baffled.

"Of course I do, silly," chuckled Kasumi. "It's my job to know."

"What *is* your job?"

"Quite the curious one, aren't you?" jested the kitsune, looking at Neila inquiringly.

In the next moment, the kettle beeped, so Neila poured the hot water into the mugs. Seeing this, the kitsune sauntered to the kitchen isle, but remained standing.

"Can I ask, why are you here?" asked Neila.

"Oh, of course! I'm here to collect you."

"'Collect' ...?" echoed Neila, even more confused now. "I'm sorry, I don't understand."

"Oh, you humans never do," waved Kasumi, glancing around and listening to every noise. "Although, I must say, your 'western region' is a nice surprise so far. I usually go to your 'east.' Such lovely peoples there!"

Neila could not withhold a smile. Loki mentioned it before that the cultures in East Asia were mostly influenced by the entities of the sixth. Proving this, Kasumi appeared as the embodiment of a fox spirit. Now, Neila started to wonder about the many different entities on the sixth, knowing about the numerous yōkai, spirits, and demons in the eastern cultures.

"Is this your original form?" the question bubbled up from her before she could prevent it.

Kasumi looked at Neila, but then gave a charming laugh.

"Well, yes. I prefer working in my original form. Much more comfortable, you know."

Neila blinked in surprise. Even more baffling was the fact that Kasumi answered everything without a second thought. Despite behaving incredibly open and friendly, a strange aura surrounded her, making Neila wary. Those inquiring eyes sent a chill down her spine.

"So," Neila broke the momentary silence, stirring her tea with the infuser then put it on a little plate. Kasumi did the same, glancing at her. "Would you tell me, what this 'collecting me' means?"

"Oh, of course," Kasumi took a sip. "Hmm, quite good. Not as good as in Japan, but almost. In any case, I'm here to take you to the fifth, where I will hand you to the fifths. They will lock you in a special facility until that Áss of yours delivers his part of the deal."

Neila blinked, pausing the mug in midair.

"I'm sorry, what?"

"Aaaw, you humans truly don't know anything, do you?" said Kasumi, tilting her head again. Somehow that charming voice now cut deeper than a knife.

"Can you enlighten me?" asked Neila, putting the mug down without taking a sip.

"I can, I suppose," Kasumi waved her tails musingly. "You were generous enough to serve me tea, so I can repay it in kind. You see, the fifth is a ... a trading point to all realms with a Bifröst. They are a kind and patient people, if a little closed-minded, unless somebody takes advantage of them. They like to make bargains, and when it is broken for some reason, their rules allow them take serious measures. Usually, they pressure the other party by taking something valuable of theirs. They outsource this job, though, since the fifths don't leave their home. At all, imagine that! Boring!" Kasumi rolled her eyes.

Neila blinked again while the kitsune took a few sips from her tea. "So ... you're a bounty hunter?" she asked.

"Yes, I suppose, you could say that," mused Kasumi. "But I prefer the term 'collector.' Sounds much less intimidating, don't you think? In any case, some of us choose to work for the fifths on such occasions. They give us the name who didn't keep their part, and we have to bring them something valuable of theirs."

"This all sounds nice, but what do I have to do with any of this?" Neila wanted to know, sipping her tea.

Kasumi glanced at her, surprised. Seeing Neila's serious features, she gave a chiming laugh.

"Oh, you really don't know what you are, do you?" the kitsune asked, laughing. Then, she placed both her elbows on the kitchen isle, resting her chin on interlinked fingers. A dangerous light appeared in her eyes while talking further. "It was incredibly easy for me to find Loki's weak point. Of all the things, a mere human female was the key to that Áss!"

Neila almost took a step back at that intense stare, but managed to stand her ground.

"That is incredibly difficult for me to believe," she scoffed. Then, she added with a shrug, "you are mistaken. I'm a nobody."

Kasumi gave another charming laugh, and finished her tea. Then, she rested her chin on one hand, while playing with the mug with the other. Her voice sounded sweet like honey, yet somehow it hid great power.

"That"—she pointed at the necklace—"proves you wrong, my dear. You know, I almost wish you would put up a fight to make this hunt entertaining. You would be interesting to track down, given your immunity to my natural charms," she said with lust flickering in her eyes. Then, she inhaled deeply and shrugged. "However, I promised to bring you unaffected," she rolled her eyes, grimacing in dislike. "Whatever Loki did, the fifths are still trying to remain on his good side. Understandable, I suppose," she mused further with a huff, drawing little circles on the counter with a claw.

Neila listened silently. Completely out of words, she waited for the kitsune to pose a question or just direct a sentence at her. In the next moment, Kasumi glanced at her with a smile.

"So, are you ready to go?"

"Erm, I guess," Neila answered.

"Marvellous!" Kasumi straightened up. Immediately, she pulled out a little fox figurine from her wide belt, placing it on the kitchen isle.

"Can I ask a few things, though?" Neila continued, watching the tiny trinket, interested.

"Sure," the kitsune rolled her eyes, bored.

"Do I need something, anything, in that ... uh ... place? Clothes, food, whatever?"

Kasumi gave her a pitiful glance.

"Aaaw, you poor soul. This is just cruel, isn't it?" she said, sounding sad, yet mocking. "The fifths will take good care of you, do not worry your little head about anything. You will have everything you could wish for, believe me. It is their job to keep the valuable in good condition. Otherwise, how could they use it for a bargain?" she asked in a condescending manner that was meant for teaching an idiot. "This is why I'm leaving a message behind. So he would know, where to find you."

Neila flashed a disapproving frown, but said nothing. Of course, she would seem like an imbecile in the eyes of a kitsune.

"Okay, sorry for existing," she growled, folding her arms defiantly.

"Don't worry," Kasumi waved dismissively. "Your beloved Áss will undoubtedly come and rescue you. Well, I think, at least," she mused. "Nobody has ever had to get a bargain against a seventh before. Now, are you ready?" she smiled, making Neila rather confused again.

At Neila's shrug, the kitsune fished out a blue stone from her kimono sleeve.

"Here, take this, please," she handed the stone to Neila, who took it with an interested look.

Kasumi started a chant that echoed in the room in whispers. After a few short sentences, the blue stone lit up, and they both disappeared from the living room.

When Neila next opened her eyes, they stood in what seemed to be the middle of a jungle.

"Where are we?" she murmured, looking around in the damp heat. Then, another phenomenon grabbed her attention. While Kasumi tried to get something from her other sleeve, muttering inaudibly, Neila glared at the strange spectre only a few metres away.

The thing resembled a column of swirling hot air. Yet, something was not quite right about it. The air itself seemed to warp around *something* that Neila could not see. All her senses buzzed, though, making her overall uncomfortable.

"Here, take this, please," Kasumi now handed her a red stone. Neila took reflexively, still just staring ahead.

"Oh, first time seeing a raw connection?" Kasumi asked, seeing her bafflement. "Wait until you can see the real one. True marvels of the node! In any case, hold your breath for a moment."

"What?" Neila asked, but the kitsune already activated the stone with a word.

The red stone lit up brightly, and Neila suddenly found herself imprisoned in a purple gem, forming a transparent crystal shell.

"What the hell?!" she cried out, tapping around the thing, sacred.

"Oh, calm down," Kasumi chided her, holding a stone herself. "This is for your safety, otherwise you could end up ... quite out of shape. You are able to breathe in there, so please, calm down."

Neila seemed miserable, yet heeded her words. After the kitsune made sure that Neila could remain calm, she created a similar gem around herself. Then, with another few enchantments, she 'glued' them together at one face. Kasumi continued chanting, her eyes seemed to shine. As a result, the gems slowly took off from the ground, hovering around half a metre above. Kasumi placed a hand on the inside of her gem with stretched fingers, seemingly driving the gems forwards. As she moved her hand, the gems followed accordingly.

They slowly approached the strange tornado. Neila stared, with mouth agape and a throbbing heart, waiting for them to enter.

Their travel took only a few seconds, and Neila could not really comprehend anything that happened 'inside' the connection. Seeing bizarre spots and flickering lights, she felt the shaking of the gem around her. Interestingly enough, the vibration did not continue into her body.

The shimmering surrounding made Neila dizzy, so she shut her eyes until feeling the gem turn still. Then, she cautiously pried open an eye.

"We're here!" said Kasumi cheerfully, tapping a certain pattern on the gems, making them shatter into a myriad pieces. Then, she spoke further, motioning around. "Welcome to the fifth realm!"

Neila found herself stepping into The Perfect Sci-Fi World. Glancing around, aghast, she only wished for more eyes to see all that surrounded her. Everything humans could have ever imagined was there. And more.

Shining, huge, and tall buildings, stretching to the sky proudly. Flying car-like things, bigger or smaller drones, sphere-shaped things, robots, and a lot Neila had no word for could be seen everywhere. The gentle hum of mechanical things vibrated in the air, yet silence still ruled the landscapes. A cry of a soaring bird could easily pierce through, and so could the breeze.

"By the gods ..." whispered Neila, spinning in a circle to see.

"Oh, I don't think they have anything to do with this," said Kasumi, musing. "In any case, here come your newest friends, so be nice," the kitsune grabbed Neila's arm and gently but firmly turned her to the right direction.

Neila's eyes would have widened even more, if that were possible, spotting the arriving fifths. When they got close enough, she reflexively took a step back from the two huge creatures.

Kasumi approached the fifths, talking to them in a strange language. They nodded and gave her what looked like a tiny golden box. Then, the sixth turned to Neila once more.

"They will take this over now, since I've finished my part," said Kasumi, smiling. "It was really nice to meet you, Neila. *Sarabada!*" she motioned to send a kiss, accompanied by a wink, then walked away without expecting a reply.

Neila felt too numb to react anything. The sight of a massive hand snapping fingers jerked her back to the present. When she glanced at him, the fifth pointed to a sign on the floor, motioning with another of its hands to stand there.

Neila obeyed; her senses too overwhelmed to do anything else. At least, she felt quite safe. After meeting an Áss, then a living kitsune, a four-armed, huge, grey thing could not shock her further.

A sudden loss of balance almost made Neila nosedive into the ground. Apparently, the sign under her feet belonged to some kind of saucer, which now detached itself from the ground. Hovering in midair, the saucer moved forwards, following the walking fifth.

The disc glided incredibly smoothly, yet the moving surroundings tricked Neila's mind enough for her to lose balance several times. After almost dizzying off the disc, she saw a grey arm appearing beside her. Stunned, Neila looked at the fifth, who just stared with those huge, almost baby-like eyes. Saying nothing, he nodded, signalling at his arm with his eyes. Obviously, he offered his arm as help, so Neila flashed a faint smile and gingerly put a hand on it.

Were it not for the immense number of things to gawk at, Neila might have found it odd to hold an alien's arm for support. However, the incredibly advanced surroundings completely occupied her attention. What struck Neila now was the complete absence of greenery anywhere in the city.

The trio approached what appeared to be a rod sticking out from the ground. Halting by the thing, one of the 'guards' put a hand on the flat top, activating a console. After tapping on a few symbols, a barely noticeable shield rose from the platform, surrounding them. Then, a white light started to scan them from the top.

Neila watched the scanner move swiftly, making the tall fifths' heads disappear. Within a second, the light arrived to her. Suddenly everything went black before her eyes, lasting only for a literal blink of an eye. When next looking around, Neila still stood inside the transparent tube, in front of the rod. Unsure about whether anything had happened at all, she glanced down. By the time she finished this simple movement, the light had just finished scanning.

"Teleport," whispered Neila under breath, looking around once again.

At the horizon, she spotted a huge, flying city. Now she understood, what seemed odd about the city. Apparently, the fifths preferred to build everything above ground, leaving the forests and every other living creature to roam free underneath.

The fifths now started forwards with her saucer gliding after them. With a sigh, Neila turned her attention to the gigantic wall ahead. When getting close enough, a part where a gate or door should have been simply dematerialised. Once inside, Neila glanced back to see, how the entrance closed. The wall simply turned solid, nothing too 'flashy.'

Neila huffed, then turned back ahead. The inside of the huge building was illuminated without any visible light source. Looking around somehow gave the impression that there was no light at all; instead, one just knew where everything was. Neila shuddered at the completely alien sensation.

After a short walk, another fifth joined their group. They conversed briefly amidst themselves, sounding, as if rocks were crushing together underwater. Then, the two, who escorted Neila there, headed back, leaving the third one to take over. He, or she, or who knows what, just glanced at Neila, nodded, then motioned the platform to hover after them.

Neila found it interesting that the grey creatures seemingly wore no clothing at all. Some might have had a harness of some kind, like the one who now escorted her. But then again, she saw only these three so far, nobody else. Which fact posed quite the riddle, since she and Kasumi had arrived in a metropolis of a city, from what Neila could tell.

Upon reaching another wall, the door opened in a similar manner as beforehand. The fifth motioned inside, so the saucer glided forwards with Neila on top. Then, the door shut behind her, leaving her alone in a smallish room.

The disc descended to the ground, allowing Neila to 'dismount.' Strangely enough, she found the solid, unmoving ground under her feet soothing. Glancing around the room, she was just about to think what could come next, when another door opened, drawing her attention.

A pear or drop-shaped metal thing hovered inside; its smooth surface gleaming. It flew silently to Neila, who watched, interested and feeling perfectly safe.

Not that I could do anything against such tech, she thought, eyeing the robot scanning her from tip to toe with a bright light.

"Greetings," said the machine with a synthetic voice, yet in perfect English.

"Uh ... hi," answered Neila, baffled.

"I will be your caretaker during your time here," continued the robot.

Neila raised a questioning eyebrow and decided to walk around the thing. It did nothing in response, speaking further. Although, since it had no signs, carvings, writings, or numbers on it anywhere, the smooth metal made it impossible to tell, if it turned with her.

"You are currently in the Correctional Facility on the fifth, under the care of the fifths. I scanned you to know your personal needs, so I can provide the perfect sustenance and look after your arising needs. After this evaluation, you will be kept with the rest of the inhabitants suited most to your properties. Do you have any questions?"

"Well, I have about a hundred," started Neila, but felt too overwhelmed to remain cynical. This day just proved to be too long. "But, let's start with, do you have a name? How can I call or locate you, if I need your assistance?"

"I have a serial number. Is that applicable for a name?" asked the robot.

"Maybe. What is it?"

"Three, one, four, one, five, nine, two—"

"Stop, please," cut in Neila, feeling miserable. Since the sequence of events started, her high adrenaline level kept up the alertness and excitement. But it dissipated by that time, leaving her rather weathered. "Wait, three, one, four?"

"Yes."

"That's Pi. Can I call you Pi?"

"I have registered that you will refer to me as ... Pi."

"Thank you. What comes now?"

The robot glided to a wall, then an 'arm' suddenly detached itself from the body, pushing a point on the wall. As a reaction, a bench appeared.

"Please, remove all your clothing and lie down for the acclimatisation process."

"I'm sorry, what?" asked Neila. "What process?"

"You will undergo a procedure that will help you acclimate to your habitation and to the other inhabitants without complications.

Your level of understanding and lack of implants suggests that you would not otherwise be able to do so and survive the endeavour."

"Well, thanks to put it nicely that I'm primitive," growled Neila.

"Please, remove all your clothing and lie down for the acclimatisation process," repeated the robot.

"Will it hurt?" she wanted to know, not moving a muscle to comply.

"The procedure will be completely harmless and reversible. When you leave the compound, everything will be restored to their original settings."

"Can't I keep whatever changes you implement?"

"Negative."

Neila gave a sad sigh.

"Please, remove all—" Pi started the third time, but she cut in.

"I heard you the first time," she snapped.

Taking a deep breath, Neila began to undress. Interestingly enough, the thought of a robot being there bothered her not. Only when lying down on that bench, some embarrassment emerged.

The robot glided beside her head, placed an 'arm' on her forehead. In the next moment, everything went dark inside Neila's mind. She faintly remembered to dream something, then she opened her eyes once again, seeing the robot beside her.

"The procedure is finished. You are free to move again."

"What the hell ..." Neila muttered, putting a hand on her forehead, feeling exactly the same as before. No headache, no fluffiness of the mind, nothing. Only the tiredness remained from the too-long day.

Sitting up, Neila spotted a folded outfit of some kind at the end of the bench.

"Please, put the provided clothing on. It will automatically adjust to your bodily needs."

"Wow, what a surprise," murmured Neila, feeling like a zombie now. Regardless, the hard part was still yet to come—facing only the gods know what in the common area, where she would be spending her days in captivity.

"How long was I sedated?" she asked while putting on the snow-white onesie. Despite having a nice material to the touch, without wearing anything else underneath, Neila felt exposed. Behaving like a second skin, it hid nothing from her body. Also, it created a cover for her feet, but not for the hands and ended just under her neck. The robot allowed her to keep every jewellery, yet they were far from the wanted distraction from the tightness of the overalls.

Blushing deeply, Neila rather turned to the robot than spending more time looking over herself.

"The procedure took thirty minutes, in your chrono-units."

"Nice," Neila said with a not-bad expression.

"Follow me, please, to the area of your habitation."

"Are you this polite with everybody else as well?" asked Neila while walking with folded arms in front of her breasts, feeling beyond exposed.

Only after a short walk, they arrived to another wall. A forming door revealed an immense arena behind.

"This is your habitation area. Please go inside. I will be back when you need sustenance," said Pi.

Yet Neila could not move a muscle for a moment, staring at the incredible space before her.

"Please go inside," repeated Pi, getting no answer. At this, it grew an arm again, and gently pushed Neila inside.

Not even this motion made her aware enough to shook off her bafflement, merely standing in place, looking around. Backing to the wall behind, Neila tried to remain calm, unsuccessful.

"What the hell did I get myself into?" she whispered, almost regretting the night when she stopped to help a man in need.

Chapter 18

Loki woke after only a few hours of sleep. Needing a little rest, he asked for a break after three days of relentless searching for the connection.

"I scanned further while you slept," Týr stepped to him, holding out a hand to help Loki up.

"Do you even need rest?" teased the other, tired, knowing well the answer.

Týr just raised a questioning eyebrow at this but said nothing. Even isolated in the wilderness, they continued to speak either in English, or in Norse, or in some kind of combination, but never in their own language. It was customary never to use one's native language in any lower-level world, under any circumstance.

Loki stretched a little bit more before summoning his visor to continue their search. Flying high in the air, they scanned the landscape. In silence, they worked, finding whatever information they needed in the other's essence. After half a day of work, Loki felt a strange cold feeling grasping his soul, making him shiver. Halting, he tried to figure out the source of the sensation.

Týr joined him a moment later, looking at him questioningly. But before he could ask anything, Loki glanced at him.

"I want to go back. Something might have happened."

The Lawmaker flashed a frown, trying to figure out his meaning. Since the words they used held almost no information apart the obvious, reading one's essence became their main communication form on lower levels. Which, without the proper signs and words, could be just as misleading as the mere words on their own.

"I'm sure, everything is fine," said the Lawmaker, watching Loki's almost vibrating essence.

"Probably. But I want to make sure."

Týr inhaled deeply, slowly swaying his head. He was against Loki going back, but could do little about it.

"I'm continuing. Join me as soon as possible."

Loki nodded, then disappeared.

Týr took another deep breath, then resumed the scan. When travelling above a populated area, he made sure that nobody would discover him. Also, he was flying fast, reading the information in his visor intently. Just when he was about to pause for a drink, Loki's voice broke into his mind.

"Come to the direct connection to the fifth!" he said, ceasing the connection immediately.

Apparently, something had *happened,* thought Týr, teleporting to get to the pathway. Loki was already there, 'pacing' above the ocean impatiently with flaring eyes. Týr looked at him calmly, waiting for him to explain. The other just held up a little statue as an answer.

"Well, it was bound to happen," said the Lawmaker, knowing exactly what the fox spirit trinket meant.

The Æsir were the ones who remained in contact with the lower realms, the other parts of Ásgarðr rather focused on their own world and realm. They had their hands full as well, they said, not wanting to burden themselves further with lower-levels.

Týr could understand their point of view. Yet, from a security perspective, it was necessary for them to keep an eye on everybody else who shared the node with them. Therefore, knowing about the energy users of the sixth was something fundamental. The sixths often offered their services to other realms when they saw fit or got bored enough. The fifths especially liked to use them as bounty hunters.

"It is their right to do so," said Týr soothingly, earning a fiery glance.

"Well, then, I have something to say about that as well," he snapped, activating his whole suit, making the motives on it glow with bright emerald light.

Without further ado, Loki stepped inside the raw connection. Týr followed with a tiny scoff. They already had enough problems on Ásgarðr, and this mess with the fifths just made everything even more complicated. They needed many things now, but an Áss falling in Love was not one of them. Especially not with a lower-level. Such relations were completely forbidden. Also, unheard of. As far as the Lawmaker knew, it had never happened before. But, even if it could happen through some miracle, Loki was the last of whom Týr thought it to be possible.

Arriving on the fifth realm, the friends needed a second to determine their specific location. At the moment, they stood in an empty-looking city.

"Of course, it's changed position and we are on the other side of their planet!" Loki burst out, ascending high in the air and looking around through his visor. "Why would ANYTHING be a little bit easier than it ought to be?!"

"At least, they didn't detect your arrival," pointed out Týr, joining him.

Loki flashed a piercing gaze, but he was looking at something in the distance.

"Oh, I spoke too soon," the Lawmaker corrected himself, watching the drones heading for them. Tilting his head, he mused further aloud. "Why haven't they got here themselves?"

"I've told you, everybody's dead. Only the city at the Bifröst is inhabited. Let's go, please," said Loki, heading in the correct direction.

Despite the drones catching up to them shortly after, they just activated their shields to block the shots.

"I've had enough of this," growled Loki, blocking another one meant for his head, then gained speed to shake the drones off. Týr followed, saying nothing. Even without words, Loki knew exactly what he thought about the situation. In truth, Loki surprised himself the most with his reaction. However, he believed that he had found the Missing Link between the power wielding and current humans. Which, potentially, could also explain why and how they had lost their position.

Loki dived into that issue as deeply as possible, yet found nothing definitive. Only, that Ásgarðr remained the same since Miðgarðr had lost its position as the sixth. As far as Loki could put the story together, Ásgarðr and Miðgarðr were the closest of the nine, leaving them to have a deeper connection to each other than to the rest. Loki believed that they developed hand in hand. How else could anybody explain why humans looked so much like them? Strip an Ásgarðrian from their mental abilities, and a human would be the end result.

Therefore, Loki was convinced that getting Miðgarðr back was the key for the future of Ásgarðr. A deep Fear inside his soul always whispered that Ásgarðr was in danger. He had no idea, from what or how, but he feared the worst. From what Loki could collect, Ásgarðr had truly remained the same since the Disconnection. Meaning stagnation for thousands of cycles, during which time no meaningful development occurred. Sure, some technological revelations had appeared, like the manufacturing of their own Bifröst. However, that was not true evolution, Loki believed.

This is why he made it his Life's Goal to help his kind in any way possible. Constantly visiting lower-levels might have seemed to be a waste of time, but it also gave Loki clues about how and where *they* could evolve further. Ásgarðrian were far too advanced compared to the other realms, forgetting things that should not have been forgotten. Trying to guide a disconnected world might just be the task Ásgarðr needed to advance.

Loki saw the Bifröst in the distance, so he gained even more speed. Also, he spotted the five fifths taking positions while the iris closed on the Connection.

"They just never learn," muttered Loki, narrowing his eyes.

Shots flew towards him, but he blocked them with an energy shield on his lower arm. Heading for the closest fifth, he crashed into the ground in an almost explosive manner.

Thanks to their armour, the fifth did not even blink at Loki's arrival. Through their visor, the fifth could even see Loki's residues, knowing where he was in the dust. Nobody cared about the arriving Týr, who just descended with folded arms, looking at the manifesting fight. The Lawmaker stayed out of the brawl, only blocked the occasional rogue shot.

Loki, in the meantime, got to work. After swiftly breaking two arms of the nearest fifth, he tore off the third limb with the weapon manifested directly from the armour. Powering the weapon himself, Loki then shot three fifths without missing. None of them got killed; the Áss would never take a life intentionally. However, one's leg was blown off at the knee, leaving the creature wailing in agony on the ground. The others received a single shot with surgical precision, rendering them harmless without dying. Only one remained standing, hiding behind the console that controlled the huge iris blocking the Bifröst.

The Áss cared not about the painful cries in the air, just broke the massive weapon on his knee. Then, with a quick jump, he landed before the still standing fifth, who stared at him with widened eyes.

"Open the iris!" demanded Loki.

The creature did not comply, though, only took aim. Loki rolled his eyes, then disarmed the other with two moves. No matter, how many arms one possessed, if they were up against an Áss. The fifth landed on his back, panting and staring at Loki, who stood on his chest.

"Open it," he repeated calmly, now kneeling down.

Loki's suit glowed intensely, reflecting his inner turmoil. Only a fifth could operate the console of the iris, it had a DNA-scanner built into it. Any kind of tempering would set off a series of events that would leave it sealed for good.

The fifth growled, but did not move. The console was in arm's length to him, it would take only a few taps to obey. Yet, he remained calm, if obviously in pain, staring into Loki's eyes.

The Áss flashed an angry grimace at this, clenching his jaw. At a mere thought, a dagger materialised in his hand. Positioning the tip on the fifth's chest right above one of his hearts, he leant closer.

Seeing this, Týr actually straightened up, ready to intervene.

"Open ... the ... iris!" hissed Loki with flaring eyes. "Open it or I will cut out your hearts, and will do the same to the rest of you until one obeys!"

Týr frowned, hearing the pure Wrath in the other's voice. Loki was one of the more emotional Æsir, yet he had never let his anger escalate to *this* level before. From the light in his eyes, he *would* do as he threatened.

The fifth must have arrived at the same conclusion, because he started to tap around the console. With a shaking hand, he tapped in the combination, still just staring at Loki and his dagger the whole time. When the iris opened, the Áss made the weapon disappear and jumped off him with a smile.

"That wasn't so hard, now, was it?" he mocked, then waved good-bye and headed for the Bifröst.

Týr watched him, troubled, yet Loki deliberately dismissed everything he sensed from the Lawmaker. Loki stepped by him without a word, right inside the Bifröst. After a glance around the destruction his friend had left behind, the Lawmaker followed.

"Welcome home," an almost chiming voice greeted the Æsir on the other side.

Loki rolled his eyes at Heimdallr, but muttered some kind of a response under his breath. Heimdallr smiled, then greeted Týr just as warmly.

"Can you sense her?" Loki now asked, turning to Týr.

Even without naming the other, it was obvious, of whom he spoke. The moment they stepped on Ásgarðr, they returned to their native language, thus no chance of misunderstanding or miscommunication remained. Everything meant exactly how and what they wanted it to, speaking as much with their essence as with their voice. Hence, they only used signs when referring to somebody.

"Yes," answered the Lawmaker. "In the palace."

Loki nodded and activated his suit to fly up to Ásgarðr. While the Bifröst had a platform on the ground, the city itself was hovering above it to operate Ásgarðr's Bifröst. Heimdallr watched over both, besides guarding the capital city of the planet Ásgarðr.

"Good luck!" the android shouted after them, joyful, making Loki grunt.

"Can you behave?" asked Týr, obviously meaning the still seething essence of the other.

"I doubt it."

The city itself stretched silently underneath as they flew to the centre where the residence of the Ruler stood. However, damaged buildings and even smoke from some parts broke the overall majestic picture. Loki watched the destruction with a frown.

"Since a cycle and a half now ..." he muttered. "Any casualties?"

"Not this time. But the attacks are getting more and more frequent."

"Just what we need," growled Loki now. "War on two fronts."

Týr nodded knowingly.

Ásgarðr always had an enemy periodically attacking and thus occupying their force. Hence, not many could be spared, should their suspicion turn true about the outsider world on the fifth.

Arriving at the palace, the Æsir descended slowly to the door. Loki closed his eyes for a moment, gathering all his strength for the task ahead. Týr grabbed his shoulder reassuringly, earning a smile. Then, with a deep breath, Loki headed inside with Týr on his heels.

In the palace atrium, they immediately heard the lively chatter nearby. Around a table gathered a varied group, with Freyja sitting in the centre, who immediately turned to the arriving Æsir, and so did the others.

"You could've made some effort to look decent," Freyja announced, looking at Loki, who flashed a disgusted grimace.

Nobody intervened or tried to smooth things out between the Vanr and the Áss. Feeling hatred for somebody was perfectly acceptable. If their essences were antagonistic to each other, nobody could do anything to change that. It was as natural for them like rain or snow. Until the parties in the hatred drew nobody else into their feud, everything was permissible.

Freyr stood behind the chair of his twin, saying nothing. Only Freyja spoke from the two of them, even in his name. Twins were an incredible rarity on Ásgarðr, currently, only two pairs existed. They always were an oddity in a sense, behaving, as though having one body and mind instead of two.

Yet, for some very strange reason, Loki never minded Freyr's presence. They were far from friends, yet he at least did not want to choke the other in his own essence.

Before Loki could answer anything, somebody else drew everybody's attention—the Ruler himself approached the group. Even Týr widened his eyes at this, exchanging a glance with Loki and Þórr. Óðinn said nothing, only halted near the group, glaring at them with a strange light in his one eye. With a nod only, he motioned Freyja to continue.

Everybody there wanted to see how Loki would deal with the issue. Not many things remained a secret in Ásgarðr, hence a few Æsir walked by just the right time to hear more about the fifths.

"Loki," Freyja broke the heavy stillness, addressing the other by his lower-level name. This was considered one of the biggest insults, of which one could ever think. "What reason can you give me to listen to you?"

Loki tried to suppress his disgust and anger towards the other, but with little success. Closing his eyes in dismay, he summoned his blades. A murmur rose from the Æsir at this, even Týr looked surprised. Þórr whispered something to another youth standing beside him.

The weapon of an Æsir was their essence taking physical form. When they chose the path of War, they all had to visit the land of the Dvergar to receive their unique weapon. During this delicate process, the future Áss or Ásynja gave up a part of their essence, which the smith then melded with technology. As a result, a complete weapon was born; perfect for the abilities of the soldier itself. Whatever form the weapon took, it forged the path of their future training.

Loki held the twin daggers on his palms, looking tormented. Then, with a lowered head, he stepped to Freyja's chair. Kneeling down, he offered the blades to her.

"Use them as you see fit," whispered Loki with a shaking voice.

Even Freyja looked completely shocked by the gesture; some of the Æsir cried out, but even Týr dropped his jaw. Only Óðinn looked calm as ever.

Taking a deep breath, the Vanr composed herself. Freyr stepped in front now, taking the daggers and putting them down on the wide armrest.

"I'm surprised, I must say," she said, eyeing the rising Loki. Then, her eyes wandered to the gorgeous weapons. Lust sparkled in her gaze, making Loki close his eyes in agony.

The Vanr gingerly touched one blade, 'entering' into it with her own essence. Closing her eyes, she gave a satisfied smile, while Loki turned paler than ever. Sweat beaded on his forehead, trying his best to withstand her.

Loki felt violated to his very core, which was the whole point of Freyja's doing, he knew that much. By caressing the daggers, she basically entered into his soul. Loki himself had several relations throughout his life, and with the right person, the collision of essences could feel ecstatic. Deeper and more intimate than any physical contact on its own, a time like that literally was the lust of the mind, soul, and body.

This, on the other hand ... all Loki felt was pure Disgust, making him sick. Plain torture, what Freyja did to him, and Loki honestly wondered why this was allowed by Týr and Óðinn. The Áss wanted to carve out his heart to make it stop, yet he clenched his jaw and dug so deep for strength like never before. All he wanted to do was vomit. Or rather, vomit *on* Freyja, just to be spiteful. Yet, he did nothing of the sort.

The length I go to, to help the fifths ... Loki thought, desperate not to break.

After a few moments, even Freyja deemed him worthy, because she pulled her hand back, releasing Loki from her 'grip.' Taking a deep breath, he now glanced at her.

However, before Freyja could say anything, Óðinn cut in.

"You will help the fifth," he declared, directing it to Freyja, making her blink in surprise. "And give them back!"

Without further ado, Óðinn turned and walked away, dismissing the baffled gazes on his back. Even Loki widened his eyes, immediately recalling his blades, earning a frown from Freyja.

"Come!" the group heard the call, and every eye turned to Loki.

The Áss hurried after Óðinn, following him to his hall at the rear end of the palace. Týr could retell everything to Freyja just as well.

Inside, Loki glanced around at the numerous animals wandering everywhere. Óðinn walked to his workstation that looked like a miniature library. Abruptly, a clapping of hooves drew Loki's attention. From the garden at the back, an eight-legged horse trotted towards him.

Arriving to Loki, the horse started to gently nibble on his hair.

"Hey, it's been a long time," smiled Loki, stroking the animal on the neck. A huge wolf joined them shortly after, almost stepping on him in joy. "You remember me!" grinned the Áss, now scratching the wolf's chest with the other hand.

"Of course they do," growled Óðinn at this. "Leave them, I have to talk."

Óðinn was not one for many words, preferring to communicate through his essence.

"You must remain here from now on. War is coming," announced the Ruler, glancing at the Áss.

"To the fifth? With whom?" he asked, solemn.

Óðinn replied nothing, yet his essence twitched, raising Loki's attention.

"You have to leave Miðgarðr for now," said the Ruler, then.

"I cannot. I've found the Missing Link."

Óðinn looked at him, musing. Loki was absolutely sure that the Ruler knew something, and could not fathom, why he kept it to himself. *Is getting Miðgarðr back only important to me!?* the Áss thought bitterly.

"It is important, but you need to do it with somebody else. You must let her go and find another."

Loki could not believe his ears. He was just about to argue, when Óðinn held a hand up.

"Go to the fifth and assist her."

"Neila is in captivity there, or did that slip by you?" asked Loki mockingly, but more lost than anything else. After what had happened with Freyja, he had no strength left to compose himself, bursting out. "We are blood brothers! You have the same nanocytes as I; we've trained together! You cannot just order me like that!"

Óðinn now looked at him with such a sad gaze, it cooled Loki down in a second.

"What do you know?" Loki suddenly asked, turning worried.

"The fact that you cannot read my essence shows, you are still unprepared to hear it."

"What? I'm just confused and—"

"Exactly," Óðinn nodded, still sounding incredibly sad. "Now, go. You have work to do."

"But ..." Loki tried to argue, yet the Ruler motioned him to go. So he left.

Outside the hall, Loki just stood there for a few moments, feeling torn and exhausted. But above all, Confusion ruled.

Chapter 19

Neila glanced around, aghast. She had braced herself for a lot of things; a hall or arena full of aliens was to be expected. Instead, only a handful of creatures wandered about, paying her no mind whatever.

"Well, this is something," Neila muttered under her breath.

Most probably, the enormous arena was meant for more than five residents, even if some of the creatures were huge. The walls could be around thirty metres high, yet without a closed ceiling. Some kind of shield had to be in place, since Neila saw a creature that could climb the walls like a gecko. The blue sky stretched above, slowly darkening, signalling that night would come soon.

Neila now felt tiredness arise again. After such a long day, with several huge surprises and shocks, her system just could not manage any more serious happenings.

"Yeah, maybe it's for the best," she mumbled, then scoffed. "Great, you're here for five minutes and you're already talking to yourself."

With a deep sigh, she moved forwards alongside a wall, without having a specific goal in mind. Perhaps, the only thing she actually tried to do was to steer clear of the other creatures. Having no idea what they were or how they would react to anything, it seemed the safest thing to do.

Therefore, Neila chose a spot beside the wall to sit down. Realising that the floor was covered with grass, she stroked it a few times to see whether it felt different than on Earth. It did not.

Sighing, Neila started to observe the nearby creatures. The closest seemed to be a combination of a male lion and a bovine. He had the colour pattern and mane of the former, but in every other regard it resembled the latter. A huge one at that, too, somewhat bigger than an African elephant.

Fortunately, he behaved peaceful enough, just walking around and sniffing the ground or the air. Settling down, he yawned, showing its huge fangs.

"A carnivorous bovine ... Nice," mumbled Neila.

Feeling no fear whatever, she watched the other inhabitants. None of them wore any clothing, which raised her attention. From their behaviour, they seemed to be more animals than 'intelligent' peoples.

Whatever 'intelligent' means in the higher realms, anyway, thought Neila grumpily. Pulling up a knee, she rested her arms and head on top. In truth, she had absolutely no idea, what to expect.

In the meantime, the sky turned dark and a huge entrance appeared, letting robots inside. Neila watched the things tending to the other inhabitants, who truly behaved like animals. No robot tried to communicate with them by any kind of audible language.

Pi arrived to her momentarily.

"Here is your evening meal," said the robot, handing her a tray.

Taking it, Neila eyed the tray, interested. Even a simple thing like that looked shiny and metallic, 'very sci-fi' in every regard. There was a bottle, filled with liquid, and a plate with some kind of ragout or soup.

"Thank you," she said and started eating. "Can I ask you some questions?"

"Yes."

"How can I use the bathroom in this thing? And where is it? Is there a shower as well, or something to clean myself with, if I want to?"

"The door on the eastern side leads to the room of such requirements," the robot said, pointing with an 'arm' towards the mentioned wall. "Your clothing answers to mental commands."

Neila raised a questioning eyebrow, but her mouth was full. Pi seemed to find the answer satisfying, and somehow Neila wanted not to seem dumber than she already was. The stew was not half bad, although, tasted very different than what she was used to. It was an interesting experience altogether, surprisingly fulfilling.

After Neila finished, Pi took the tray and hovered back to wherever he stationed in the meantime. The other robots seemed to finish their chores as well, feeding, grooming, and picking up after the beasts whenever needed. Every animal had their own drone, just like Neila.

When they were left alone again, she started to think about what Pi had said. Remembering to have a zip, she tried to locate it at the neck, yet found nothing. Neila gave a huff at this, feeling the smooth fabric. Yet, Pi said it can respond to mental commands.

"All right, let's try something, then," she mumbled, thinking of ... Neila had just realised that she had no idea about how to 'command' something mentally.

Sighing, Neila could not shake the thought of going to the bathroom when nature called. If she were unable to figure out how to 'command' the overalls by then, it might end badly.

Just when she finished this thought, she felt something strange, so she glanced at her lap. The overalls freed everything up in *that* area, making her cry out and close her legs to cover herself up. Blushing deeply, Neila stared at her lap, looking, as though having a longer shirt on with hosiery ending at her thighs, and nothing in between.

Whimpering miserably, Neila tried to undo whatever she did. Desperately thinking about complete overalls again, she exhaled loudly when they suddenly 'came back.' The overalls melded themselves on her body in a similar way to Loki's outfit.

Leaning back, she panted; heart still throbbing, feeling utterly humiliated. Fortunately, nobody was there to notice her little 'accident.' Even if the fifths were monitoring the inhabitants of the arena, they would not even blink at seeing her fully naked.

Why would they? I wouldn't, if the situation were reversed. Gods, I must have seen them naked the whole time. Did it matter? Of course not, she argued inside her head. *You keep forgetting that this is NOT Earth, and these are NOT humans.*

Forcefully breathing steadily, Neila tried to ease up, forming a plan to start small, avoiding any similar accident. Holding up a hand, she attempted to make a glove on it. *I want a glove!* she said in her mind 'to her hand,' staring at it piercingly.

Nothing had happened.

Neila now summoned a picture of a glove into her head. Still nothing. Since the obvious choices failed, Neila gave a miserable sigh.

"Of course, it has to come from deeper," she muttered haggardly.

Even before the strange accident with Týr, she was conscious about the many layers of her mind. All could 'talk,' or, rather, communicate with her 'wake mind' in their unique way. One merely had to learn how to listen.

With closed eyes, Neila now tried to access one of these deeper levels. However, 'ordering' those 'inside voices' was a tricky and difficult thing. Unlike the waking mind, these layers communicated through pure feelings, impressions, or trains of thought. With an incredible amount and speed, too.

Nevertheless, it did the trick. Feeling something, Neila opened her eyes, looking at her right hand. The overalls now covered it with the most perfect and comfortable glove she had ever experienced.

"YES!" she cried out, triumphant, only to remember—she loathed gloves.

Neila blinked. As incredible and high-tech the overalls were, they still behaved like clothing. Meaning, she lost most of her sense of touch. Grunting, she now tried to turn it back. But, fatigue set in, rendering her efforts fruitless.

Neila leant back again, sighing and giving up for the moment. The sky turned completely dark by that time, yet Neila somehow still could perceive the other creatures. *Something* lit the inside of the arena, almost imperceptible, allowing the creatures to rest peacefully.

Regardless, Neila did not think that sleep would come in a strange alien stadium with only the gods know what creatures mingling around. Fatigue cared not, though, making Neila's blinks longer and longer until she lay down in an almost fetal position. Despite her heart throbbing, she fell asleep with surprising ease.

Neila was startled awake by a loud snort of some kind. Sitting up, she blinked to see what was happening. The lion-bovine thing was lying almost on top of her, only missing her with those horns by a hair.

"What the hell?!" Neila cried out, scooting backwards on the ground.

"No need to worry, he's just being friendly," said a new voice, making Neila turn to the stranger.

However, another snort drew her attention back to the animal. The creature was just waking up, hence the stretching and snorting, sometimes scratching his side with his huge horn. From a safe distance, the animal truly looked peaceful, so Neila turned to the stranger sitting nearby.

"I cannot tell you how great it is to finally have somebody here who can have a conversation!" said the man cheerfully. "I mean, these creatures are adorable, but do not talk much, you know."

"Huh?" exhaled Neila.

Sleep still held her mind, making comprehension rather slow. When realisation finally struck, Neila merely blinked unbelievingly. The man looked exactly like an elf from a fantasy book or computer game—long, blond hair, light blue eyes, slightly pointed ears, and, of course, a charming voice.

The person wore the same kind of overalls as Neila, emphasising his strong, slender body. Seeing this, Neila just sighed, not wanting to think about how *she* looked compared to *that*.

"But, where are my manners, the name's Helios," the man stood up, walking to Neila, who leant away. Seeing this, he halted with a smile.

"Isn't he a titan in Greek mythology?"

"I have absolutely no idea," the man shrugged, folding his arms. "It's just my name."

"Uh-huh," exhaled Neila, still feeling a tad fuzzy from waking up like that. Scrambling to her feet, she glanced around in the almost complete daylight.

Somehow the fact that an alien spoke English with only a faint accent could not surprise her anymore. Then, another feeling came forwards, making Neila grimace and look at the wall at the far side.

"Well, nice to meet you," she said, trying to repress a blush. "But, with the very real possibility of making a complete fool out of myself as a first impression, could you tell me, where to find and how to use the bathroom?"

Helios nodded without the slightest hint of a cynical smile or surprise. Turning, he motioned her to follow to the other side of the arena. It took them a few minutes to get to the rear end. There, Helios pointed at what seemed to be an ordinary wall.

"The door will open for you automatically, so will any other inside. There are places to relieve oneself, and, in a separate part, to clean if one would want to."

"Thank you," said Neila, heading for the wall.

Upon reaching the spot, she glanced around for any type of sensor. Abruptly, the wall faded away, allowing her to walk inside a spacious room, split into two parts.

The first appeared to be the toilet section of the place, having several booths next to each other. Beside them, a lot of things stood in a fair distance to each other. Some looked like futuristic toilets, so Neila drew the conclusion that they were just that.

Going to a booth, the entrance 'opened' immediately. Inside, there was a thing that could be sat on and had a hole in the middle. Neila grimaced, but decided to use the strange, avant-garde toilet. The 'door' closed behind her, providing privacy.

Fortunately, the overalls seemed to have a good day, and obeyed her 'wish' to be exposed down there. After finishing, she glanced around to find something, anything to flush, or disintegrate, or whatever the 'result.' She even tapped around the toilet and the walls, thinking that there might be a button. After no such luck, she tried to order the toilet mentally to do its thing. It took Neila several attempts, but succeeded in the end. When she intended to leave, the door opened on its own.

Deciding to check out the showers, Neila walked to the other side, separated by a wall. There, a few 'free-standing' showers stood in a row. However, from where the water might have come, remained a mystery. Neila measured the ceiling to find the outlet, when she heard a voice.

"Is everything all right?" asked Helios from the door.

"Yes, I'm just trying to figure out the shower," Neila answered.

Helios joined her inside.

"Just stand there and use it," he said with a glance that showed, he did not understand the problem.

"Well, let's assume that I'm a complete idiot, who doesn't know the first thing," said Neila mockingly.

"Everything works the same way. If you've managed so far, I cannot see how the shower would pose a problem."

Neila now took a deep breath, trying to calm herself. There was no hint of mockery in Helios's voice, or any kind of edge when talking. Yet, the whole situation felt infuriating to Neila, making her believe to become the Biggest Idiot of the Universe.

Her internal struggle must have shown, because Helios suddenly seemed to understand.

"You are a bargain!" he gasped.

"I don't know what that means," Neila shrugged, still looking at the shower with folded arms.

"Well, that explains a lot, actually," he said, looking at her measuring, making Neila blush and fold her arms in front of her breasts. "My apologies, I know what's the problem now."

Helios fell silent for a moment, thinking. When Neila glanced at him questioningly, he gave a huge sigh.

"All right, here's the deal," he began, stepping behind her and pointing at the ceiling. "As you know already, any kind of 'door' is technically the retraction of the wall itself. It's the same with everything, even when it comes to the showers. The water will fall, if you manage to command it."

"Okay. How?" asked Neila, taking a step away from the other. Helios raised a questioning eyebrow at this, but mentioned nothing.

"Well, the same way you can do anything else. The fifths' tech is incredibly advanced, they can pick up even your waves."

Neila shot him a gee-thanks look, then sighed.

"This is fine, but what's the command, exactly? What word, what thought?"

"What's your thought about the blue sky?" Helios asked instead of answering. Shrugging, he continued. "It's the same thing. I cannot really tell you, since my thoughts are different, even about the same thing."

Neila rolled her eyes, still looking puzzled and miserable.

"Just, stand there and keep your intention in mind. Don't *think* too much, though."

With a huff, she stood where Helios pointed. At first, nothing happened.

"Ease up," he suggested with a soothing smile. Neila rolled her eyes again, but then inhaled and exhaled deeply.

At the third breath, water started to pour on her from above, making her cry out in surprise.

"Hey, you did it!" cheered Helios, watching her getting soaked while trying to get the wet hair out of her face.

"Hurray me," she growled, spitting out a little water. "How do I make it stop?"

"Same way."

"Ugh!"

Neila felt like a lost pup sitting in a puddle caught in the pouring rain. At least, the water was comfortably warm. She tried to make the shower stop, but felt too agitated to manage. Interestingly enough, the fact that Helios stood there, watching, slipped her mind for the time being. Despite feeling exposed in that snug outfit, Helios's gaze did not linger on anything 'inappropriate.' In fact, he looked just as 'naked.' That white outfit hid little of his physical attributes.

Suddenly, the 'rain' stopped, and Neila wiped the water out of her eyes. Helios stood beside her, also soaking wet.

"Sorry, didn't mean to intervene," he said with a calming smile. Obviously, it was *his* command that stopped the shower.

"No worries," Neila muttered, stepping away again while squeezing the water from her hair. "How to dry?" she asked.

"Same way," answered Helios almost apologetically. "Think about getting rid of the water."

Abruptly, his outfit became full of water droplets, as if the cloth of the overalls suddenly turned water repellent. Then, he formed gloves from the outfit, and stroke his hair a few times. The gloves seemed to suck every drop of water out, releasing it as he shook his hand. Only after a minute, Helios stood before her completely dried, now getting rid of the gloves. Finally, he tied his hair back the way it was before.

Neila mouthed a wow at this, then took a deep breath, wanting to try as well. Immediately, Doubt rose inside her soul, casting misery. *How could I even think that I can do this?* she thought. With tears stinging her eyes, Neila quickly turned away from Helios, who just flashed a confused frown.

"It's going to be all right, relax," he said, putting a hand on her shoulder.

"How could you possibly know?" Neila snapped, then bit her lip and dropped her gaze.

"Because you've managed so far," continued Helios, still calm. "And, believe me, I've seen worse. Humans sometimes manage to wander to the higher realms, but this doesn't mean, they would be able to use anything just like that. You're doing well."

Neila rolled her eyes, still fighting with tears. Dripping and soaked, she obviously tried to believe. But Doubt was just too strong.

Helios sensed her turmoil, but he could not really help. He, too, knew what a powerful foe Doubt was. Maybe the greatest of all; even facing Fear seemed easy in hindsight when dealing with Doubt.

"Look," he started, grasping her shoulder reassuringly. "You won't get sick or anything alike. The drones will bring our meal momentarily, just wait for them and they will dry you."

Helios tried to sound as warm and calming as possible. When she nodded, he thought about trying to ease her mood, but then decided against it. Failure was not something that could be forced away by telling a joke.

"UGH!" Neila grunted while they headed back to the arena. "I hate being wet!"

This, however, gave Helios an idea.

"Maybe, focus on what you *want* to achieve, instead of what you *don't* want."

Neila gave a blunt glance at this. Then, she finally understood; the realisation almost audible. With a scoff, she managed to dry herself in an instant. Yet, her half glove remained. Growling disapprovingly, she used it to dry her hair, but even after, it remained.

"Well, at least I'm dry now," growled Neila, thudding down beside the wall, then made a bun out of her hair.

Helios joined him, settling down in a distance Neila seemed to judge appropriate.

"So, what's the story there?" he asked, glancing at the glove on her right hand. Of course, he knew the answer, especially after what happened during the shower.

"Proof of my idiocy, that's all," she replied mockingly; her cynicism aimed towards herself.

"You shouldn't be so hard on yourself," Helios said.

"Meh," Neila shrugged, looking at the lion-bovine scratching against something. When it walked away, the huge brush melded back into the wall, making Neila frown, then scoff disbelievingly.

"See? Even an animal can do this without a problem!" she cried out, hurt.

"You should know the story before you judge," Helios noted, earning an interested glance.

But before he could continue, the robots entered the arena, heading for the inhabitants with their breakfasts. Neila ate silently, being lost in thought, and Helios wanted not to disturb her. However, he could not feel anything but amazed whenever he looked at her.

Knowing that she was a bargain, it could mean only one thing. Despite working when Neila was brought in, Helios had heard about the mission that was given to the spirit from the sixth. Both of them applied, but the fifths chose the kitsune. In a way, he now understood, why.

Incredible! A trinket of an Áss! This's just gotten much more interesting, he thought, smiling in his mind. Helios just could not believe his luck.

Chapter 20

Helios nibbled on his breakfast, lost in thought. Forming plan after plan, he needed to proceed with caution. He still could not believe his luck, though. Having such an opportunity would not come very often, and he decided to make the best of it.

Despite being born on the fourth, Helios had managed to ascend to the fifth at a young age. This was a huge accomplishment on its own, since only a few could do so overall. Having associations with higher levels did not guarantee the same depth of understanding.

However, reaching the fifth was just the beginning in Helios's eyes, having no doubt whatever in his abilities to be able to do *that*. Being one of the finest among his kind, he had always yearned for more, testing the very limits. Remaining realistic, his ultimate goal was to reach the seventh. Not even Helios believed that anything higher would be achievable.

For his dream to come true, he required an incredible amount of luck, or the Æsir to learn from them. To have it both was something Helios had never anticipated. Therefore, he needed to tread carefully, winning Neila over to his side to get close to the Áss. Whoever that might be. Sadly, the specifics were not revealed before the fifths gave the job away.

A question brought him back to the present.

"Could you tell me more about this place, please?" asked Neila, finishing the last of her breakfast. Shortly after, she gave the tray back to the waiting Pi.

"Of course. But first, you could tell me your name."

Neila blinked in surprise.

"Haven't I?" she mused, so Helios shook his head. "Oh, my apologies. I'm Neila."

"That doesn't sound like a usual name for a third," he raised an eyebrow.

"I have no idea. It's just a name," she shrugged, glancing at a robot who tended to something on a huge shelf high above. Whatever animal was up there, it seemed to be even lazier than the rest, not coming down since Neila was there. She now could have a glimpse at a feathered wing, then a stretched lion paws.

"Is that a ... *griffin*?" she gasped.

"Huh, that's how you call them?" Helios mused aloud, also looking at it. "Whatever," he shrugged. "So, what do you want to know?"

Neila shook off her surprise and turned back to Helios, picking up the conversation again.

"Well, what is this place, exactly? And why am I here?"

"This is the Correctional Facility of the fifth realm."

"You mean a prison?" Neila widened her eyes.

"Not exactly. Although, a section of it functions like that. In a way. Maybe," Helios answered, looking a tad troubled. "There is no real prison above the fourth, so I wouldn't really call it that."

"How come?"

"Do you want the answers or just want to ask about random things?" he mocked, earning a measuring gaze at this. "The fifths make a lot of deals, both with each other and with other races. Thus, they have very strict regulations when it comes to deals, having a rule to every situation, eventuality, and outcome."

"And you say, *I* was saying random things," Neila now cut in, also mocking.

"I have to start *somewhere*," said Helios with a faked hurt in his tone. "And from what I know of you, I'd better start that at the beginning. Or wouldn't you think so?" he asked with a cynical half-smile.

Despite mocking, he still sounded less hurtful than a human would in the same situation. Neila flashed a smile at this and motioned him to continue.

"So, as I was saying," he resumed, without an edge in his voice now. "They have an extensive set of rules. Which makes it too easy to break them, to be honest. Obviously, the biggest break of contract, so to speak, is when one party does not deliver on their part. When this happens, the fifth have the right to take more serious actions.

First, they try to take the other into their custody, forcing them to keep the deal. If this is not possible, they then take something incredibly valuable as a bargain, forcing the other party to react."

"Are you serious?" asked Neila, baffled. "This is just pure black-mail."

"Well, yes and no," Helios mused. "It rarely happens, to be honest, and when it does, it's kind of justified. After all, why would anybody want to avoid the consequences? The fifths are fair. They simply want you to keep your word."

"All right, so why are you here, then? Whose ... what did you call me? Bargain? Whose bargain are you?"

Helios gave a half-smile.

"I'm here because I broke the rules myself, hence now serving the punishment."

"What did you do?" Neila wanted to know, genuinely interested.

"I stole some technology," he shrugged.

"What? Why?"

Helios gave a laugh at this.

"Why would anybody steal anything? Because I needed it."

"Couldn't you buy the thing?"

"Not a chance. Everything is extremely expensive here, and I don't have the time to gather that much energy."

"Energy?" Neila echoed, sounding and looking a bit lost. Helios gave a sigh.

"You humans truly don't know anything," he swayed his head. "The fifth is the last place, where a remnant of currency still exists. Given their society's reliance on technology, it makes sense. In truth, they accept any kind of payment, in the sense that you have to have something they want. Which might be tricky as well. Anyway, energy is the currency here, if you can even say such a thing."

"Wow," she huffed, thinking. "It kinda makes sense, I guess."

"Of course it does," snorted Helios.

"All right, so couldn't you just give the thing back?"

"Oh, no, it's a healing tech, and I already integrated it inside my body. Since I turned myself in and accepted punishment, the fifths don't really care about getting it back."

"YOU GAVE YOURSELF UP?!" Neila burst out. "If you could get away, why would you do so?"

Helios burst into laughter, until tears poured down on his cheeks. Completely baffled, Neila merely stared at him. Feeling her gaze, the fourth tried to settle down.

"I'm sorry, sohorry," he held up a hand apologetically, still chuckling. "I just ... I mean, this is truly hilarious. Why *wouldn't* you give yourself up?"

"What?" Neila blinked, completely lost.

"Look, I had what I wanted, and I knew, the punishment wouldn't be bad. So of course, I turned myself in. Afterwards, all will be good, as if nothing has happened. It's the right thing to do, isn't it?"

From her baffled look, it was not. A momentary silence fell on them, broken only by the animals.

"All right," said Neila, still sounding doubtful and stunned. "So why did they put you here, then? Is this the place where any kind of ... uh ... bargain or 'criminal' would go?"

"No. As I mentioned before, there is a prison-like section of this facility. I, of course, was put there first. The fifths don't mix valuable things like the bargains with 'criminals.' Otherwise, they could be damaged, which the fifths cannot allow."

"What happened, then?"

"Oh, I've killed three of the inhabitants."

Neila froze. Helios admitted this so calmly, as if it were the most natural thing in the Universe.

Suddenly, Neila realised what seemed so controversial about him. From the moment she first met Helios, he seemed peculiar somehow. His voice never carried malice, not even when mocking; he also had been kind enough to help her by providing information. Yet, *something* in his eyes did not add up with this 'nice elf' mentality.

For Neila, it all came down to the eyes.

One's gaze told a lot about the person; and it was always the truth about somebody's personality. Neila had long discovered the very disturbing fact about herself, that she was drawn to dangerous people. Even during her youth, she befriended some boys who had a questionable reputation, at best. Some tried to warn her off from such young men, saying that they were 'bad news,' mingling with 'dangerous crowds.'

However, no such person had ever hurt Neila. They, in fact, always behaved naturally around her, accepting her as she was. Unlike anybody else, who tortured her on the simple premise that she was different.

Helios had the same predatory gaze, Neila suddenly realised. Those sky-blue eyes might look kind at first, especially with his charming character. But nothing could be further from the truth.

Helios now glanced at her; that strange light flickering in his eyes. Taking a deep breath, Neila continued leisurely. In truth, she cared little about sitting next to a killer.

"Was it an accident?" she inquired.

"No, but in self-defence. That's why my sentence was not amended, and why I was brought here."

"Sounds fair, then," she bobbed her head. "So, how long will you stay here?"

"Well," Helios sighed, looking troubled. "I'm here for a full circle now. A ... erm ... year, I think you call it. I had a specific number of tasks to do for the fifths, and I only have two jobs left. But, with everything that's going on with them, it might take longer than I anticipated."

"Why, what's happening to them?" she now wanted to know.

"Nah, it's politics and I wouldn't want to go into that right now. I don't know any specifics, you know."

Neila accepted the answer and fell silent for a moment. Then, a question struck like lightning, making her burst out again.

"Wait, how long will *I* stay here?"

"Oh, just until your party delivers their side of the deal. I wouldn't worry about it," he waved a hand dismissively.

"Great," growled Neila, suddenly looking gloomy. "I'm going to die here."

This, however, drew the fourth's attention. Opening his mouth, Helios was just about to ask something, but then closed it without uttering a word. Seeing her troubled gaze, he rather tried to soothe her.

"No, you won't. After a full circle here, you can go free, even if the deal is still broken."

Hearing this, spark of hope appeared in her eyes, although, it extinguished just as quickly.

"Great ... I'm going to die here," she muttered almost acceptably. "Well, there could be worse places to spend one's remaining life, I guess. I just wish for something to do! I'm booored!"

"Yeah, you humans always want to do something," agreed Helios, mocking, then lay back on the grassy ground with an arm under his head. "I, on the other hand, don't mind a bit of rest."

"Reeeally?" asked Neila, glancing at him with a raised eyebrow. "As I recall, you were happy to see somebody, whom you could talk to."

Helios gave a well-yeah grimace.

"That was because I'm here, alone, for half a circle now. I like to be alone with my thoughts, but *that* was too much, even for me."

"Yeah, I know what you mean," muttered Neila, glancing around.

Suddenly, the life of an animal seemed rather appealing. They looked content to just dilly-dally through life, existing without the urge to feel useful or to prove something.

Sighing, Neila rose to stand and stretched.

"What are you doing?" asked Helios, glancing up at her.

"Well, if all I can do is think, then I might as well do it while moving," she said, starting to stroll around the huge arena.

Helios watched her inquiringly, but replied nothing. Closing his eyes, he decided to take a nap.

Chapter 21

Neila had been on a walk for a little while now, musing on nothing in particular. In a comfortable speed, she sauntered around on a sinuous route.

Suddenly, she heard stumping from behind. Turning, she saw Helios running towards her, pursued by the lion-bovine, whose relentless chase made up for the lack of speed.

"What the ..." gasped Neila.

When reaching her, Helios just grabbed her hand and pulled her after himself.

"Come, come, he's not too fast, but fast enough," he panted. Neila began to trot beside him towards the edge of the arena.

"What happened?" she asked, feeling out of wind already.

Neila hated running altogether, but the animal continued his steady pursuit, looking like a tank.

"Let's split and see whom he follows," suggested Helios, darting to the left.

Neila halted for a moment, heavily breathing and confused. The lion-bovine got closer and closer, looking quite scary with his mass. Neila turned to the right and started trotting again. Instantly, the creature turned to chase after her.

"Of course it's me," panted Neila, glimpsing back from time to time.

Helios saw this, too, now heading back. Too far to be able to influence the creature, he watched as Neila was getting dangerously close to the edge.

Reaching the wall, Neila halted, thinking about her next move. The creature behind moved slow enough for her to have a tiny break, yet too fast to just dilly-dally.

With a painful grimace, Neila straightened, holding her aching side whilst looking around.

"Climb, I would really need to climb," she mumbled. But the wall was smooth as glass, with nothing to grasp.

Then the thought of the lion-bovine creating a scratch post for himself popped into her mind. Without thinking further, she touched the wall, willing steps to form upwards to safety. Immediately, a flat surface emerged from the wall.

Neila's eyes widened, but she had no time to ponder with the lion-bovine closing in. With a huge breath, she stepped on the new surface. Immediately, another step appeared a little bit higher, then another, creating an ordinary staircase.

Climbing upwards carefully, Neila felt insecure with the lack of rails. The creature was around four metres tall, thus she needed at least five to be safe. Preferably even more. Fortunately, the steps appeared synchronised with her momentum, so by the time the lion-bovine had arrived at the wall, she already reached enough height.

"Platform!" she now exhaled, winded from the running and climbing. "I need a platform."

Obeying, the next step became wider, creating a big-enough surface for her to sit down comfortably. Resting, Neila looked down and around.

The lion-bovine reached the wall with what sounded a happy snort, then started to scratch itself on the staircase. With a raised eyebrow, she watched the animal.

"Hey, good job!" shouted Helios to her from the background, waving excitedly and with a huge grin on his face. If not for that strange light in his eyes, Helios would look as kind as any fairy tale creature. Pure Good, even.

But he's a psychopath, so there's that, Neila thought, looking at him. His shouting drew the lion-bovine's attention. With a lot of snorting and other sounds, the creature turned and trotted towards him.

Helios started running again, chased by the animal, while Neila watched them from her platform. The animal seemed to behave rather playfully during this game of catch. Watching Helios, he bobbed his huge head happily.

Since the fun could last for ages, Helios decided to end it after a certain point. Heading for the wall Neila was at, he quickly climbed the stairs to the platform. Panting, he then simply thudded down, almost on Neila, who cried out in protest.

"Hey! There is not enough space for the two of us!" she complained.

"Then make it bigger," Helios suggested between breaths.

Neila shot a disapproving glance at his back. However, if she did not want to be sat on or huddle with the man, she ought to comply. On the first try, they now had enough space to rest comfortably.

"You're getting really good at this," noted Helios, leaning against the wall.

Neila sat at the edge, dangling her legs and watching the lion-bovine scratching himself on the stairs again.

"So, what was all this?" she broke the momentary silence.

"You said you wanted to do something," Helios answered with a playful half-smile.

"Well, being almost trampled to death would not be my first choice."

"Oh, we were perfectly fine," he waved a hand dismissively. "It's a game we played many times before."

"Oh?" Neila's eyes widened.

"Yeah. They are intelligent enough to train. I could teach him to create a scratch post as well."

"You TRAINED him to do that?" Neila gasped, earning a cynical side-look.

"Told you not to judge before knowing the story."

Neila huffed, then pulled up a knee, glancing at the huge shelf at the far side, near the 'ceiling.' There, the griffin stationed. The creature remained in hiding, as if did not exist.

"What happens, if we are not picked up by anybody?" she asked, suddenly solemn.

Helios followed her glance.

"He's fine, you know. Griffins have a ... a ... I don't know the word. A silent period, when they basically do nothing but sleep for a long time."

"They hibernate?" asked Neila, dubious.

"Erm ... I have no idea what that means."

"Some animals survive extreme seasons by basically sleeping through it."

"Well then, yeah, that's it," he smiled.

"So, what happens to those, then?"

Helios flashed a grimace, as if displeased. Obviously feeling the change in her mood, he tried to avoid answering. But, she let him not.

"Well," he took a deep breath. "They remain here, since the fifths are not very concerned to get them back to wherever. But, it rarely happens, you know. The value of the bargain always ensures that *somebody* would come, sooner or later."

Neila just gave a scoff, glancing again to the griffin's platform.

"Would the robots intervene, if somebody would fall from that height?"

Helios blinked, almost frozen. An ice-cold feeling crawled up his spine, seeing the immense Pain that lived in that tricolour gaze. He wanted to change the subject again, but she glanced at him, prompting for an answer.

"Uh ..." Helios stuttered. "They would not come in advance, if that is what you're asking. But, if one can survive the fall, they would be treated. Why are you thinking about such things?"

"I'm thinking about a lot of things," Neila answered with a huge sigh. "For example, have you noticed that there is no echo in here? We're in an arena, and everything sounds like, as if the whole place were soundproofed. Also, there are no vibrations through the wall. That bovine-thing is huge, yet I felt nothing of his doings through the platform. And, now I'm thinking about a drink. I'm feeling very thirsty after all that running."

"The water in the bathroom is perfectly fine for drinking," replied Helios, still not looking very convinced.

Before she could respond, a robot entered into the arena approaching them. Flying through the air, it halted right beside Neila, giving a cup to her.

"What's this?" she asked, looking at the water-like liquid inside.

"Your brain chemistry is out of balance," answered Pi, hovering beside the platform in the air.

Neila just stared at the drink.

"What's wrong?" asked Helios, sliding to the edge beside her.

"It's probably some kind of anti-depressant drink," she mumbled. "So?"

"So, I don't use such medication. It's just for managing symptoms, nothing more, and I don't think that's good. Masking symptoms doesn't solve the underlying issue."

"Uh-huh, logical," nodded Helios, mocking. "You'd rather suffer constantly and experience a distorted reality through the sickness, spiralling downwards."

Neila flashed a piercing gaze at him.

"Come on, what could it hurt?" Helios nudged, patting her on the shoulder. "Don't forget that the fifths are incredibly sophisticated."

"Yeah, that's the problem," sighed Neila, tormented. "I'm *actually* curious about this thing!"

"Then drink it and see what happens."

"But then I would abandon my principles."

"Principles change, as you yourself change," Helios smiled. "Don't throw away hope just because of stubbornness."

"Hope?" scoffed Neila mockingly. "What are you, four?"

"Hey!" he cried out, sounding hurt. "That was uncalled for! True, but uncalled for."

Exhaling, she nodded apologetically.

"You're right, I'm sorry. Still ... just don't."

Helios gave a well-all-right grimace. In truth, her reaction caught him by surprise. From the times he visited the third, Helios knew that a lot of humans were about 'positive thinking,' and 'hope.' They liked to hear about such things, wrapped into nice sounding lies. With such veil on their eyes, they asked permission to ignore everything they disliked, wanting somebody else or a pill to do the work *for them.*

In any case, Neila seemed to understand how things worked in this regard.

Maybe the Æsir are onto something with her, Helios mused, watching her pondering about the drink. *I really need to get closer to her, and fast,* Helios decided, wanting information like where to find her on the third. It was a huge planet to scan for one person, alone.

Helios was about to open his mouth and ask, when she suddenly drank the whole cup.

"Oh, so you've decided to join the sunny side?" he jested.

"Gods, no!" replied Neila while wiping her mouth and giving the cup to Pi, who then retreated. "I was just too curious about this thing."

"And?"

Neila shrugged.

"Don't feel anything yet. Maybe it's placebo."

"What?"

"Never mind," Neila fluttered a hand, then she glanced down at the lion-bovine. "He seems to have settled down. Wanna head down? It might be more comfortable."

Helios could not even answer, she already stood up and started to go down on the stairs. Scrambling to his feet, he quickly joined her.

"When will we get lunch?" Neila inquired while sauntering by the wall, looking for a spot to sit down.

"It's still a while away," replied Helios, glancing at the sky. "Are you sure, you're all right?"

"Yeah, sure," she shrugged. "What do you want to do until then?"

"I was thinking about sleeping, to be honest. I have the feeling that the fifths will work me through the night again."

"Okay," she acknowledged, musing. "What do you do for them, by the way?"

"Well, not much, since I cannot use any of my abilities in this realm."

"What kind of abilities?" Neila wanted to know with sparkling eyes.

"Eh, I don't know, the usual, I guess," replied Helios, feeling a bit confused about her enthusiasm.

"Telepathy? Or telekinesis?" she asked.

"I don't know, what those mean. This is far enough," he decided, and thudded down on the ground, leaning against the wall. Neila joined him, explaining.

"The former is when you can read somebody's mind, their thoughts; the latter is when you can move objects with your mind."

"Okay. The second yes, and some more. I can manipulate some elements as well."

"Really?" Neila asked, sounding like a child hearing a fairy tale for the first time. "Like what? Creating fire balls? Magical weapons?"

Helios blinked in confusion.

"Uh ... I can light fire without wood or lighter, yes. And, if I understand you correctly, I can also use it as a weapon. So, yes, things like this."

"Wow, you are an actual mage! Cool," she exclaimed, excited.

"I'm—" he wanted to argue, then just took a deep breath. "Yes, perhaps you can call me a mage. A very skilled one at that, too, of course," he added with a playful grin.

"Of course," Neila agreed, also smiling. "So, you wandered around the realms, haven't you?" she asked, changing the subject.

Helios raised a questioning eyebrow, but nodded. Neila did not inquire about his origins so far, probably wanted to figure out herself.

"Is there a planet where there are more than one ... uh ... dominant species?"

"If by dominant, you mean beings like us, then no. As far as I can tell, only one such race exists on each of the planets in the node. Even on the sixth."

Neila bobbed her head, obviously thinking. Helios watched her, but since she remained silent, he decided to take that nap.

"If you don't want to ask anything else, I would sleep now," he said, yawning.

"Okay, sweet dreams," she answered with a smile.

Helios raised a questioning eyebrow, but replied nothing just closed his eyes. Only two more jobs remained of his sentence, and he wanted them done as soon as possible.

Chapter 22

Helios woke to an excited scoff. Hearing some mumbling, he glanced around to see what was happening.

Neila was standing nearby, staring at the wall and muttering almost constantly. Her excited look prompted Helios to get up. Joining Neila, he too, looked at the wall to see what was so intriguing about it.

Helios now dropped his mouth in surprise.

"What *are* you doing?" he gasped, staring at the motives all over the wall as high as she could reach, and some even higher.

"Well, I occupied myself," she replied, sounding almost bursting with energy.

"I can see that much," he agreed. "What is all this?"

"I tested what I could do with the wall."

Helios blinked at her, confused. Neila explained, sounding almost fanatically excited.

"The bovine and those steps gave me the idea. So I tried to test the limits," Neila began, getting gradually louder and more energetic; her gaze almost sparkled feverishly. "At first, I've started with easy things, you know, like another step, or a vertical thing. Then, I thought, can I bend this? Can I create only a lump, or something spherical?"

Neila talked, as though this was the most fascinating topic throughout the nine realms—filled with enthusiasm, eyes wide and sparkling with pure joy.

"It turns out, I can!" she almost squealed, grabbing Helios's arm and shaking him a little. Then, she interlinked her arm with his, talking further whilst gesticulating. "Then, I started to create patterns, you know, just for fun. I also wanted to know whether I needed direct contact with the wall during, or can I sculpt from afar? If yes, from how far away?

"It turns out, there's a metre or so, in which the wall responds perfectly. Of course, the farther you go, the stronger and simpler the command has to be. Then I thought, how long would they stay on the wall if I walk away?"

"I would say, you have to walk pretty far?" said Helios in her momentary break when she caught up with breathing. Looking around, the wall there was full with motives.

"Yeah," she nodded with a grin. "The first ones are still there. I'd bet, I have to go to the other side of the arena for them to disappear. Then, I started to think about the limitations of formations. You know, how much they can hold and so on. So I created a horizontal rod, and I could easily pull on it with all my weight. Even more impressive was that I could thin its base to a hair, and it still didn't break! A literal thread kept everything steady, even WITH my weight pulling on the END! And I could create a pole almost as long as the arena!"

"Did you do all this while I was sleeping?" asked Helios, baffled.

"Yeah," she smiled, still hyped. "Why?"

"Nothing, it's good," he replied quickly. "You have a good mood, at least."

"Yeah," Neila agreed. "I have no idea, what they put into that drink, but I feel ... Fine! Completely fine! No fear, no anxiety, I can just ... be. It's almost like after a couple of drinks, just enough to take the edge away, you know, to have a nice time."

"Well, I'm happy that you're happy," Helios smiled, tapping the other on the back. Before, she always avoided his touch, but now she almost seemed to want it. Not too much, or in a clingy way, but she did not mind it, at least.

"Well, I wouldn't go that far. BUT, I haven't even got to the best part yet," she continued, grinning. "Did you know that you can *remove* parts from the wall?"

"What?" Helios gasped, suddenly realising, *exactly what* Neila was talking about.

Up until that point, he mostly watched Neila's body language and tone. Talking about jumping down from the top of the arena raised his awareness about her internal struggle. Since Helios needed her to get to the Æsir, it was wise to keep her in a good state of mind.

Now, however, Neila talked about some truly fascinating facts. Helios had no idea about the things she discovered. Despite knowing how advanced the fifths were, he had never thought about 'researching' the facility like that. Thus, from that point on, he listened intently.

"Look," Neila said and hurried to the wall, where a staff stood. Picking it up and showing it to Helios, she continued. "It's there since I put it there. However, the one I plunged into the ground a few metres away, disappeared after like ... ten minutes or so."

Helios flashed a frown, looking at the rod.

"How far can you take it?" he inquired.

Neila gave a knowing laugh, implying some surprises yet to come.

"If it's with you, then it remains," she explained, grinning. At his questioning glance, she now fished out a tiny sphere from a pocket. Helios flashed a confused frown again.

"Yeah, you can make pockets as well," Neila said, still enthusiastic. "You can do whatever you want with the outfit, I think."

"Yet, the glove remains," noted now Helios, eyeing her right hand.

"Yeah, you got me there," Neila admitted. "But, I think that's just my brain screwing with me, as usual. Or, the outfit just likes my hand that much. But, this is not even the most interesting part," she continued, stepping over the shame that the glove represented. "You can modify these objects. Look," she said, holding the sphere in a palm. With a thought, she made it into a cube, then into a saucer.

Helios widened his eyes at this.

"You really had no idea about any of this?" Neila inquired.

"No," he admitted, glancing at the wall again. "You can also make the wall hollow. Huh!"

"Oh, yeah," Neila nodded, looking where she experimented with 'carving into' the wall. "This place is so awesome!"

"You've truly done very well, yes," Helios remarked with a smile.

"You think so? I was just curious," she argued, although, her gaze still sparkled joyfully.

"I don't think that too many prisoners know these things."

Neila wanted to say something, but then just dropped her head shyly. Perhaps, for the first time in her life, she actually could accept a compliment. Finally, occupying her curious mind with experiments ended in something good.

Neila felt thrilled, without the slightest hint of Anxiety or Doubt. Sure, she made mistakes at the beginning, when the wall did the opposite or nothing of what she wanted. However, she felt those failures as normal steps in learning. Finding the right command was always difficult, but the more she 'played,' the easier it became.

Somehow, Neila felt bursting with energy, *wanting* to do things instead of just dragging herself through a day. Curiosity took over her brain, guiding her to wonder about all the marvellous things a technologically advanced world could give. Finally, she wanted to *experience* things, and collect memories.

"Oh, you slept through lunch, though," she suddenly remembered. "I asked Pi whether I could take your meal and give it to you, but he said no."

"Pi?"

"I named my robot Pi," Neila admitted. "Ooo, do you think that *they* could take any shape, like the wall?" she now mused, excited again.

"I have no idea," Helios shook his head. "But, you can ask next time."

Neila shrugged, smiling.

"If they could," she wondered, sitting down in the grass. "That would make a great story."

"Story?" asked Helios, joining her.

"Yeah. I'm a writer, and I have gathered so many ideas about what to write next."

"A storyteller?" he grinned. "I'd have never imagined," he teased with a measuring look.

"Hey!" Neila cried out, laughing, pushing the other by shoulder, almost tipping him over. Helios straightened, still with a wide grin.

Abruptly, a door opened at the side, drawing their attention. A robot stood there, now escorting a person inside. Looking at the newcomer, Helios's expression darkened. Jumping to his feet, he quickly pulled Neila up and ushered her to the wall.

"What's wrong? Who's that?" she asked, confused, almost stumbling over her own legs. Neila tried to take a peek at the newcomer, but Helios always positioned himself in between her and the stranger for some reason.

"*That* is trouble," he answered, looking fierce as ever.

The new arrival was a tall, humanoid creature, covered with some kind of exoskeleton. Bigger and smaller spikes placed in patterns gave some 'decoration.' He glanced around with quite big, red eyes, looking akin to a compound eye. Despite his overall bug-like features, he had distinct human-esque mouth and hands, although, the legs resembled those of a bird.

What captured Neila's attention were the rows of sharp-looking spikes adorning the lower arms. He, too, wore overalls, only grey instead of white.

"What is *that*?" Neila gasped, eyeing the spikes poking through his outfit.

The creature glanced at the pair, pausing for a moment. Immediately, Helios tensed up and got ready to jump. Then, the newcomer simply gave a disgusted grimace and started walking again, settling down at the far side.

"He is from the third, a member of a very aggressive species."

"Wait, the third? That's impossible! He's not from Earth by any means!"

Helios took a deep breath and settled down by the wall, keeping a keen an eye on the creature.

"He is from another solar system than yours; from a planet that is outside our node. If humanity has never encountered them, consider yourselves lucky. Somehow, they've managed to get to our world, and since then, we are at war with them."

"WHAT?!" Neila cried out. The creature raised his head at the sound, so Helios motioned her to calm down.

"You might have guessed that they have evolved from some kind of insect. Hence they have a good hearing, if not like ours. Keep your voice down and stay calm."

Helios's tone made Neila worried; fear sparkled in her eyes. Yet, she obeyed, settling down beside him.

"How could they go to the fourth in the first place?" she then asked, tense.

Abruptly, the door opened again and a robot entered, heading for them. Halting before Helios, it started talking in a strange language.

The fourth gave a grimace, but answered something. Then, he turned to Neila.

"Look, I have to go, and will be gone probably for the whole night. Try to avoid *it*. Hopefully, it'll behave. It's wearing grey, which means that it won't be able to follow you into the bathroom. Sleep there. I'll find you when I return."

Neila turned ashen, utterly stunned, and was just about to say something but the robot was faster. Helios snapped at it, yet started moving for the door.

The robot escorted Helios to a little room where he could change back to his own attire, just like when getting any other job beforehand. Then, they headed outside, where a teleportation console took them to their destination. It might have been in another city, Helios would not be able to tell.

Since he had been visiting the fifth for a long time now, he did not spare a glance at the marvels greeting from everywhere. Furthermore, Helios thought that even the fifth would look mundane in comparison when looking down from the seventh.

As far as anybody knew, no lower-level could ever manage to get there, yet. This was one of the reasons, Helios wanted to be the first. It would also be a true fairy tale—somebody from the fourth managed to evolve all the way to the seventh. *Why not?* Helios asked himself with a half-smile. *You have to dream big.*

A drone darted by them now, drawing his attention. Heading in the same direction as they, Helios eyed the huge curved building upfront. All mental abilities were rendered useless on the fifth; the planet possessed no energies. *What could I possibly do here, then?* Helios mused.

The robot guided him inside the building, then into a room, full of ...

"Æsir ...!" gasped Helios, frozen in place.

The room clearly was some kind of laboratory, or something or other. There, at least five sevenths stood in front of consoles or monitors, wholly submerged in their work. Sparing no glance at Helios, they focused on their tasks, looking incredibly tense.

In his astonishment, Helios noticed only vaguely when the robot glided to a woman, saying something, who then sauntered to Helios.

A gorgeous woman, she was; her long blond hair tied in an incredible braid and adorned with gold jewellery. Her green eyes seemed to almost shine in the brightly lit laboratory; each of her movements emitted regal grace. Wearing a gold-and-silver dress, she simply looked transcendent.

"Welcome," she greeted charmingly, speaking in Helios's native language. "I believe, you will be our helper. Please, follow me and we will assign you to a task."

Helios just blinked, feeling in a trance. Shaking it off, he trotted a few steps to catch up to her. Despite the woman being a tad shorter, her behaviour and overall power made her seem much taller.

"In here, please," she gestured towards a room, full with blinking computers, monitors, other types of consoles, and a lot of things Helios could not even identify. Here, a second group of sevenths worked, looking just as immersed and tense as their brethren.

"Your job will be easy. You simply need to help whomever with anything they ask. How can we call you?" asked the woman.

"My name is Helios."

"Very nice," said the woman leniently. "You can call me Freyja."

"Yes, Ásynja," Helios bowed his head a little, thinking that flattery would not hurt.

"I am not one of the Ásynjur," she corrected him immediately. "I am a Vanr, and I come from Álfheimr. Now, there is a lot to be done and little time, so please, stay alert."

With this, Freyja walked away. Helios glanced after her, puzzled. Even such a morsel of information was more than most knew about the sevenths. Then, he turned to the ones scattered around in the room. Nobody seemed to even acknowledge his presence, so Helios took a deep breath and found a chair.

Apparently, the fifths wanted to get rid of him as soon as possible, hence this ridiculous 'job.' Nothing had to do anything with his abilities whatever; he was there to do the bidding of the sevenths. A gofer.

Well, it's still a chance to watch them, Helios though, suppressing a yawn. Hoping that Neila would be fine in the meantime, he started to muse about how long this specific 'job' would take.

Chapter 23

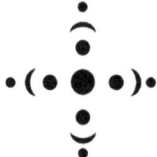

Neila was woken by Pi gently shaking her shoulder.

"Huh? What's wrong?" asked Neila drowsily, rubbing her eyes, moody from sleeping on a makeshift 'platform bed' in the showers.

"You are being collected. Follow me, please," said Pi, heading for the door.

Neila blinked, but scrambled to her feet. Stepping out to the arena, though, they nearly bumped into that strange bug-creature. Staring at them, those creepy eyes sent a chill up and down Neila's spine, making her walk as close to Pi as possible. There was no way of telling, what he could be thinking because of the lack of facial expressions. Neila felt that piercing glare on her back right until the door shut behind them as they left the arena.

Pi led her to a smallish room once again, where Neila had to lie down for reverting whatever procedure they did at the beginning. Afterwards, she got back her own clothing. When Pi wanted to escort her out, Neila held the robot back.

"Could you give a message to Helios? You know, the man I've been with these last couple of days?"

"I know, of whom you speak. I can deliver any kind of information to anyone within the compound."

"Great. It's a private message, so please make sure that nobody else hears it. Please tell him that, if or when he's on the third, I would be happy to have him for a visit," she said, adding her address at the end of the message.

Overall, Neila felt vulnerable for handing out her address to a relative stranger, yet she wanted to see Helios again.

"Oh, and tell him I said goodbye, and I hope to see him again."

"Is this all?"

"Yes, thank you."

"I will deliver the message as soon as possible. Now, follow me, please."

It was just about daybreak, yet Neila could never mistake the man who waited for her at the main entrance.

"Týr," she smiled, trotting to him. The Áss greeted her with a smile as well.

"Are you well?" he asked, looking over her from top to bottom.

"Yes, I'm perfectly fine," Neila nodded, then glanced around. "Where's Loki?"

"He is otherwise occupied, hence I'm taking you home," answered Týr, sounding a bit tense.

Neila picked up on the strange tone.

"Is he all right?" she asked, worried.

"Yes, he is perfectly well. Now, please stand next to me," he motioned beside him, so Neila obeyed. "Heimdallr, whenever you are ready."

"Please, fasten your seat belts and keep your arms inside during the whole ride," a cheerful voice now said in Neila's head, making her widen her eyes and glance at the Lawmaker.

"Don't mind him," Týr muttered. "He has a peculiar sense of humour."

In the next moment, Neila felt an odd energy engulf her, quite literally submerging then picking her up like a powerful wave. Before comprehension could set in, it was already over. In a blink of an eye, the landscape in front of her changed to what seemed to be a forest on a hilltop.

Týr now touched her, teleporting both of them back to her apartment. There, Neila stumbled a few steps, feeling misery like never before. It started off akin to the pain as when one accidentally hit their funny bone. The numbness quickly escalated to her mind and body, making her growl. Fortunately, the sensation lasted for only a few moments.

"I'm not sure that I like teleporting by magic," Neila muttered, stepping to the kitchen isle and sitting down on a stool.

Týr just eyed her inquiringly.

"You've handled yourself very well. You've grown stronger on the fifth," he noted.

"You think so?" she asked doubtfully. "I don't feel any different. But, there's nothing a good tea cannot solve. Want some? Do you have the time?" she asked, rising to fill the kettle.

The Lawmaker remained silent for a moment, looking preoccupied, but then said yes and took a seat on a stool.

"Is Loki truly okay?" asked Neila again, as though sensing something herself.

"Yes, he is," Týr reassured her patiently, then tilted his head slightly, asking, "you truly worry about him, don't you?"

"Yes," Neila admitted with a shrug. "I know, it's silly, but I just do. I hope, he's okay."

"What makes you think he wouldn't be?"

When kettle beeped, so Neila poured the water into a pot big enough for both of them.

"I don't know," she mumbled, shrugging again. "He has a natural talent for getting into trouble, I guess. Which reminds me, can you tell me NOW, what was this deal he made with the fifths? How long was I even gone?" she mused, suddenly remembering that time moved faster on Miðgarðr.

"Miðgarðr is slowing down, so I doubt that too much time has passed," mused Týr.

Neila hurried to her room, returning with her smartphone in hand. She checked everything important while sauntering back to the kitchen.

"A week?" Neila gasped. "Oh, gods, my editor is outraged!"

"*Only* a week, you mean? Consider yourself fortunate."

"Well, you wouldn't say that if you'd seen her messages," she said with a grimace. "Oh, this will be ugly to deal with," she sighed, putting the phone down. "But, she can wait a little longer. So, what's the deal with the deal?"

Týr mused about the answer for a few seconds, deciding how to deal with Loki 'hiding' in the next room. The Áss should have been on a mission, yet he probably wanted to say goodbye in person. *So let's see, what* she *has to say in the matter,* the Lawmaker thought, allowing no chance for them to do so. Thus, Týr chose to stay for a chat.

"Well, Loki asked for a very rare piece of material for us, and in return, he promised the help of one of our experts. He made the deal before informing us, though, so when the fifths sent the piece, he could not deliver on his part, breaking the deal."

"Huh, classic," mumbled Neila, bobbing her head. "I assume, he's managed to convince that expert to help, otherwise I wouldn't be home."

"Indeed. Are you all right, though? After everything that happened? It must have been scary for you."

"Nah," Neila fluttered a hand, then poured tea for herself. "I'm fine. It was all right. Just the kind of crazy I was expecting after knowing Loki, you know," she smiled.

"Really?" asked Týr now, measuring. "What *do* you think of Loki, then?"

Suddenly, Týr felt the growing tension in the apartment, emitted by the eavesdropping Loki. Even Neila must have picked it up on some level, because she glanced towards the room.

But she couldn't possibly know, could she? Týr asked himself, looking at her intensely.

Whatever happened in that facility, it started a growth spurt in Neila's dormant abilities. Just after a day and a half, her essence had changed drastically. As a proof, she did not even wince under his touch; and the teleportation should have exhausted her more than a little numbness.

She's adapting incredibly fast, unlike anything I've seen before amidst low-levels, Týr mused, listening to her answer. Neila talked almost longingly, with the pain in her tone that came from loss.

"He's incredible, you know, the best thing that ever happened to me."

"So you are not angry about being taken against your will?"

"Oh, no," Neila waved dismissively. After a few sips, she continued. "In my interpretation, Loki represents Chaos itself. Of course, something or other would happen around him. It's just who he is; it's completely natural, isn't it?"

"Perhaps," agreed Týr, musing. "But it still doesn't make it right. You could have been hurt."

"But I wasn't," she smiled. "And, to be honest, I'm more worried about *him* getting hurt, with all those 'misunderstandings' and 'broken deals.' He's reckless! He clearly means well, but honestly, he's like a naïve, super smart teenager sometimes. I cannot even imagine, how much ... uh ... more, better, enlightened, or evolved, or whatever word you want to use, you all are on that seventh level. You are ... well, gods," she shrugged, sounding a tad too forgiving. "But, this also means that ... you know ... you might forget how a less evolved creature thinks."

"Oh?" Týr raised an eyebrow, interested.

"Well, with all due respect, but it's like ..."—she tried to think of a good metaphor—"Like parents forgetting what it was to be a child or teenager. Is it truly *that* difficult to remember, how THEY thought when they were young? When THEY were seven or nine years old, what a boy or girl thought about the world? Or, what answers they just HATED to hear from *their* parents as a teenager? Yet, they say the exact same stupid things, making their child angry with those typical 'adult' answers, then get upset when the teenager is enraged. I mean ... You've gotta remember!" she sighed, sipping from her mug.

"I think, I understand," nodded Týr, also drinking his tea.

"I'd say, Loki's the same. No wonder, he gets into trouble. That spike through his chest? THAT was scary. I don't care about spending a couple of nights in an alien prison, to be honest. It was actually pretty cool. I just don't want to see *him* getting hurt."

"You really care about him," noted the Áss softly.

"Well, yeah," Neila admitted with a tiny shrug. "He's my friend, and I trust him, strangely enough," she said with an unbelieving grimace, sipping her tea again.

"That's interesting."

"No, not really," Neila argued. "I consider *you* my friend, too, and trust you. And I barely know you," she said, shrugging again. "I think, it's for the mere reason that neither of you are human. So, this might be simple naïveté from my part, believing that everybody from the higher levels is good and trustworthy."

Týr gave a well-yeah head bob, hearing Loki mutter something in his room.

"This is all well, but it was not what I asked," the Lawmaker said; his stern indigo gaze locked on the tricolour pair of eyes, not letting them go.

In the end, Neila dropped her gaze with a faint blush.

"I know."

"So?"

"So what?" she snapped painfully. "What does it matter, to be honest? I'm sure, in a couple of days, he wouldn't even remember that I exist."

"Why would you think that?" asked Týr, surprised. "He cares, you must know that."

"Oh, of course he 'cares,' I know that," agreed Neila, still sounding in pain. Talking further, her voice sometimes choked, as though fighting with tears. "But, I am a nobody, and I *know* that I'm a nobody. A tiny little speck, compared to the Universe, you know. And he ... *He* is a god."

"You know, that's untrue," argued the Lawmaker solemnly.

"Is it?" she asked with a shaky smile. "Yeah, sure, he had a little fun. But I don't think, I matter in the grand scheme of things. Even if Loki would visit frequently, he'd soon grow bored of me; or would find another human to toy with. And it's fine, it's just who he is. I understand this, believe me, I *do*.

"He showed me incredible things, you know; showed me a little piece of what's Out There. For which I'm incredibly grateful. And, this is why I would selfishly want him around," she gave a chuckle, but it almost turned into a sob. "You know, I actually use *him*, not the other way around. And I would want to continue doing so for as long as Loki lets me."

"You cannot possibly believe all this to be true," replied the Lawmaker with a disbelieving frown.

"I have to," Neila said with choking voice, averting her gaze. "Otherwise it's just too painful."

With a trembling hand, she finished her tea, then quickly put the mug in the sink. Yet, she could not turn around fast enough for Týr to miss the tears.

Even Loki vanished from the apartment, leaving the Lawmaker in a particularly tough position. He *would* have to punish his friend for all the trouble caused. Severely. Even if it meant causing collateral damage.

Eventually, the Áss broke the heavy stillness.

"Well, I have to go now."

"Yeah, sure, you have important matters to tend to," Neila turned around, still sad but composed enough. "Will I see you again? Either of you?"

"I can come visit from time to time," promised Týr with a smile. "And Loki?"

The Áss would want to say what she wanted to hear, but it was just not the way.

"We'll see," he said in the end, standing up.

"Well, take care, and I wish you all the best," Neila stepped closer, but halted. "I cannot even hug you to say goodbye, can I?" she scoffed.

"Perhaps, that would be unwise."

"You know what, I don't care," she shrugged, swiftly embracing him in a quick, tight hug.

Týr had managed just in time to withdraw his powers. To his utmost surprise, Neila remained conscious and quite unharmed, even if suffering visibly afterwards. Hugging herself, pain distorted her features, yet nothing too severe.

"Go easy on Loki when you sentence him, please," said Neila with a painful smile, wincing randomly.

"That would not be just."

"I know," she sighed, shivering. "Tell Loki I said goodbye," she muttered with cluttering teeth. "Farewell!"

Týr nodded, then disappeared without further ado.

Chapter 24

Stepping out from the Bifröst, Loki sighed. Arriving to the sixth, he glanced around to see who greeted him. The wilderness surrounding the Bifröst stretched endlessly, broken by no structure of any kind. Nature ruled above all, it looked, undisturbed.

The inhabitants of the sixth realm were masters of mental abilities, being able to fool even a seventh. Apart from the Vanir and Æsir, they could hide from anybody, should they want to.

Loki glanced around in the huge and lively city. For him, little difference existed between sensing and physically seeing. Despite having an abysmal mood, he forced a smile when an elderly kitsune approached him.

"It is an honour to have an Áss visiting us," he said in their native language, which Loki understood.

"It is an honour to be here," Loki replied, just respectful enough. "I came here with the news that the Bifröst is closed on the fifth. You cannot travel there until further notice. All, who have been left behind and want to come home, will be allowed to do so under our supervision."

The kitsune greeted the news calmly, yet tense; murmur rose from the bystanders.

"May I ask, why?"

"Until we know more, we have to assume that war is imminent. Closing the Bifröst is the safest for the node."

"Understood," the elder nodded. "I wish you a successful defence, Loki from Ásgarðr."

"Thank you. Until we say otherwise, please keep an eye out as well. Just to be sure," Loki continued, earning another nod. "I, now, bid you a good day!" he said, then teleported to a faraway location.

Since the Bifröst was closed on the fifth, Heimdallr needed to transport him to wherever Óðinn and Týr commanded. Which was best done away from a populated area.

"Please remain seated until the seat belt light is turned off," Heimdallr's voice said in Loki's head, making him flash a frown.

"Where do you even learn these?" asked Loki, but he was cut off by the Bifröst, transporting him back to Ásgarðr.

"Our beloved Ruler wants to see you in his hall," announced the android cheerfully, earning a sigh.

"Thanks," mumbled Loki, starting to walk.

For some reason, he felt no urgency to comply, knowing perfectly well, why he was summoned. Týr himself said that he would face judgement after settling the deal with the fifths. It actually surprised Loki that Týr delayed his punishment for this long.

Instead, he was given the job of informing the fourth and the sixth about the closed Bifröst. Alongside the Vanir and Álfar, the Æsir also got involved in the happenings on the fifth. While the former had the responsibility of helping the fifths avoid extinction, the latter scouted for hostile activities. For security reasons, the Bifröst had been closed with the iris, separating the realms from one another.

In reality, this only impacted the fourth and the sixth, since the eighth and ninth remained silent in any matter. The logical assumption was that they possessed their own transportation system, just like Ásgarðr.

"So why would they care?" mumbled Loki grumpily, recalling the fourth's reaction. "Leaving me stuck with the responsibility of telling those idiots."

Truth be told, the fourth was considered only a little bit more advanced than Miðgarðr in the node. Loki even preferred humans to them.

Just because they can mingle inside their own solar system, they think that they know everything better. I mean, the tantrum they threw when I told about the closed Bifröst ... Unbelievable! And they dared to tell ME what to do about it?! Loki remembered, angry.

Anticipating something like this, he started there. In comparison, the kitsune understood everything perfectly, being able to read between the lines. Their language allowed more precision as well.

They knew, if the Æsir were involved, something massive was happening. Which *should* be enough warning on its own.

And speaking of warning signs... Loki now mused about the upcoming meeting with Týr and Óðinn. Suddenly, an ice cold void started to form inside his soul; his heart pounding. Somehow he knew that *this* judgement would be a truly serious one.

"Well, let's get this over with, then," mumbled Loki under his breath and started to fly to the hall. Ásgarðr was a huge city; just by walking it would take a fair amount of time to reach the centre. Still, he preferred flying over teleportation, mostly because of the view.

Arriving at the palace, Loki saw nobody inside the atrium. With everything that was happening, nearly all forces were mobilised. Regardless, his sentence would be made known almost immediately; there was no real reason for anybody to be there in person.

Stepping inside the hall, the huge wolf immediately jumped to him for a stroke or two.

"Hey, boy, good to see you again," smiled Loki, scratching the animal.

"Come, we need to talk and time is short," Óðinn cut in, motioning him to step closer. Loki did so with a lump in his throat.

Beside the Rule, only Týr was present, eyeing him with a strange gaze. Mostly, he looked troubled, restraining his essence to stillness. This, however, raised Loki's interest in the others' prior conversation.

Loki stood tall, facing the two Æsir calmly.

"It is time for your judgement," started Óðinn huskily.

"I understand," replied Loki.

"This was one of the more serious matters lately," continued Týr sternly, making Loki clench his jaw. "You allowed Ásgarðrian technology to remain in a lower-level world. To make it worse, a *disconnected* world! Also, you've created a situation in which a human was taken as a trinket."

"In my defence, that was a misunderstanding," Loki cut in.

"You should have known better!" Týr thundered at this, making him drop his head. "Whenever you deal with a lower-level, YOU bear the responsibility, nobody else! You could have dealt with it before it got out of hand, but chose not to. These are very serious offences!"

"I understand," Loki said solemnly. The wolf crawled beside him on the ground, poking Loki's hand with his nose. The Áss scratched the wolf's head while Óðinn continued.

"You're lucky that you are our finest scout, otherwise I would have you immobilised to finally learn your lesson. THIS time, you *will* have a severe punishment, despite the approaching war. Firstly, you are banned from Miðgarðr."

Loki gasped, but Týr cut in.

"No," the Lawmaker said, tense.

Loki's horrified expression now turned into a stunned one, while Óðinn just looked simply sad. Dismissing all reactions, the indigo gaze only hung on his friend as Týr continued.

"In this, *I* will rule."

Loki widened his eyes even more, utterly confused. Óðinn merely swayed his head, looking more tired and sad than anything else.

Týr had the authority to overrule Óðinn's decision, if deemed necessary. Which possibility happened only once before, making this situation even more complicated than it seemed.

The Lawmaker took a deep breath, then continued.

"You will be stripped from all technology, removing even the implants. *Everything* but your daggers," he declared, making Loki ashen. "Then, you will have to live on Miðgarðr until further notice."

"NO!" Óðinn cried out at this, grabbing Týr's arm. "Did you fail to *listen?*"

"I did listen," he argued, still calm like an immovable object facing the tempest. Seeing his essence, Óðinn leant away, taking a step back.

"You don't know what you are doing!" the Ruler hissed, sounding somewhere in between horrified and exhausted.

"We will see," said Týr, composed.

In the meantime, Loki merely stared at them, not understanding a thing anymore.

"Do you accept?" asked the Lawmaker, drawing Loki's gaze.

"I really have no choice now, do I?" he answered faintly.

"Indeed not. Go, and have it done," Týr instructed, motioning at the door with a hand.

Loki took a deep breath, gave a little bow, then left with his head held high. Týr was just about to follow, but Óðinn held him back by an arm.

"I hope, you know what you're doing," he said. "His presence is crucial against what's coming."

The Lawmaker took a deep breath.

"Perhaps. Should the situation turn to the worst, we can summon him. However, right now I have the feeling that this is the road we must take. I lack the exact understanding why, I'll admit that. I am unable to see the pattern."

"Unfortunately, I can," muttered Óðinn, releasing the other. "At least, I can see the beginning. What you have done now ..." he swayed his head, sounding incredibly sad.

Týr watched his essence with narrowed eyes.

"Perhaps, we have avoided to face these events long enough. But, you know her, too. Believe me, Loki is the person for this."

"For everybody's sake, I truly hope you're right," Óðinn muttered, leaning on his spear wearily.

"This is what I have decided."

Óðinn nodded, then turned away and slowly walked towards the garden at the rear of the hall.

Chapter 25

Neila walked along the street, lost in thought. Hearing only a small amount of the surrounding noise through the headphones, she could remain calm enough. Neila was about to arrive at the café for the meeting with her editor. Tracy already sat at a table, looking over the menu. When spotting Neila, she rose for a brief hug.

"It's good to finally see you," Tracy greeted, sitting down again, then ordered a frappé for herself and a green tea blend for Neila.

While putting away her headphones and settling down, Neila listened and nodded as required to Tracy's chatter. In truth, she was in no mood for this, but they had a deal, and Neila managed to honour it so far.

"You are looking good!" Tracy exclaimed loud and excited enough to capture Neila's attention.

"Really?" she asked, doubtful. The dark circles she had noticed under her eyes in the mirror did not support this statement.

"Yes!" the other said, measuring her. "As your friend, I must tell you, whatever you did, it agrees with you."

"If you say so," muttered Neila with a fake smile.

Nothing could have been further from the truth than she being 'fine.' A month had elapsed since Týr's departure, taking everything interesting from her life. Nearly heartbroken, Neila barely found the energy to deal with Tracy and Richard. They demanded some kind of explanation for her silence very aggressively. Clearly, neither of them took her week-long disappearance lightly.

"I do say so," Tracy bobbed her head. "Look, I got it, break-ups are hard. But look at you! Sometimes, it's what we need, even if it hurts."

Neila flashed another smile at this, then thanked the waiter when bringing their drinks. Since she told absolutely nobody, what had really occurred, Neila had to come up with something. Behaving elusively had led the others believe that there was a man involved, who was 'not around anymore.' Technically, it was no lie. Neila just 'forgot' to correct their assumptions about the romantic aspect of the situation.

"But, I must say," Tracy continued, "I'm still kinda hurt that you didn't tell me about your boyfriend! We're friends!"

"Yes, I'm sorry. It's just …" Neila tried to explain, but could not. "It's just complicated."

"Well, it must have been; you looked abysmal when you finally answered," she continued, gabbing away. "But, what did I tell you? Work is the solution. You know *my* last break up. It was a complete mess, but I've managed to turn it around. I've stopped editing and started to work as an agent!"

"I remember," Neila bobbed her head with a faint smile. "But, it was over a year ago."

"So? It still hurts. I thought, she was my soulmate! But, instead of breaking down, I dove into work. And now look at me!" she smiled, making Neila smile as well. "Eat THIS and choke on it, Ruth!"

"But, shouldn't Ms Cho be here by now?" Neila asked, not wanting to hear about Ruth for the hundredth time.

"Oh, I told her to be here a half an hour later," Tracy waved a hand. "She sounds firm, though, doesn't beat around the bush. I like that, especially in a lawyer. In any case, I wanted to talk to you first, you know, to see how's it going and so on?"

"As I said, I'm fine," echoed Neila with a glued-on smile.

"Well, your work shows how well you're doing. I just love, love, LOVE it!"

"Really?"

"Yes! You know, I don't lie to you. I love everything, that's why I'm still working as an editor for you. But, this? It's your best thing yet!"

Tracy seemed genuinely excited, chatting about this or that between sips of her coffee. Neila listened only half-heartedly. Feeling abysmal, she wished this charade to be over for good. All of it; Life, in general. Neila wanted nothing to do with it.

Longing for the safety of her home, Neila mustered every remaining strength to deal with these issues. The half hour flew by while Tracy chattered, cut off by the attorney's arrival. They now sailed onto waters of business. After Neila properly introduced Tracy to her attorney, Haley Cho, they settled down once again.

"I know, you are still hurting, Neila," Tracy began, switching to her 'business tone.' "But, this work shows that you've managed to channel it well. You have to deal with the offers we're having. I know, this is difficult for you, but we can get through it."

Neila nodded, feeling already exhausted.

"So, about the movie—" Tracy continued, now turning to Ms Cho, but Neila cut in.

"Wait, what? A movie?" she asked, baffled.

"You haven't even looked at my mails!" Tracy snapped. "We got a serious offer from a production office. This is why Ms Cho is here, so we can draft an official reply."

Neila just blinked, confused.

"Maybe, we should start at the beginning," suggested the attorney. "Ms Bricks briefed me on this contract. It's promising, but we must assert our terms as soon as possible."

"I still don't understand," said Neila. "Why would anybody want to make a movie about anything I wrote?"

"Oh, honey, haven't you heard?" Tracy asked expectedly. However, when seeing Neila's blunt eyes, she turned serious. "Oh, my Lord, you really don't know, do you?"

"Know what?"

"You're absolutely sky-rocketing right now! You're a huge hit!"

"Say what now?" blinked Neila. "Since when?"

"For about two months, or so," Tracy replied, looking at Ms Cho for confirmation. "After that awesome post from Loki Leifsson, you're trending! He said that your books are his favourite, and since then, you became Da-Next-Thing! Isn't this marvellous?" cried out Tracy, excited.

Neila just blinked, feeling frozen and hearing only half of what she said afterwards.

"I have no idea, how somebody like him came across your books, but I'm incredibly happy about it!" chattered Tracy. "I've been FLOODED with e-mails ever since! Offer after offer! Although, I've respectfully declined every attempt to snatch you away from me," she admitted with a faint blush. "I know, you wouldn't want to part from yours truly," she said with a joyful teasing, meaning herself.

Neila gave a faint chuckle at this, feeling a tad nauseated. *Loki, what did you do?* she asked herself. Apparently, giving her a new apartment with enough money to support her through three lifetimes, was not enough. Fame just had to be the tip of the iceberg.

Noticing her turning ashen, Tracy and Ms Cho exchanged a worried look.

"Oh, honey, it's a good thing," said the agent, trying to sound soothing.

"Yes, indeed," Neila whispered weakly.

With an aching heart, she just glanced around, listening not to the other two. Misinterpreting the happenings, they ordered another tea with some cake or muffin. However, she was not anxious in particular, just heartbroken.

You cannot be heartbroken, if you were never together, Neila chided herself. By any means, she was not in love with Loki. Nevertheless, the thought of never seeing him again just tore her soul apart. The most agonizing part in all of this was the uncertainty. *Maybe he's not allowed to visit, but how should I know?* she thought, feeling the tears welling up. Not to mention the fact that Miðgarðr was fast, compared to the connected realms. Years might pass for her, until Loki returns. If ever.

Neila took a deep breath, starting to eat the cake Tracy ordered for her. She meant well, so Neila tried to behave as expected.

"Thank you, it's really good," she mumbled between bites, flashing another fake smile.

"It's just what you needed, I knew it," Tracy declared victoriously.

"Mm-hmm," nodded Neila.

"So, do you have any special requests, regarding the movie?" asked Ms Cho.

"Yes," Neila replied, but her attention wandered, as if drawn away.

While setting her terms, she glanced around. As though somebody was watching her; a mind clearly was focused on her. Alas, Neila had found nobody who would notice their little group, let alone stare. Not even the waiters gave them more than a quick glance; the pedestrians rather eyed the tables where somebody ordered a complete meal.

Yet, Neila felt her skin almost crawl. Then, she spotted a deep-blue gaze, now locking eyes with hers.

"Loki ..." Neila whispered, turning pale.

"What?" Tracy asked, then followed her look. "Oh ... my ... word ...!" she burst out with poorly restrained excitement, turning to Ms Cho, who just flashed a frown. "That is Loki Leifsson! THE Loki Leifsson! I can't believe it!"

While Tracy almost squealed in excitement, Ms Cho just sipped her coffee unaffected, and Neila still sat, completely frozen. Loki's arrival at the table made even Tracy fall mute.

"Good afternoon, ladies," he greeted charmingly.

"Mr Leifsson," Ms Cho acknowledges. "Care to join us?"

Tracy just dropped her mouth at this, unable to believe that this was happening.

"Oh, I couldn't possibly disturb you," Loki argued faintly, now glancing at the still stunned Neila. Those deep-blue eyes managed to bring her back to the present.

"You are not disturbing. Please, join us," said Ms Cho.

"Well, if you insist," he yielded, but only after Neila nodded. Despite not speaking, her essence told everything. "But, I must freshen up first. Please, continue."

Loki walked inside the café, making Tracy almost explode in excitement.

"I had no idea, you knew Loki Leifsson!" she burst out. "How do you know Loki Leifsson?"

"I'm his attorney as well as Ms Saraven's," replied Ms Cho ever so calmly.

"Seriously?" gasped Tracy, then turned to Neila, who still had a faint blush on her cheeks, now staring longingly into the distance. Leaning closer and lowering her voice, she asked, "wait, is HE the one? Is HE, who broke your heart?"

"Uh ..." stammered Neila, dropping her gaze, turning deeper red.

"HOW did you manage to get a guy like THAT?!" Tracy demanded, completely shocked. Ms Cho flashed a disapproving frown at her tone, so she quickly corrected herself. "You know, I didn't mean it like *that*!" she clarified, directing her words at the attorney. "It's easy to see why *he* fell for you. I mean, you're obviously hot," Tracy babbled, gesticulating at Neila, who just raised a questioning eyebrow. "All I meant was that he's known as a party guy, and you're ... Well, not. How did you two even meet?"

Neila had just opened her mouth to answer, but Loki returned, making Tracy straighten up with a frantic grin. After asking the passing-by waiter, he fetched a chair from another table for himself, sitting down beside Neila.

"So, what are you lovely ladies talking about?"

"That Ms Saraven has been delayed in making important decisions," Ms Cho stated almost like a robot. Apparently, she preferred to get straight to the point, talking only when she had something to say. Tracy, however, immediately got defensive at this, babbling nonsense answers.

"Well, I'm sure that I'm to blame for that," Loki flashed a smile, making Tracy wave almost theatrically while stammering further.

"Oh, it was nothing, really, I was too strict and demanding," she said, too loud and excited.

Neila just swayed hear head at the facade, still silent. It was quite difficult to say anything with the talkative Tracy around under normal circumstances, let alone now, when she was just head over heels to be in Loki's presence.

"In any case, can you handle this?" asked the Áss, turning to Ms Cho, since he hired her to begin with. Ms Cho looked over the notes she took about Neila's terms.

"Provided that we can settle a few minor details soon, yes."

"Splendid," he smiled, making Tracy babble nonsense again.

Neila glanced at him, puzzled. Loki sounded off, accompanied by a certain miss in his appearance. As though *something* about him was just not quite right, or as it should be. Unsure about what she felt exactly, the only certain thing was that he wanted to get out of there as much as she.

"Ms Cho," Neila now cut in, "could we postpone this discussion? You can send me whatever question is still undecided, and I'll answer as soon as possible."

Tracy started to protest, but the attorney understood the hidden meaning.

"Yes, I can write up a draft according to what I have. We can refine everything later," she said, then turned to Tracy. "If we can stay a little bit longer, perhaps?"

"Thank you, that would be a great help," said Neila, cutting before the agent. "We really have to go now, I'm sorry," she apologised just genuinely enough, standing up.

Loki followed, smiling, yet his mind seemed to be far away. Saying just enough of a goodbye not to be considered rude, he followed Neila to a smaller street nearby.

"Can you take us home?" she posed the question, looking around to see, if somebody were nearby.

The Áss nodded, then teleported them straight to the apartment. Inside, Neila threw her purse down wherever and kicked off her shoes.

"Are you all right? What happened?" she asked immediately, worried.

"I'm well enough," answered Loki, walking to the bar for a drink.

Neila just scoffed, folding her arms. With an almost boiling essence, she clearly wanted to demand for answers, but managed to stay silent. After a glance at her, Loki gave a sigh.

"I'm fine, you needn't worry," he echoed, but something sounded off.

"You're lying!" Neila said, baffled.

"I don't lie."

"Maybe not intentionally, but you're not telling the truth either," argued Neila, stepping closer to him.

"You've truly grown stronger," smiled the Áss at this, settling down on the sofa. Neila joined him, waiting for him to continue. "As you might have figured, I have had my punishment," he raised his drink as 'cheers,' then took a sip.

Neila inhaled deeply at this, wanting to ask, but stayed silent. Loki truly appreciated her concern and the silent offer of support. While sipping his whisky, he gave a small snort at the situation. Behaving like a human, he faced it by pouring alcohol to ease his soul. Truth be told, it was a terrific whisky; one that Loki particularly enjoyed. As for the alcohol part, nothing so weak could ever affect him.

Sensing the expecting tricolour glance, he took a deep breath and explained.

"I've been stripped from every technology I owned, leaving only my abilities," the Áss started, avoiding to look at her. For some reason, he could not face that gaze just yet. "I also have to live on Miðgarðr for the time being," he finished, taking a huge gulp.

Neila greeted this with widened eyes.

"For how long?" she asked.

"Until I'm told otherwise," he sighed, then forced a smile. "It's not that bad, given the circumstances. It reminds me of my early training days. I had no tech, back in the day, only myself. Perhaps, it will be nice to reconnect with that part of myself," he mused, finishing his drink.

"What will you do? Or how should this work?" Neila wanted to know, confused.

Pure pain shone in her eyes, which was why Loki averted his. He needed no pity, yet she behaved, as though he were sentenced to give up his daggers.

"It'll be fine," the Áss reassured, glancing at her. "Although, I might have to begin anew. I didn't get many rules about this, but I'm guessing, the whole point is to live like a human. Therefore, nothing I've accomplished should matter or be used. An interesting challenge," he mused aloud.

"Didn't you object, at all?"

"Why would I? Týr is fair. I *did* break the rules. Major ones, at that."

"But, he's your friend, isn't he? How could he do this to you?"

Loki scoffed, insulted.

"What do you think, he's done to me? Friendship, or any kind of relationship, means nothing when there is a ruling. He is our Lawmaker, Justice itself. If he saw this to be fit, it is fair and just, believe me. He isn't a lesser friend to me by any means, and he will come to my aid, should I need it."

"So, you're not angry with him?" Neila asked, baffled.

"Of course not," he smiled. "If I want to be angry with anybody, it should be with myself. *I* chose the path I took, nobody else. However, anger is useless in a situation like this."

"That makes sense," she admitted, albeit unsure, but then added with a smile, "well, in any case, you're more than welcome to stay here with me."

"I don't think, that would be allowed."

"You said that there are no specific guidelines on how to do this. So, I'm offering, as a friend, helping another friend in need."

The Áss narrowed his eyes at this.

"Finding the loopholes isn't my purpose."

"Be that as it may, why punish yourself more than you already have been?" Neila asked. "Believe me, visiting Midgard is one thing, but living here is another. It's punishment enough. Take the help when it's offered."

Loki twisted his mouth, so she continued coldly.

"Or, you can sleep outside. Despite the warm weather, it's still cold during the nights. And the ground is still hard. But, I'm sure an Áss like yourself finds survival in the wilderness a piece of cake. Your choice."

With this, she stood up and went to her room to change, leaving Loki alone on the sofa.

"When did she start making sense ...?" he mumbled to himself, watching her leave.

Chapter 26

When Neila returned to the living room, Loki stood at the bar again, pouring another glass of whisky for himself. At this, she raised a questioning eyebrow, but said nothing.

"So, will you move back in, then?" Neila broke the silence.

"I don't see how, to be honest."

"What do you mean, you don't see how?"

"Look," Loki explained. "The whole point is to experience how humans live. I already have a huge advantage, just because I'm from a higher level. It makes life easy, but that's not the human way, is it?"

"You *have* seen my former apartment, so ..." said Neila, leaving the sentence unfinished.

"My point exactly. All I need to do is find a job and all that."

"Famous last words," she muttered grumpily, walking to the kitchen and starting to unload the dishwasher.

"Why are you doing that?" asked Loki, leaning against the kitchen isle with the glass in his hand.

"What do you mean? Who should?"

"The housekeeper."

"Oh, she doesn't really come here anymore," Neila admitted, clattering with the plates.

"Why not?"

"Because I don't need her."

Loki glanced around, dubious. From his look, the place could have used a housekeeper. Seeing this, Neila turned to him with sparking eyes and a hand on her hip.

"YOU weren't here. Don't dare to judge!"

"I'm not. I just don't understand," he said, sipping his drink.

"I don't need a housekeeper. I don't like anybody coming to my home, you know that."

"But you hate cleaning."

"Who doesn't? But, if you're going to be a pain about it, then pick up the vacuum yourself!" she growled, starting to put away the cutlery. Then, she added with a grin, "think of it as rent for the room."

This, however, now gave Neila an idea. Loki did not seem very present, but glanced at her when felt her gaze.

"Would *that* be acceptable?" she asked.

"Oh, I'm not going to be your maid," said Loki, making her exhale sharply and sway her head.

"Seriously, pull yourself together and understand what I'm saying," Neila snapped. "Would it be acceptable for you, if I were to *rent* you the room? Think about it as if ..."—she tried to think on her foot— "As if my brother would have moved out or something, leaving his room empty. Why couldn't you use it? And, you can pay rent when you are able to. What do you think?"

"That might be acceptable, yes," mused Loki, looking preoccupied. Whatever he might have said, he was definitely not fine, by any means.

"It's settled, then," smiled Neila, seeing perfectly his conundrum, yet unable to do anything about it. "You can use the phones and such as well, since I don't. Although, I must warn you that Richard *did* borrow a suit a week ago."

"What was he doing here?" asked the Áss, suddenly fully present.

"We're friends, he was over for pizza night," answered Neila, looking over a brochure to decide what to order.

"To what purpose?" he inquired, intense, earning a questioning look.

"Why do friends come together for a pizza? I seriously don't understand you sometimes."

"Only sometimes?" he mocked, still tense. "What are you two doing together?"

Neila had opened her mouth to snap back, but after a glance at him, she just exhaled sharply.

"Nothing, believe me."

"Really?" asked again the Áss with a strange tone. "You really want me to believe that you *don't* want to use him?"

Neila leant against the kitchen table, confused now.

He's not asking about romantic stuff, so what, then ...? she asked herself. The Áss stood her inquiring glance, probably teaching her some lesson right then and there. Letting her mind ease up, Neila allowed her subconscious to take the lead and whisper the answer.

When realisation struck her, Loki motioned at that.

"Finally," he muttered. "You *are* getting stronger, but you have to do better than that."

"Well, sorry for having NO IDEA about what I am doing in the first place," Neila scoffed. "And, as for the answer, no. I didn't tell him anything, and I didn't know, that he could be ... how did you put it? Useful to you, or me, or us, or whatever."

"Perhaps, you should pay a little more attention to such people," suggested Loki, finishing his drink.

"I don't care for humans."

With that, Neila immersed herself in the brochure once again. Silence fell on the apartment for the time being. Loki mused about how he would do things, while Neila tried to decide what to eat.

In the end, the Áss broke the stillness, standing by the window, looking out.

"Are you expecting company?" he asked, drawing Neila's attention.

"What? No. Why?"

"Because somebody's coming," answered Loki calmly.

Neila raised both eyebrows in surprise. Without asking, she glanced around in the apartment, waiting for somebody to just appear out of nowhere. Since Loki reacted nothing more, it was safe to assume that the newcomer brought no danger.

When the 'guest' finally arrived, Neila just grinned and hurried to him. To Loki's biggest surprise, she then gave him a big hug. When the newcomer noticed Loki, he dropped his mouth.

"Loki?" gasped the man, turning to Neila beside him. "Of all Æsir, you're the trinket of LOKI?" he asked, grinning from ear to ear.

"I'm nobody's anything, thank you very much," replied Neila with a smile, glancing at the approaching Áss. "But, how do you know Loki?"

"Oh, everybody, who has a little interest in the Bifröst, knows him," smiled the man, making the Áss narrow his eyes. "The name's Helios," he continued, holding out a hand. "It's an honour."

Loki raised a questioning eyebrow at his move, then grabbed the other's lower arm firmly whilst glaring into those sky-blue eyes. Since Helios did not even flinch at his full power, he scoffed and released the other.

"What is a fourth even doing here?" growled the Áss, almost rude.

"I invited him here," said Neila.

"Obviously, but why?"

Neila just blinked, but Helios only laughed.

"Don't mind him, he notoriously hates us. It's fine," he fluttered a hand, minding not that Loki still just stared at him intensely.

"Well, that's just lovely," mumbled Neila. "However, I'm starting to get really hungry, so I'd want to order something. Is Greek food acceptable for everybody?" she glanced at the men.

"I don't need anything, thank you," growled Loki.

"Mediterranean isn't really my preference, but it's fine," Helios shrugged. "Whatever you want is perfect," he smiled at Neila, who thudded down on the sofa where she left her laptop.

A momentary silence fell on the apartment, in which Helios sauntered around the room, looking at everything, measuring. Loki followed his every move, still staring hostilely.

"Nice try, Áss, but don't be rude," Helios noted, not sparing a glance at Loki.

Neila glanced at them, but stayed out of their squabble. Only her sparkling eyes told, how curious she was about their interaction. After finishing the online order, she just leant on the backrest of the sofa, glancing from one man to the other, listening intently.

"There is something about you ..." Loki murmured, eyeing the fourth intently. "I'm fairly sure that I know you from somewhere."

Helios gave a chuckle.

"We have encountered each other a few times," he replied while measuring the necklace from the sixth. "But, we have never spoken or anything alike. I just saw you from time to time."

Loki seemed unconvinced, still bothered.

"No, there is something else. Why were you imprisoned?" he wanted to know.

Neila glanced at the 'elf' questioningly, suddenly realising that he wore his 'normal' attire. Biting her lips not to chuckle, Helios looked even more like an elf than before. *What's not to like about him, I wonder?* she mused, knowing that simply disliking his race would not justify Loki's hostile behaviour.

"I broke some rules, same as anybody else," Helios shrugged, then flashed a grimace. "Look, I appreciate the attention, but please, stop. I've modified the spell the sixths use; you won't be able to break through this easily."

"Impressive," Loki acknowledged, sounding genuine enough. "But it's not nearly enough for you to get to the seventh."

This comment made Helios straighten up, tense. Seeing this, Loki continued with a half-smile.

"Repelling such elemental prying is impressive for your kind, I will admit that. And, I will even apologise for my rudeness of doing so. But do not get cheeky, fourth; you still have much to learn. However, you might have what it takes," he measured the other from tip to toe. "In a couple of thousand cycles, you may even succeed," Loki finished with a wry smile.

Neila widened her eyes, quietly laughing at the 'rivalry.' This, however, now earned a disapproving glance from Helios. Mouthing sorry, she dropped her gaze.

"Very amusing," growled the fourth, unclear to whom, Neila or Loki. "I've managed this far, I can be the first to succeed."

Loki just gave a well-you-can-try nod. Before they continued, Neila cut in.

"So, did anything happen after I was gone?" she turned to Helios, who thudded down right next to her on the sofa.

This, however, earned him a warning glance from Loki, which he dismissed as if not seen. The Áss settled down in one of the comfortable armchairs.

"Apart from me becoming the servant of the Vanir, nothing," he sighed. "I mean, those people are incredibly smug. I could only bear it for six days, which is quite the record, in my opinion," he told Neila, seemingly forgetting about Loki's presence altogether.

When they heard the disapproving growl from him, Helios flashed a charming smile.

"Oh, no offence intended, of course," he said with feigned innocence.

"I'm sure," Loki replied grumpily.

"But, I see, you managed to lose the glove," Helios took Neila's right hand playfully, which she pulled away with a chuckle.

Their private jest only made Loki's anger rise. Feeling the urge to intervene, he immediately composed himself, not truly understanding his reaction. In truth, having such an advanced fourth around Neila helped his own cause even more. Especially, if they were on friendly turf.

But do they have to be that *friendly?* Loki growled inside his head, watching Neila laugh about something Helios said. Obviously, she liked his closeness, which showcased an already existing connection between them. Clearly, *something* must have happened in the Correctional Facility.

Stewing in his anger, Loki tried to analyse and thus understand the situation. No other human had ever looked at him the way Neila did—as an equal. Despite their obvious differences, she treated him, and now Helios, perfectly normal. As though knowing higher-levels would be the most natural thing in the Universe. Without a trace of the expected enchantment, she instantly bonded with both of them.

Something almost drew Loki towards her, which should not have been possible with a mere human. From Óðinn's will to ban him from Miðgarðr, it became obvious that Neila truly *was* special; in ways the Áss had yet to understand. At the moment, he believed that she was the Missing Link, who could actually catalyse the changes needed for Miðgarðr's reconnection. Loki just could not let her fall into the wrong hands.

Laughter broke Loki's train of thought, bringing him back to the present. Not listening to the conversation, he now tried to pick it up once again.

"So, how does this travelling through the Bifröst work exactly?" asked Neila, puzzled. "Why can't you just go wherever?"

Helios glanced at Loki, who just rolled his eyes, so the fourth started to explain.

"You see, unlike a raw connection, the Bifröst ... uh ... knows your level of understanding."

"You mean it can determine how primitive one is?" Neila tried to clarify.

"Yes, although, I wouldn't put it that way," said Helios with a lenient smile. "In any case, you can only travel to a realm which has the matching level to your understanding. If you manage to evolve, you can go higher, but until then, you're stuck below a specific realm."

"Okay, but how does the Bifröst determine this? Is it a sentient thing? You've mentioned before,"—she glanced at Loki—"that it is basically one pathway, not several to each realms. So, if it's one ... uh ... big tube, are there lanes inside, for the different levels of understanding? How does it even know, where you want to go, as in 'up' or 'down?'"

"Okay, let me think a little," said Helios, trying to order his thoughts, but an agitated grunt drew his attention to Loki.

"I better explain this, since it is unlikely for a fourth to understand the mechanism of the Bifröst," he mocked, earning a piercing glare from the other. Seeing this, the Áss added in a less sharp tone, "even if he's managed to visit the sixth already. They know little as well."

Neila glimpsed from one man to the other, waiting for them to settle down.

Loki stayed silent for a little while, deciding what to tell and how. His eyes caught the paper and pen on the coffee table before him, so he grabbed it. While drawing, he explained. Neila slid closer, but Helios just leant back comfortably, as if not interested. The sparkling sky-blue eyes told otherwise, though.

"Let us say, that this is the fifths' planet," he began, drawing a circle, from which he drew eight parallel straight lines upwards. Above this circle, he drew eight more circles beside each other in a line, connecting them to the first one. "These are the other planets. Each is connected to the fifth first. Meaning, if you step into the Bifröst, you can only travel there, as a mandatory stop. From there, you can go wherever you are able to."

"Um ... Loki?" said now Neila, staring at the drawing. "Hate to break it to you, but *that* really looks like a tree ..."

The Áss glanced at the drawing, puzzled, so Neila turned it upside down for him.

"Huh," he scoffed. "That's on me, then."

"Anyway," Neila continued with a shaking voice from withheld laughter, "how does the Bifröst 'know' things, like who wants or is allowed to go where?"

"Well, I do not know the specifics. But, this is a mere simplification anyway. Imagine these paths piercing realities and dimensions;

entangled with each other since nothing is in a straight line, of course. To put it simply, the Bifröst is a collection of many, many small pathways. Each goes either to or from a realm, being able to do only that specific function. The higher level you are on, the more you feel the energies inside, thus you can guide yourself into the right pathway. Much like in a huge highway with many lanes on both sides."

"So, the Bifröst itself 'knows' nothing, cannot scan you or something to make sure, you are going into the 'right lane,' so to speak," summarised Neila, bobbing her head.

"You may say it like that, yes."

"Okay, nice," smiled Neila, but before anybody could say anything else, the intercom buzzed, signalling that the food had arrived.

Neila jumped up and hurried to the door, followed by Loki's interested gaze. Beforehand, she would have had great difficulties with answering the intercom, or with interacting with the delivery boy. Neila still seemed anxious while doing so, but managed far easier.

"She's learning incredibly fast for a human," muttered Helios, glancing at Loki knowingly.

"You wouldn't know," the Áss growled, clearly not liking the fourth's familiarity when speaking of her.

"If you insist," the other shrugged, still speaking silently so Neila would not hear them. "You needn't behave so protectively of her, you know. I wouldn't want to hurt her either."

Loki just gave a snort.

"That is a tall order from somebody who literally drains the energy out of living things. No wonder, the sixths refuse to do anything with you."

"They refuse me for a different reason, and you know that as well," argued Helios.

"Oh? Is it, perhaps, because you steal techniques as well as technology?" the Áss taunted. "I wonder, what she would say, if she knew your true nature."

"And what would *that* be?" replied the fourth, just as sharply. "Is it any different from you, whose only goal is to get Miðgarðr connected again? No matter the cost?"

Loki flashed a frown at this, making Helios smile.

"That's right, I know *of you* just as much. So, don't even try to take the moral high ground on this one. At least I own my intentions."

The Áss gave a piercing look at this.

"She knows enough," he growled, glancing at her in the kitchen. "She just doesn't evolve fast enough, and I don't know why."

"If *you* would have been born amidst the humans, seventh level or no seventh level, *you* would be a caveman as well. Give her a break," said Helios, earning a well-yeah grimace. A moment later, he mused further, "I wouldn't mind to have a taste of that ancient blood, though," Helios sighed longingly.

"You *haven't* yet?" asked Loki, almost surprised.

"I've told you, I'm not like the others. I don't do that," announced the fourth. "How do you think, I could get to the sixth?"

Loki now looked rather interested in the matter. However, Neila finished plating the dining table beside the bar, and now called for Helios to join him. Even Loki got up, but he only fetched a bowl of fruit from the fridge.

The trio ate quietly, until Loki broke the silence.

"Are you interested in vampires, Neila?" he asked, casually surveying the fruits for his next selection.

Hearing the question, Helios suddenly missed a swallow and started coughing. Then, he flashed a piercing gaze at the Áss, who minded him not.

"Of course! Love them, why?" she asked, but Loki just glanced at Helios mindfully, accompanied by a small smile. Neila followed his gaze with widened eyes.

"That's YOU?" she gasped, pleasantly surprised.

"Nooohooo," replied Helios immediately, still coughing. "Not me, no."

"Then?" she wanted to know, excited.

"Not me, personally. But my race, yes," explained the fourth, flashing a killing look at Loki. Then, he quickly added, "but we are not blood sucking vampires, by any means!"

"Was it a misunderstanding?" asked Neila innocently, although, nobody could miss the mocking.

Helios nodded with a half-smile, continuing with eating.

"How did that happen, by the way?" she inquired further.

"Well, some made a few bad choices when visiting, that's all," replied Helios, avoiding her gaze.

"Everybody talks about visiting Midgard a lot. Is this why *you* want Midgard to be connected again so much? To have your spa-realm back?" Neila now scoffed, taking another bite.

Helios and Loki exchanged a glance.

"You can say that, yes," admitted the Áss. "But it's not that simple."

"Of course not," agreed Neila, teasing. "It never is with you guys."

A momentary silence fell on the room, which Neila broke.

"Why don't you call the realms on their names instead of their position?" she asked. "But, only some, since even you"—she glanced at Helios—"refer to Earth as Midgard almost every time. Yet, I've never heard the name of your own realm, or even the name of your race. Is everybody just a number in this whole system?"

"We refer to things by their position for clarity," replied Helios. "It's just easier, since everybody knows what this means. Not all would know the sixth's name."

"How come? If this whole connection thing is open knowledge, why wouldn't everybody know everything's name?"

"Does every human know every country on Earth? Or know the languages?" asked Helios instead of answering. "Of course not. It is the same on the other realms. Only those know this, who are truly involved with the other realms. Mostly those, who live around the Bifröst, or can travel through. Other parts would not even talk a lower-level language, or know what Miðgarðr is."

"But everybody knows about Asgard, don't they? You even called Loki by name immediately," Neila remarked, confused, finishing her meal.

"Well, yes, because I travel a lot and actually wanted to know as much about them as possible. Which is close to nothing, to be honest," he continued, glancing at the Áss, who just raised an eyebrow at this. "Everybody learns about Ásgarðr, because they are the highest level actually engaging with us. Sort of like a big brother, who sometimes mediates disputes. But, believe me, we don't know much about them. It was just a few days ago, when I heard the name Vanir for the first time."

"That cannot be right," Loki cut in with a frown.

"Well, it is," said Helios, looking at him. "Why do you think, everybody wants to go there? Or, to be fair, to any kind of higher level? Nobody tells you much about them when you just happen to live on the fourth."

"Is there really this little communication amidst the realms?" asked Neila, sipping her lime-infused water. "But, I thought, there were a lot of trades and such."

"There is not much trading, until you can go to a higher level. Which is fair, in a way," Helios shrugged. "But in truth, if you're born on the fourth, you have little to no chance of meeting a higher-level person, unless you linger around the Bifröst constantly."

"That's just sad," noted Neila. "Humans would go crazy like that for sure."

"They are not much better when they stumble upon a higher-level, believe me," Helios disagreed. "We had to go through great lengths to tame them; behaving like scared animals."

"Wait, what?" gasped Neila. "There are humans on the fourth?"

Even Loki looked interested, yet he still stayed silent, deep in thought.

"Yes," nodded Helios. "A few times it happened that a sizeable group managed to attract a path and get to the fourth. We welcomed them, of course, gave them land to live on. Helped them integrate and so on."

"Who are they?" Neila wanted to know, still stunned.

"I believe, the last such group called themselves Mayans. I don't really know; never spent much time with them."

"Huh," she exhaled, baffled. "I've always believed that they actually managed to go somewhere else, but I thought, it was another dimension. Why don't they come back, then? And try to help the rest?"

"Because they can't," Loki cut in suddenly, sounding sad, yet still preoccupied. Obviously, he was thinking deeply about something while keeping track of the conversation.

"What? Why?"

"I've already mentioned that one needs strong abilities or advanced technology to be able to travel through a rogue path. If one managed to attract one, they might even survive. But it's a one-way voyage in reality. Until they learn to control those wild energies, they are unable to travel back. However, nobody under the fifth can do so."

"So, these humans are now stranded on the fourth?" Neila glanced at Helios, who nodded.

"Indeed. But, they made a home for themselves on the fourth, living happily as far as I know. Even help us with the ongoing war."

"What war?" asked Loki, suddenly fully present and alert.

"I don't think, you have heard of them," said Helios, glancing at him. "They call themselves hograx."

"That's impossible!" gasped Loki. Rising to stand, he leant on the table, glaring at Helios piercingly.

"Why, what's wrong?" asked Neila, worried.

"They live on the *fifth* realm, in a neighbouring planet to the fifths, *outside* our node. How could they attack *you*?"

"I don't know," replied Helios, turning serious as well.

"Answer me!" Loki boomed, smashing a fist into the table, making it vibrate. His gaze sparked in anger, his whole body turned tense.

Neila and Helios also jumped to their feet, fearful. Helios summoned a shield around himself, glancing worriedly at Neila at the other side of the table. She backed to a wall, but seemed composed enough.

"Answer me, fourth!" Loki demanded, taking a step towards him.

"I don't know!" Helios cried out, talking fast now. "They just appeared one day, never in too many ships or troops. Their technological level is above ours, but we could repel them so far because of our numbers and some stolen tech. I cannot tell you anything else, since we could hardly capture one alive. We thought that they came from the third! That's what they said, anyway. Alas, they almost always managed to kill themselves before we could try anything. We don't know, why they attacked, or what they even want. It's all I know, I swear!"

Loki suddenly straightened up, calm; his features troubled.

"What does this mean?" asked Neila, stepping beside the Áss.

"That I have to break the rules again," he answered, taking a deep breath. "I have to get this information to Týr."

"Can't you rather call him down?" she suggested, but he just shook his head.

"It might take too long. Why didn't you say anything to us?" Loki turned to Helios again, who just gave a scoff.

"Would you have even cared?" he asked cynically. "As you lovingly said several times now, it's not your job to save us. How should we 'inform' you, then?"

Neila glanced from Helios to Loki, whose gaze just darkened even more.

"What does this mean?" Helios inquired, lowering his defences as the Áss calmed down.

"I don't know," mumbled Loki, looking incredibly troubled. "Nothing makes sense anymore."

The chime of Neila's phone made her jump. In the momentary silence, it almost sounded like a loud bell; an inappropriate one at that, too.

"Ugh," she grunted, hurrying to the phone.

"Who's that?" asked Loki when he heard Neila's swear.

"I completely forgot about my trip three days from now."

"What trip?" the Áss wanted to know.

"I've ..." she started but trailed off. "I've booked a two-week long holiday on Crete. I thought, I could use the break from all this, and I wanted to visit a different mythology than the Norse," she explained with a faint blush. "I didn't know you were coming back."

Helios now opened his mouth, but then both he and Loki became tense.

"What? What's going on?" Neila asked, watching the men. Loki eased up almost immediately, even smiled faintly, but Helios remained wary. "Who's coming this time?"

"Apparently, I'm being watched," noted Loki, folding his arms.

In the next moment, Týr appeared in the apartment, drawing all glances. After looking around, he rested his gaze on Helios for a moment, who stared at him with widened eyes.

"What are you up to, Loki?" the Lawmaker asked, calm as ever, although, annoyed.

"For once, I had nothing to do with *this*," he answered, motioning at Helios with his head. "It's all Neila's doing."

"Oh?" Týr turned to her.

"You know," she mused, insulted. "You guys are truly behaving like meddling big brothers."

Týr flashed a confused frown, then glanced at Helios again.

"But, you couldn't have come in a better time," Loki cut in. "Tell him," he motioned at Helios, who seemed to be having trouble with shaking off his surprise.

"Speak, then!" Týr turned to the fourth, who shook his head at this, confused, as if fighting with something in his mind.

After a moment, Helios seemed to have returned to the present, looking at the Lawmaker, who exchanged a glance with Loki. Neila, in the meantime, just thudded down on the sofa, listening but staying out of their business.

Helios told again what little he actually knew—he fought against the hograxes at the beginning, the fourth said, confessing that this war was the main reason for him to steal from the fifths. However, since the hograxes ceased their attack afterwards, Helios decided to give himself up. Hence, he got to know Neila in the prison.

Týr mused about the heard information for a moment, then glanced at Loki. For a few seconds more, he just glared at his friend, pondering. Whatever he was about to do, he did not like it, though. In the end, the Lawmaker pulled out a little badge-like thing from a pocket, throwing it to Loki, who caught it with one hand.

They understood each other without words, so Týr turned to Neila.

"It was good to see you again. Take care," said the Lawmaker, then disappeared without further ado.

A momentary silence fell on the apartment, which Helios broke in the end.

"Is this going to be a regular thing?" he asked, looking at Loki.

Chapter 27

Loki and Neila had just arrived home. After kicking her shoes off, she walked straight into the kitchen to boil some water for tea.

"That bad, huh?" asked Helios from the sofa, watching something on the TV.

Loki stepped to him and simply turned the TV off, earning a disapproving cry from the fourth. But the Áss minded him not, sauntering to the bar and poured himself a glass of whisky. In the end, Loki settled down in one of the armchairs.

Neila watched them, leaning on the counter and waiting for the kettle. At the moment, she felt glad that Richard would not drop by unannounced, as he sometimes did. It was bad enough that her editor already thought of Loki and Neila as an item. Dealing with offers, or bank accounts, or testaments together in front of Ms Cho helped little in this regard as well. Therefore, Neila kept Richard at bay through messaging, always making it clear that she needed solitude for work. *All I need now is for him to find another man living with me,* she thought, massaging her forehead haggardly.

"You cannot even begin to imagine," Neila growled when Helios glanced at her for an answer. "Humans make life so much more difficult than it should be!" she sighed, pouring the water in her preferred glass pot with an infuser. Then, grabbing her favourite mug and the teapot, she joined the men.

"Was your mission successful, at least?" wanted to know the fourth.

"Oh, yeah, we've managed to modify everything, finalise the drafts and all that."

Neila felt somewhat satisfied with their accomplishments. *Even if all of this made sure, nobody would ever believe that Loki and I are not together,* she thought.

This whole thing started with Loki still determined to start anew. Therefore, he transferred his original bank account to Neila, who then adjusted her will accordingly, and so on. The Áss thought of such precautions to be an overreaction, yet Neila listened not, for once. For some very strange reason, she felt an urge to settle these matters rather sooner than later.

Neila had made sure that every dime was accounted for after her death. Her original account would be divided among her few friends, including Tracy and Richard. What Loki now transferred to her would go to charity; to organisations focusing on science and technology for a more sustainable future. Last but not least, Neila finalised everything regarding the film adaptation of her book.

All of these tasks consumed quite some time, leaving Neila feel like a zombie now.

"Please, somebody tell me that there is an alternate reality where I don't have to deal with such things!" she lamented, leaning back comfortably.

"What do you mean by that?" asked Helios.

"You know, other realities," Neila explained, but he did not seem to understand. "Other lives, you might have lived, choices you did not take. For example, if I have never met Loki, I'd still be living the glorious life of a starving artist."

"Well, apologies for that," growled the Áss, earning a frown from Neila.

Whatever is the matter with him, seriously? Neila mused, not understanding Loki's behaviour. Although, his spiky mood could have been caused by Helios. Loki never concealed his dislike for the fourths. Helios, of course, only poured oil on the fire, constantly teasing the Áss whenever he got the chance. Nothing too disrespectful, but just enough.

"You are forgiven," smiled Neila soothingly, pouring tea into her mug. "In any case, I might be a vampire in a different reality. That would be cool."

"You want to be a vampire?" Helios raised a questioning eyebrow.

"Yeah, why not," she shrugged. "Anything is better than being a human. But, is it possible?"

"It is possible, if your essence permits," muttered Loki, seemingly staring into his drink.

"I was kinda joking, but now I'm interested," said Neila, tucking her legs under herself in the chair.

"It's difficult to explain. I shouldn't have said anything," Loki mumbled, averting very uncharacteristically for himself.

"Then why did you?" teased Helios, earning a disapproving glance from the Áss.

"Don't be mean," chided Neila. "However, now I'm truly interested about this."

Loki took a deep breath.

"I don't even know, where to start, to be honest. Even we know very little about 'other realities,' as you called them. But, try to imagine that your essence is like a pool. You can draw some out and form a body with that in a world like this one. This being is you, since they have part of your essence. But, the pool is so vast, you can form many others as well. All would be you, yet different."

Neila just blinked, but even Helios seemed a tad lost.

"You have to find a better metaphor, please. This sounds deeper than I anticipated," said Neila apologetically.

Loki fell silent for a little while, sipping from his drink.

"Try candles," suggested Helios, earning a side look from the Áss.

"It's as good as any, I guess," sighed Loki. "All right, imagine that your essence is a pool of wax, from which you can form various types of candles. Round, big, small, twisted, with multiple wicks or just one, or even none. These are all you; living, breathing persons, like the one who's sitting in front of me right now."

"Okay, but how could I be a vampire candle, then?" Neila asked.

"This is when it gets truly complicated. Everything, even perhaps Miðgarðr itself, has a pool like this. Or, Miðgarðr would have a different material altogether, and it also has to be compatible with yours, whatever that may be. Otherwise, that specific person would be out of place, probably unable to live properly, if at all. Just as if you would want to light a candle underwater."

"Oookay ..." Neila exhaled, looking more and more confused.

"For a working and viable life, everything has to be compatible," Loki continued. "But, circling back to vampires, IF the world has it in *its* essence, AND your essence would be compatible with said world, you very well might be a vampire."

"Uh-huh," Neila nodded. "I've lost it completely."

"I told you, it's complicated," teased Loki with a faint smile. "As I mentioned before, not even we understand this exactly."

"Or just *you* don't," mumbled Helios loud enough.

"I'm a soldier. It is not my job to understand such things," growled Loki. "In any case, not even the other nations of Ásgarðr understand. Otherwise, we would be able to replicate Heimdallr."

Helios scoffed at this, earning a questioning look from both Neila and Loki.

"Is there something the matter?" asked the Áss.

"Nothing, nothing," replied the fourth. "It's just ... interesting to hear you admit to such a thing, that's all."

"Why wouldn't I? It doesn't make me any less."

Helios gave a well-yeah grimace.

"True," he admitted bitterly. "It's just ..." he was looking for a word, but then just scoffed and left the sentence unfinished.

Neila glanced from one to the other, listening and sipping her tea.

"Just what?" Loki pressed, tense.

"Given what we know about the seventh through the Æsir, it's difficult to imagine that you don't know something, that's all," answered Helios, averting his gaze.

Before anybody could respond, the chime of Neila's phone broke the serious atmosphere. Blushing, she fetched it.

"Richard again, I presume?" asked Loki.

"Yeah, he wished me a safe travels," said Neila with a sigh, sitting back into the armchair. "Which reminds me, I know it's close, but would you want to come with me?" she glanced at the others.

"No, thanks," Helios shook his head. "I'm not going to step foot on that island, ever again."

Neila just opened her mouth to ask, but then changed her mind, turning to Loki instead.

"And you? You'd really need a vacation. I'm sure, we can still arrange it."

Loki nodded in agreement, although, seemed less than thrilled about the prospect. Nevertheless, he did everything in his power to modify the hotel reservation at such a short notice.

"Are you sure, you don't want to come?" Neila asked Helios while Loki was outside the balcony, speaking on the phone, arranging the change of plans.

"Absolutely," he nodded. "I think I'll go to the fifth, trying to find out more about the hograxes. Maybe even offer my help."

"That's oddly nice of you," teased Neila, but his serious gaze silenced every further jest.

"If the hograxes are, indeed, behind this, the entire node is in grave danger. I'm a skilled warrior; I won't let them take over anything without putting up a fight."

"Just, be careful, okay?" she said, patting him on the shoulder. Helios grabbed her hand and drew her in for a hug.

"Take care yourself," the fourth muttered into her ears, then stepped back. "I'll be back, don't worry," he smiled, then gave a playful bow and disappeared.

Neila just sighed, hoping that he would be fine. Then, she tried to distract herself with packing.

Chapter 28

Neila stood at the balcony railing, gazing into the distance.

They had just arrived to the private house of the hotel on Crete. Right after their helper put down the suitcases, she changed to a more appropriate outfit, matching the weather. Now wearing a sleeveless top with loose linen trousers, she walked out to the balcony barefoot, looking around the gorgeous landscape.

At that time of year, the weather was fairly warm on Crete. The almost constant breeze caressed everything soothingly; the afternoon Sun shone comfortably warm.

Inhaling deeply, Neila closed her eyes, listening to the wind, birds, and the ocean. Shortly after, Loki joined her, placing two glasses and the complimentary wine on the table. He, too, had changed, wearing comfortable and airy linen trousers and shirt.

"Isn't this magnificent?" sighed Neila, opening her eyes.

Loki hardly recognised her, though. Neila seemed completely calm; her essence waving to the sound of the ocean. With a faraway gaze, she looked into the distance, probably seeing nothing of the landscape itself. Her every feature showed perfect stillness. Peace itself ruled her.

The energies on Crete were quite pleasant, if intense, making it one of the best places for relaxation on Miðgarðr. This was one of the reasons, the Áss had used to visit the island. Yet, he would have never anticipated it to cause such a drastic change in anybody.

Loki could not believe his eyes. Literally from the moment they disembarked the airplane, Neila had transformed into a completely different person. Emitting nothing but peace and calm, she walked with fluid motions; a constant faint smile ruled her features. As if she felt at home there, or at the very least, safe.

A wave of her essence now brushed against his hand, sending an almost ecstatic shiver down his spine. With a sudden decision, he embraced her from behind. Neila did not even flinch, only brushed her cheek against his.

Immersing into her essence, Loki felt himself becoming lost. He had never encountered such incredible calmness that now enveloped both of them. Closing his eyes, the Áss surrendered to this perfect Peace, letting his mind find rest at last. In that moment, feeling the breeze and hearing the crashing of waves filled Loki's mind. Anything else, like the thought of war or his punishment, faded into the background.

Loki did not notice his head sliding lower. Only when his lips brushed against the skin of her shoulder, he realised the happenings. With eyes still closed, Loki inhaled deeply, taking in Neila's essence as well as her perfume. He even felt her heartbeat now, a slow and calming rhythm in his mind, like a lullaby.

Complete and utter Peace.

Unconsciously, Loki embraced Neila tighter, feeling her hand caress his cheek; her fingers then weaved through his hair. Suddenly, his heart began to throb, aching from the perfection of the situation. Still not fully self-aware, Loki exhaled with lips caressing her shoulder. As he reached her neck, a sudden surge of her essence made everything feel explosive.

Abruptly, Loki became horribly aware of the situation; his heart nearly skipping a beat. Breathing heavily, he backed away, as though burnt, stumbling to the door for support. Neila turned to him immediately, puzzled.

"Are you okay? What happened?" she asked, worried.

Panting, Loki just turned his head away, desperately trying to pull himself together. Concerned, Neila now stepped closer and put a hand on his shoulder, making him feel almost ablaze once again.

"Loki? Are you okay?" she repeated, trying to get any kind of response.

"Yes," he managed to exhale, fighting to get his own mind and feelings under control. "Yes. I just ... I just need to go."

With a thought, the Áss vanished to a nearby beach. There, he could finally breathe; gulping air, as though drowning beforehand. Feeling the salty air filling his lungs, the fire inside succumbed.

Loki could not believe, what had happened ... or nearly did. No Ásgarðrian had ever fallen in Love with a lower-level before. No person from those realms could offer enough, hence even a simple friendship had its emotional limitations.

Yet, the impossible had happened, plunging Loki in agony. With an aching soul, mind, and body, he wanted not to think about how close he came to breaking their strongest rule. Any physical relation was forbidden with a lower-level, since not even they could foretell the consequences. Naturally, this rule was for everybody's safety.

However ... Loki thought, closing his eyes in agony.

That perfect Calmness; that unyielding Peace, that Neila somehow generated, tormented his mind even from afar. He *wanted* to go back; *wanted* to be submerged in that ocean, unconcerned about having no way out.

Then, an ice-cold chill ran down his spine, making him spin around and look at the direction of the house.

"No ..." he whispered with widened eyes, disappearing immediately.

Loki arrived just in time to witness a hograx pull back his energy knife from Neila's heart.

"NO!" the Áss cried out, jumping to catch her fall.

The hograx vanished without further ado, but Loki could not care less. Kneeling down, he gently cradled Neila while placing his right hand on her chest. By activating the remaining nanocytes in her system, he managed to slow the bleeding, keeping her somewhat conscious. But there was nothing more Loki could do there.

Wrath seized his mind, forcing sanity into a corner.

"HEIMDALLR!" the Áss boomed; his eyes glowing blue; his powers shaking the walls around them.

In the next moment, the Bifröst activated, blowing the house apart as it transported them to Ásgarðr, where Loki glanced around for help.

Óðinn and Týr were already there; their expression a mix of horror and concern. Loki still knelt on the ground, holding Neila in one arm, while the other rested on her chest, controlling the nanocytes. Blood streamed from the wound, and from her foggy gaze, she was barely aware of the happenings, if at all.

Týr stepped closer to the pair, still stunned, while Óðinn struck the ground with his spear, activating the shield around the Bifröst platform, sealing them inside. If any Æsir found this strange, nobody dared to intervene.

"What have you done ...?" whispered Týr, aghast. "It is forbidden to bring a lower-level here!"

"I don't care!" Loki shouted, glancing up. Tears gathered in his eyes now. "Help her, please!"

"We cannot," Óðinn stepped beside Týr, looking down at Neila almost sadly.

"Cannot, or will not?" demanded Loki, angry.

"Both."

A twitch of his mouth was Loki's answer to this.

"Then, I'll find help elsewhere," he hissed, starting to rise with the clear intention of leaving.

Heimdallr watched the scene with widened eyes, but said or did nothing until ordered otherwise.

"You are not allowed to leave," Óðinn called after Loki, making him halt. "Also, nobody would be able to help her."

At this, Loki slumped back to the ground, cradling Neila's body and looking utterly lost.

"I'm sorry," said the Ruler.

"Why can't you just save her?" Loki burst out, glancing at Týr, then at Óðinn.

The Lawmaker dropped his gaze when their eyes met, but the Ruler could withstand even that immense pain.

"Even if we could save her body, her essence is already lost. It is too late; the shock was too great."

"But you *can* save her?" asked Loki, almost begging.

"Perhaps," Óðinn admitted, looking at the foggy tricolour gaze.

Neila remained alive and was somewhat aware of their conversation. As they spoke in English, she could even understand them. Comprehension, however, was a different matter.

"Then do it!" demanded Loki desperately.

"Her essence would be broken beyond repair. Do you really wish that on her?" asked Óðinn with a strange tone, nearly breaking Loki.

"If ... If there is a way ..." he muttered, glancing at her and seeing her essence literally fade away before his eyes. "If there is a chance ..."

Óðinn was just about to answer, but a faint huff from Neila drew their attention. Loki carefully repositioned his arm to better support her head. Neila blinked, then seemed to glance almost directly at him; her life had yet to slip away completely.

"No ..." she lamented inaudibly, but the Æsir understood.

Loki turned ashen, while Týr dropped his head. Óðinn merely straightened himself, looking down at her almost coldly.

"You heard her," the Ruler announced.

"No, no, Neila, no," mumbled Loki, speaking softly to her. "Everything would be fine, you have to allow us to help. You *have to!*"

"No ..." she whispered, barely managing to look into his eyes. "I ... cannot ... live ... broken ... I'm ... sorry ..."

"But, you would live here, with us, then," pleaded Loki, tears streaming down his cheeks. "It will be fine, you'd still have a full life. Please, you cannot ... Just cannot ..."

"My ... choice ..." Neila whispered; her consciousness slipping away.

Summoning every remaining strength she could muster, Neila reached for his hand on her chest with the obvious intention of moving it. However, that simple motion took everything, leaving her hand thud back to the ground. A single tear streamed down her cheek, saying goodbye with one last look.

All remaining intellect faded from the tricolour gaze; the body sustained solely by Loki's nanocytes. Only a faint flicker of essence remained.

"It's time," Óðinn said solemnly, making Loki shake his head defiantly.

"I cannot," he whispered shakily.

"Allow me the honour, please," Týr offered, kneeling down beside them. Holding out a hand, he was about to take control over of the nanocytes, but Loki shook his head again.

"No," he said softly. "I will do it."

The Lawmaker nodded, stepping back respectfully. However, worry shone in his indigo gaze.

Everybody knew the fact that Loki had never taken a life before, neither by accident, nor in battle. Yet now, he was prepared to break that; for a lower-level, nonetheless. For Love.

Týr himself knew all too well, how difficult it truly was to take a life, including in battle. Killing intentionally, even if it was for mercy, could take a great toll on anyone, even on the strongest Æsir. Never getting used to that feeling, losing a friend in such a manner nearly broke him once before. Regardless, the Lawmaker still could not begin to imagine, what Loki was going through now.

The first time was always the hardest.

Loki closed his eyes and exhaled a kiss to Neila's forehead, then rested his head against hers. Withholding a breath, even his essence disappeared as he withdrew his hand, deactivating the nanocytes.

Death hovered above, taking away the last drop of her essence. Upon Their departure, an incredible silence engulfed the platform. Nobody moved or said a word; all paid respect to the dead.

Loki remained kneeling on the ground, holding the body in his arms. With his exhale, his essence seemed to turn into a pitch-black abyss, swirling around them. In the next moment, this immense darkness lit up, drawing Óðinn's and Týr's attention immediately.

As Wrath seized Loki's mind, his eyes glowed with a bluish light, seemingly burning from the inside. Loki cried out in agony; his strange blue powers expanding like wildfire wanting to burn everything to the ground, shaking the foundation of the city of Ásgarðr. The flames disintegrated anything they touched, including the lifeless body in his arms.

The incredible burst of energy shattered the shield around the platform, nearly wiping away Óðinn and Týr. Only the Lawmaker's quick reflexes saved them from those intense flames, jumping before the Ruler and forming a protective barrier around them. Heimdallr seemed to be able to handle himself, too, leaping behind the Lawmaker just in time.

As devastating the blue flames proved to be, they vanished after a moment, leaving only the steaming black stones. Still kneeling on the ground, Loki now gasped for air. Then, he slowly rose to stand. When he next glanced up, even Týr took a step back from that look. Pure Wrath lived in those blue eyes, holding hand with Pain.

"I want my tech back!" whispered Loki with a deathly tone.

Óðinn watched him with widened eyes, completely stunned. After getting a nod as an answer, Loki started for the palace, not even glancing at his friends when passing by them.

• • ● END OF VOLUME I ● • •

Glossary and Pronunciation Guide

A note on entries in this glossary. As many readers may not be familiar with Norse mythology and the Old Norse language, below is a very simplified guide. The idea of this collection is not scholarly precision, but to be a usable guide for the story.

The definitions and pronunciations listed here are specific to this book. Therefore, they might differ from the real-life mythologies, or from the original Old Norse usage.

Pronunciation

Á, á (Áss) A slightly longer version of the known vowel found at the beginning of words like 'ice' or 'eye.'

Æ, æ (Æsir) A longer version of the known vowel found in words like 'get,' 'head,' or 'less.'

Ð, ð (Miðgarðr) Usually written as 'd' (seldom 'dh') in anglicised texts, however, it is closer to the beginning of the word 'this' or 'that.' One could also think of it as a 'soft-d' in contrast to the 'hard-d' used in the word 'end.'

Ó, ó (Óðinn) A longer version of the known vowel found at the beginning of words like 'of', 'object', 'organ.' Closely mimicked by 'oar' or 'ore.'

Ö, ö (Jötnar) Somewhat resembling a very short version of the vowel found in 'bird' or 'circle.'

Ǫ, ǫ (Jǫtnar) A shorter version of the known vowel found at the beginning of words like 'of', 'object', 'organ.' Somewhat mimicked by 'flop' or 'drop.' In anglicised texts usually transcribed as 'ö' instead.

Þ, þ (Þórr) Usually written as 'th' (or simply 't') in anglicised texts, however, it is closer to the beginning of the word 'think' or the end of 'path.' One could also think of it as a 'soft-t' in contrast to the 'hard-t' used in for example the word 'time.'

Ý, ý (Týr) A longer version of the vowel known found in words like 'cease' or 'tease.'

-r (Heimdallr) An 'r' at the end of Ásgarðrian words denotes a 'hard stop' of the word. This could be approximated by a not trilled 'r.'

Characters

Freyja and Freyr Sevenths, one of the two currently living twin pairs on Ásgarðr. Born in Vanaheimr. They are members of the Vanir. Freyja is one of the strongest Vanr, lives in Álfheimr, and never goes anywhere without her twin brother.

Freyr does not speak.

Freyja is also known on Miðgarðr (falsely) as: Goddess of Love, Goddess of Lust, Goddess of War.

Freyr is also known on Miðgarðr (falsely) as: God of Fertility, God of Peace.

Heimdallr Seventh, was created by several Ásgarðrian scientists, as a sentient android. He is currently the oldest of the Ásgarðrians, and the Lookout of Ásgarðr, having the ability to see into other realms without leaving his post. He is also responsible for overseeing both Bifrösts on Ásgarðr—the natural Connection and the one built by Ásgarðrians. He raises the alarm if there is an attack on Ásgarðr.

Also known as Miðgarðr (falsely) as: An enigmatic god, without a clear-cut description.

Helios Fourth. The first fourth, who could reach the level of the sixth. He is a skilled fighter and 'mage,' often works as a bounty hunter.

Kasumi Sixth, a kitsune (fox spirit). She works as a bounty hunter. As a sixth, she mostly visited the eastern parts of Miðgarðr.

Loki Seventh, born in Jǫtunheimr. One of the strongest of the Æsir, a skilled soldier, who also likes to keep up good relations with the other realms. He frequently visited Miðgarðr in the past. As an Áss, he is also responsible for training the next generation of Æsir. His Ásgarðrian weapon is a pair of twin daggers. Týr is his best friend, and has a close relationship with Þórr.

Also known on Miðgarðr (falsely) as: Father of Lies, God of Lies, God of Mischief.

Neila Third, born on Miðgarðr. Working as a fiction writer.

Óðinn Seventh, the current Ruler of Ásgarðr, born in the nation of Ásgarðr. Leader of the Æsir, although, became (in)famous for his uncanny logic and tactical abilities. He can see patterns like none other, thus calculate the possibility of different outcomes of the happenings. He used to be on good terms with Loki and Týr, however, turned away from them when he became the Ruler. Since then, he usually spends his time alone, collecting knowledge. By an accident, his body became broken and now looks like an old man, even though he is the same age as Loki. Also, he lost an eye, choosing to wear an eye patch instead of letting it replaced. He resides in his palace hall in the city of Ásgarðr, where he collects rare animals (for example Fenrir, the giant wolf). His Ásgarðrian weapon is a spear.

Also known on Miðgarðr (falsely) as: Allfather; God of Wisdom, War, Poetry, and many more.

Richard Third, born on Miðgarðr. Working as a bank liaison for Loki and later befriends Neila.

Tracy Third, born on Miðgarðr. Worked as an editor, currently is the agent and editor of Neila.

Týr Seventh, born in Jǫtunheimr. The strongest of the Æsir, who is also the Lawmaker of Ásgarðr. He functions as the judge in disputes, and have the power to overrule the Ruler of Ásgarðr, if deemed necessary. As the strongest Áss, he is responsible for mobilising the military forces (for example the Æsir) during an attack or defence. He also trains the next generation of Æsir. His best friend is Loki, and has a good relationship with Þórr.

Also known on Miðgarðr (falsely) as: God of War, God of Victory.

Þórr Seventh, son of Óðinn (and Jǫrð). As a trainee, he is under the care of Loki and Týr. As a young teenager, he liked to visit Miðgarðr, spreading tales amidst humans, giving base for most of their mythology. His Ásgarðrian weapon is a war hammer.

Also known on Miðgarðr (falsely) as: Lord of Thunder, God of Thunder.

Terminology

The node Is a folded space phenomenon that contains several planets. The node in this story has nine planets, also known as the nine realms. These worlds are connected through the Bifröst, with the fifth realm as the centre 'station.'

The planets are ranked from least to most evolved, starting with the first. The first three planets are the Disconnected Worlds, which have broken off from the rest, having no Bifröst of their own anymore.

The planets inside a node influence each other, therefore, their habitation is cross-compatible. The inhabitants can visit other realms through the Bifröst, but can go only as 'high' as their own level of understanding allows.

For clarity inside the node, it is customary to call both the planet and their inhabitants by their rank.

Bifröst Also known as Connection. It is the stable pathway that connects the planets inside the node. Anything can travel through the Bifröst, from living beings, through inanimate objects, to thoughts or even feelings.

Through the Bifröst, the planets can influence each other, so their overall environment remains similar, allowing the inhabitants to travel with relative ease. When using the Bifröst, one must make a mandatory stop on the fifth. The highest levelled world that still communicates with the lower-levels is the seventh, Ásgarðr.

The Disconnection The chain of events when a planet gets separated from the rest of its node and its Bifröst breaks. From that moment on, such planets are not tightly connected to the rest of the node; their time frames are independent from the rest.

The nine realms of the node

The seventh Also known as Ásgarðr, the highest ranked planet that still actively communicates with the rest. It has nine nations, for example Álfheimr, Ásgarðr, Jǫtunheimr, Vanaheimr. Ásgarðr protects the node with their military force (for example the Æsir). The capital of Ásgarðr is the city also named Ásgarðr.

It is home to Ásgarðrians.

The sixth Home to the pure energy users inside the node. They often work as bounty hunters, and liked visiting the eastern parts of Miðgarðr, giving birth to the many stories and legends about shape-shifting animals, demons, spirits, and deities.

It is home to the sixths.

The fifth The central junction inside the node, as a mandatory halting point when travelling through the natural Bifröst. It is a popular trading hub, and they possess very advanced technology, with which they compensate the lack of natural energies on their planet. They are the only ones, who have a protective iris that can close the Bifröst, so nobody can travel through, unless having their own, separate transportation system.

It is home to the fifths.

The fourth The lowest of the connected worlds inside the node. The inhabitants are not liked by higher levels because of their abilities. They are considered by others only slightly more advanced than the humans of Miðgarðr.

It is home to the fourths.

The third Also known as Miðgarðr, or Earth. The highest ranked of the disconnected worlds inside the node, having no Bifröst of its own. Because of the rich energies the planet possesses, many from the higher realms like to visit it, even though this is considered inadvisable.

It is home to humans.

Miscellaneous

Álfar (singular Álfr) The people living in Álfheimr (a nation on Ásgarðr), led by Freyja.

Æsir One branch of the Ásgarðrian military forces. A male soldier is called an Áss (plural also Æsir), a female soldier is an Ásynja (plural Ásynjur). They excel in combat, and each of them has their own special weapon, forged by the Dvergar.

The strongest of the Æsir currently is Týr, their leader is Óðinn.

Dvergar (singular Dvergr) The ones who forge the weapons and create technology for the military of Ásgarðr.

Essence Everything a person was, is, will be, or could be. The experiences one goes through, their memories, their thought process, their views of the world. 'Using' the essence can manifest in abilities, such as flying or manipulating elements. Also, emotions or thoughts can show in the person's essence, so it is used in every-day communication by the higher-levels to 'speak' clearly and avoid misunderstandings.

Jǫtnar (singular Jǫtunn) The people living in Jǫtunheimr (a nation on Ásgarðr). Most Æsir are actually Jǫtnar, including Týr and Loki.

Vanir (singular Vanr) A special division of fighters of Ásgarðr. They excel at using mental abilities instead of weapons.

Yggdrasill A metaphor, misunderstood by humans, based on when Loki tried to teach them about the node and the nine realms. It is best to avoid mentioning it, when dealing with him.

A note from the author

For an indie author, such as myself, each and every review
means a lot. If you enjoyed this book, please spread the word,
recommend it to your friends, or leave a review on any
platform you prefer.

In case you would want to reach out to me privately,
you can do that via www.saraven.net